Praise for *The Three Lives of St. Ciarán*

Weaving together history, myth, and dark visions of the future, Labarta creates a strange and beguiling exploration of Spanish and Irish identities. This is a beautifully written, subversive, and endlessly inventive novel.

Naomi Krüger,
author of *May*

The Three Lives of St Ciarán manages to be a transgressive, page-turning read – & at the same time, a deep meditation on gender, daughterhood, the climate crisis & the deep psycho-mythological connections between Ireland & Spain. Bearing meaning through time like *Cloud Atlas*, as disruptive of gender as *The Passion of New Eve*, the ground tilled by St Ciaran's multiple narrators is the urgent cultural interface of religion & the body.

Eoghan Walls,
author of *The Gospel of Orla*

Exciting and Provocative.

Intricate, compelling and clever – I loved this book.

The Three Lives of St. Ciarán

INÉS G. LABARTA

A Blackwater Press book

First published in the United States of America by
Blackwater Press, LLC

Library of Congress Control Number: 2023950823

ISBN: 978-1-963614-19-0

Cover design by Eilidh Muldoon
Illustrations by Inés G. Labarta

Blackwater Press
120 Capitol Street
Charleston, WV 25301
United States

blackwaterpress.com

To my mother and my sister – thanks for always believing in my writing.

The Bull's Betrothed

The Three Baptisms of
la Niña de Irlanda

by
Ciarán de la Cierva*

* Extract of what is left from the novelette titled The Three Baptisms of La Niña de Irlanda. The story was published periodically in 1936 BF in the literary magazine Cruz y Raya, founded by José Bergamín. Three chapters – now lost – preceded this extract. Little is known about the author, Ciarán de la Cierva, one of the most obscure writers from the Second Spanish Republic.

Spain, 1931

I.

The ship from Ireland arrived in the Land of Everlasting Sun, where the clouds were yellow and the skies a kindly blue. The warm wind smelt of olive trees and shellfish. Sunlight melted on the sand, forming a crust of sparkling crystal. The white houses in front of the port glowed. Storks watched the deck from their perches on the masts. They flew down to the beach to snatch crabs and fish that had fallen from the fishmongers' boxes, competing with the seagulls for the best bite.

The sailors took the cows, the bulls, and the girl out of the hold. She was not a corpse, but she wasn't alive, either. She had been the Girl with Apple Cheeks before, but now her body was soulless. She was a statue. She had turned into La Niña. The sailors were so afraid of her that they left her on the pier and ran away. And there she lay, dressed in a black tunic and a white scapular, surrounded by a herd of monstrous black bulls with fierce metal eyes, and horns like crescent moons. They bellowed at anyone who dared to come close. The shadow of a hook hanging from the top of a crane circled around them like a vulture.

People came for the cows. Cattle keepers armed with cedar canes took the bulls, too. But nobody came for La Niña, who lay among wet pieces of rope and fish carcasses.

A man passed by her side.

"Eh, niña, niña…" He bent over, shaking her arm. He tried to take her scapular off, thinking that she was suffocating in the heat of such a stifling day.

"What are you doing?" A woman approached them. "Let the girl alone."

A small crowd gathered around the girl, who lay stiff as a figure made from alabaster. "Is he bothering the girl?"

"Why is she on the floor?"

"There's a man here molesting a girl…"

"I haven't done anything, you bastards." The man put his flat hat on and stalked away. "Come here, niña… what's the matter?" A fishmonger woman tried to help her stand. "Water?"

"Give her this." Another woman took a hip flask from her bosom.

Then, the most extraordinary event took place. The iron hook came loose and fell. The hook was heavy and sharp, like a bull's horn. It landed on La Niña's tender face. The women screamed but La Niña remained voiceless.

"La Vírgen purísima…"

"God help us."

"Is she dead?"

"Let me see, let me see!" The woman with the hip flask knelt at the girl's side. With her gloved hands, dirty with salt, dried blood and fish entrails, she held the hook. The girl's nose was red and had started to swell, its bridge slightly bent to the left side. La Niña let out a small breath. Not a single drop of blood came from the wound. The fishmonger stepped back, murmuring a prayer.

"Padre nuestro, que estás en los cielos…" A short

man appeared behind her.

"My uncle is a doctor." The short man wore an old striped suit and an expensive leather ivy cap. "He'll take care of her." His eyes were yellow and cunning, like those of an old greyhound.

Nobody objected.

And that's how La Niña ended up in the back of a cart pulled by a one-eyed horse, sitting on boxes of smuggled Jerez liquor. The sea became a thin line on the horizon. The afternoon sun roasted the track, which was edged with prickly, grey bushes and small olive trees.

The Man with Yellow Dog Eyes didn't take her to a doctor but to an orchard of almond trees. Red, green, and blue wagons were stationed there. Horses grazed in the shade, whilst people swam and washed clothes in the nearby stream. They were all part of Madame Mariposa's Maravilloso Circus: that is why three sinuous golden Ms were painted on the side of every wagon. The Man with Yellow Dog Eyes took La Niña to a wagon separated from the rest. Next to it, five little brown girls played with the almond flowers that carpeted the ground, tossing them in the air and letting them fall on their heads as if they were snow. The man knocked down the castle they had built from several tin-plated buckets.

"Go and get some water," he shouted at them.

He knocked on the door. A smell of kohl and tobacco came from inside. "Who is this?" a nicotine-rough voice asked.

"Me. I bring you something."

Madame Mariposa stepped out. She had ebony skin and ringlets that fell down her back like a cascade of midnight. She wore a bulky red dress and a single pearl earring. Her ample bosom rested on her rounded belly. She stared at La Niña, who had no apple-like cheeks anymore, but empty eyes the colour of a squall. La Niña's nose was black and swollen like a rotten potato.

"What does she do?"

"Well, she…"

"What's your name, niña?" Madame Mariposa grabbed La Niña's chin.

"She doesn't speak."

"What?"

The Man with Yellow Dog Eyes slapped La Niña twice. She collapsed onto the floor.

"Did you see that? She doesn't feel it. And…" He pointed out the black nose. "She doesn't bleed or scream or…"

Madame Mariposa frowned, playing with her pearl earring. They tried everything to make the girl react. The Man with Yellow Dog Eyes poked La Niña's arm with his slender knife. Madame Mariposa pricked her lips with the earring's screw. The Man with Yellow Dog Eyes stabbed the prong of his belt into the girl's inner elbow. Madame Mariposa pushed needles into La Niña's burnt fingertips. Not a single drop of blood.

And that's how La Niña gained her third name. The Maiden of Squall Eyes.

The circus people were sure the Maiden of Squall Eyes was a stray martyr, like the ones they had seen at church in the form of carved statues, but because they all knew there was no space in heaven for artists and acrobats, they were not scared of using her to make money. Thus, they got rid of her nun-like clothes and dressed her in a raggedy bridal dress, once used by the clowns.

Madame Mariposa turned one of her old silk handker-chiefs into a veil to cover her face. Whenever they arrived at any village, they made the Maiden of Squall Eyes stand inside a wooden receptacle as narrow as a coffin. Around her they placed flowers, wrinkled mass cards, red candles and small figures of San Antonio and baby Jesus.

"We bring the Maiden of Squall Eyes," the Man with Yellow Dog Eyes shouted. "We bring the Maid of Squall Eyes, who saw La Vírgen and was forgiven the sin of blood. Who wants to see the Maiden of Squall Eyes? She'll ask La Vírgen to heal you!"

The curious gathered around. Anxious parents spent a peseta so their sick infants could touch the girl's frozen feet. Old women kissed the Maid of Squall Eye's dry wounds, praying for daughters and sons living in faraway lands. Young men peeked under her veil: a pattern of blue and purple veins played under her skin. Her broken nose was an aggressive mountain in the calm geography of her face. Black circles of dried skin surrounded her eyelids. The Maiden of Squall Eyes never cried.

II.

Madame Mariposa's Maravilloso Circus arrived in the largest city in the Land of Everlasting Sun, Madrid. The yellow buildings were tall and full of eyes and mouths. The city didn't smell of manure and holm oaks, but of asphalt and gasoline. Waves of iridescent pigeons occupied the streets, feeding on food waste.

It was La Inmaculada Day, the yearly celebration of the Virgin Mary, and everyone from miles around had gathered in La Plaza de la Constitución. The circus had secured a small stand in the square, where they brought the Maiden of Squall Eyes. La Plaza was surrounded by porticoes, with the afternoon sun shining on the painted façade of the Bakery House. Hawkers pushed handcarts stacked with caramelised apples, fried chorizo, and creamy buñuelos. Nuns walked in couples, selling candles to the devoted. Drunken students followed them, trying to lift their brown habits. An old lady covered morcillas in pig's blood before roasting them on her portable stove. Families sat on the benches drinking sour hot chocolate and peeling roasted chestnuts. A bunch of girls climbed onto the bronze statue of King Felipe II, and rode his horse, while they sang and drank Moscatel.

"The Maiden of Squall Eyes is here, she's here!" The Man with Yellow Dog Eyes passed his leather ivy cap around. People threw cents in it and queued in front of the wooden box. During La Inmaculada day, everyone was rich.

"The Maiden of Squall Eyes is here! The Maiden of Squall Eyes is here!"

A group of school kids from La Institución paused in front of the girl's box. Their teacher, Profesor Yebra, had organised a special field trip. All carried portable blackboards and small chisels.

"What's that?" one of the kids asked, pointing out the ghostly figure inside the box.

Before Profesor Yebra could answer, some other kids ran towards the stand, ignoring the complaints coming from farther back in the queue. One ripped the silky veil aside, to find a cadaveric face beneath. He screamed. The brown scabs on the Maiden of Squall Eyes' fingertips, and the movement in her chest were her only signs of life. Another school kid poked a large grey scar on the girl's arm, but she just blinked. This encouraged one of his classmates, who took a candle to burn the Maiden of Squall Eye's forearm. Another used his chisel on her shoulder.

The Man of Yellow Dog Eyes was too busy counting money, and when he realised what was happening, it was too late to contain the mob of excited schoolboys. "Rufianes! Go away!"

"Boys, come back here, come back." Profesor Yebra shouted, grabbing an arm here, an ear there. People started laughing when one child tried to introduce a baby Jesus figure into the girl's blueish mouth. They threw chestnut peelings at her. The boys hauled the girl out from the box, pulling her hair and ripping her dress.

The Maiden of Squall Eyes reacted slowly to the pain. The blond hairs on her forearms, and her burnt fingertips remembered El Toro. Her nostrils retained small particles of his tar stench and she could still hear his bellows.

Grasping hands.

Poking fingers.

The Maiden of Squall Eyes was about to fall into pieces. Sharp biting teeth

A sour flash climbed up the girl's throat and her body bent when she retched.

Red splatters on the boys' white shirts. Screeches.

The Maiden of Squall Eyes kept throwing up blood. "Good grief, what's going on here?"

A woman with lustrous dark curls, wearing a calfskin overcoat, pushed the kids out of her way. She kicked their naked calves with her high heels until they cried and hid behind Profesor Yebra.

"What's all this about?" She was young, and moved around La Plaza like she owned it. But a certain dimness in her eyes, the pallor of her face, partially covered by carmine blush, and the thin wrists poking out the coat suggested she had been marked by something dark.

The Maiden of Squall Eyes, covered in blood and sweat, collapsed on the floor.

"She…" The Man with Yellow Dog Eyes tried to take charge of the situation, but the woman blocked his way and knelt in front of the Maiden of Squall Eyes. The girl was thin as a skeleton and the dirt on her skin was indistinguishable from ulcers. Her white dress stuck to her limbs like placenta. She smelt of blood and sick. The woman patted the girl's face gently, but she didn't open her eyes.

"Get off her!"

"What?" She faced Madame Mariposa's man.

"Who are you?" He insisted.

"I'm the person who's going to call the police right now so they can send this little business of yours to hell." The woman spat while she spoke. She was used to making herself heard.

"Three pesetas and she's yours," he said.

The woman checked her pockets and threw a few copper cents at him.

"Go away now, you bastard, or I'll call the police."

The Man with Yellow Dog Eyes took the coins and stepped back. He considered shouting back at the woman, hitting her even, but his canine instinct told him there was something dangerous in that brunette. Perhaps it was the way her small hands seemed rough and strong, or the way her red lips stood out on the youthful, yet wrinkled, face. He had already made a lot of money from the Maiden of Squall Eyes, but now that she was bleeding again, there was no business. Every meteoric career in the circus had a quick end, and the Maiden of Squall Eyes had reached hers. He let her go.

The woman whispered calming words and held the girl's hands. She took her calfskin overcoat off and covered the girl to keep her warm in that December afternoon.

"My name is Carmen," the woman whispered, leaning over the Maiden of Squall Eyes.

Something moved under the woman's skirt. Perhaps it was the wind.

Or the black, hairy tail of the bull. El Toro.

The Delightful Garden
1931-1932

Lesson 1: Yo soy, tú eres, yo me quedo, tú te quedas, ven. ¡Aquí!

"Yo soy Carmen," said the woman, kneeling in front of the body hunched under the set of black bookshelves that encircled the space like mute giants. The only light came from the street lamps outside and the dying embers on the fireplace, so it was difficult to see the girl. A dense smell of roasted lamb and fresh seafood drifted from the dining room. Carmen coughed to cover up her nausea.

"Yo soy Carmen," she repeated, this time pointing at herself. The girl didn't move.

Carmen bent forwards. The girl held her bony knees against her chest. She was wearing Carmen's old hospital nightgown, but it was too tight and short.

"Yo...soy...Carmen," the woman said a third time, knocking on the marble floor, sweat dripping between her breasts enclosed in the new dress. Her feet were swelling inside the lacquered high heels and the pearl necklace felt too heavy. "Yo soy Carmen, and you, ¿Tú eres...?"

Carmen grabbed the girls' hands – Dios, they were large, and so cold – and shook them. "¿Tú eres...?"

The girl turned her face to the shadows and pulled her hands from Carmen's.

"¿Tú eres...tú eres...tú...?"

Pedro, wearing his battered evening suit, entered the room. "People are coming." He didn't look at the girl.

"Is she deaf?" Carmen took the glass of Tempranillo wine he offered her.

"Well, we just need to drop something when she's not looking to see if she reacts." Pedro took a sip from his own glass.

"Ven, come here." Carmen put her wine on the floor and stood up, pulling the girl to the corner of the room. The girl was as tall as Pedro, so it was tricky to move her around. She remained where she was, looking at the wall.

Pedro took a big tome from the bookshelf, but Carmen hissed.

"Don't you dare to spoil my Bernini catalogue. Use your Old Testament."

Pedro grabbed *El Quijote* and threw the heavy book against the floor. The covers splattered open and the girl turned back, scratching the fresh scars on her hands.

"See?" he said. "Now make sure she stays inside the room, or else think of something creative to tell our guests if they see her wandering around."

Pedro left.

"Tú te quedas en la habitación. You stay in the room, hear me?" Carmen made the girl sit on the divan facing the window. "Tú te quedas en la habitación. Yo me quedo out there. Stop scratching. And if you hear any noise, if someone tries to open the door or if they knock, you stay here. Aquí."

Carmen knocked on the floor. "Aquí. Here. Do you understand?" The girl kept scratching.

Christmas songs started playing in the living room. People were cheering for the one-year-old Spanish Republic. Carmen stood up but cringed, holding her belly. She was not in the mood for parties.

"Damn it." She didn't bother with smoothing out her dress. Instead, she pointed to the chamber pot under the divan. "You know what to do with that. Josefa will come to check on you at some point. I won't be too late. Pedro has promised everyone will be out by midnight."

Lesson 2: Ven, quieta, mira, no tengas miedo

On a sunny February afternoon, Carmen brought the girl to the studio. She hadn't been there in the last few months. She preferred to lie on the living room sofa, the sketches made by her students surrounding her like autumn leaves. She barely looked at the pages as she marked them. The young girls she taught were so annoying; they knew nothing about art. They just wanted to model figures of their ugly pet dogs or make flowery pots to keep their jewellery in. They hadn't experienced any harshness in their short, unoriginal lives. No one could expect them to tame stone.

Carmen had lain on that sofa during the weeks after she came home from the hospital. The pillows that Pedro had stuffed under her – filled with lamb's wool – hurt as if they were made of marble. Her insides were sour. She was like a walnut someone had emptied with a knife. She had tried to explain that feeling to others, but words didn't come to her lips during the first weeks. Pedro fed her and took her to the lavatory because she refused to use the chamber pot. Whenever he held her so she could sit straight on the toilet, she cried from the pain but hid her face from him. At some point, he suggested praying together. She screamed at him until he was gone. Now the soreness remained, but her body had rebuilt itself around it. Although she hadn't recovered the weight she'd lost after the surgery. Thin wrists, and a face with more lines and shadows than she was comfortable with. Had her cheeks always looked that hollow? Had she always had those dark marks under her eyes? She didn't want people to look at her and think she was ill. She was fine, now, even if it was difficult to leave the sofa. Her well-deserved throne of agony.

The studio was crammed full of shelves, books, statues, clay, and stone dust. It opened up to a balcony offering a view of Madrid's orange tiled roofs. Pieces from a broken mirror hung outside to scare the pigeons. The pots of money plants and the calabash were still green – Pedro must have been watering them.

"Ven." She asked the girl to stay on the stand placed in the middle of the room. "Quieta," Carmen ordered once the girl was up there. "I'm going to sketch you."

She pinned a piece of paper to the board and took the charcoal. The sunshine filtering through the balcony illuminated the snowflakes of dust falling about the girl. She wore Pedro's nightgown and was barefoot. Her legs were covered in a dark fur, which contrasted with her blond, almost white mane of hair. Her blue eyes looked beyond the walls, face pale as winter clouds. Like an apparition, the girl didn't match any of the objects in the room. She didn't belong there.

"Quieta. Very good." Carmen drafted the tall, angular body, paying special attention to the large hands.

"You are going to be my model for my St. Ciarán statue, are you okay with that?" Carmen liked to chat when she was drawing. "When I got that commission from the Irish college I thought it was shit, I don't even give a fuck about Dios, all the saints and…But I needed the money, after the…And then I found you, and St.

Ciarán was kind of a funny thing, I bet you didn't know he was always riding a cow, ha! Now, we're in Spain so I thought it'd be funny if he rode a bull instead. Wait, I'll show you."

She started looking through the pieces of paper she kept in boxes until she found the big rolled canvas that depicted a large bull's head. "Mira."

She opened it out.

The girl started screaming.

Carmen thought she was in a dream. The girl had never made any sound at all, not since the day she had rescued her, not even when she was treating her wounds.

The girl leapt down from the platform and ran towards the locked door. She tried to open it. She kept on screaming, kicking the door, banging her head against it. Carmen watched her, fascinated. Finally, she came to her side and grabbed the girl's wide shoulders.

"No tengas miedo, don't be afraid," Carmen whispered. Then she slapped the girl's face. The screams died.

Lesson 3: Hazlo, desnúdate, no tengas vergüenza

Carmen hid the picture of the bull before bringing the girl back to the studio. She didn't quite understand how the girl tolerated Éboli, Carmen's one-eyed cat, but was terrified by a picture of an animal.

She made the girl pose. Sitting on her knees.

Lying on the floor, head twisted towards the balcony. Standing, staring at the floor, embracing herself.

Carmen's favourite parts were the girl's large, bony hands and feet, robust like the roots of an oak. Her face was fascinating too: a wide forehead, small eyes the colour of a sunless day, broken nose, full cheeks and a modest mouth of thin lips. It was as if an artist had started carving a classic Greek bust – such as the ones Carmen had copied at the San Fernando's Royal Academy of Fine Arts – but one night had decided, drunk, to add the features of unrequited love. You could still feel the rage. The mixture didn't work, but that's what made it appealing.

Carmen left the sketchbook on the side and got the scissors. The girl didn't move. The scars on her arms and hands proved she was well used to sharp objects.

"That's better," Carmen mumbled after trimming the locks of hair that shadowed the girl's face. She kept sketching, marvelling at the girl's figure, which was just vaguely alive, like the best- carved statues. This girl, she couldn't be more than seventeen. A peasant, perhaps, or a nun. Or a prostitute. Carmen didn't care.

By the twelfth day, Carmen had enough studies of the face, hands, legs and feet.

"Desnúdate. Take your clothes off." She mimicked the action. "I need to see the whole thing."

The girl, sitting on the platform, blinked.

"Good grief." Carmen started unbuttoning the girl's nightgown, but she crossed her arms over her breasts and curled in on herself, tight as a stone.

"¿Tienes vergüenza? Are you ashamed?" Carmen stopped pulling at the girl's clothes. "You can't, look, you're my model. I need this."

She tried to grab her again, but the girl rolled on the floor and started banging her head against the marble.

"Stop that." Carmen stood up, showing her hands. "I'm not touching you, okay?"

The girl went back to her original curled up position. This was like trying to convince Éboli to get into the basket, when she'd moved from her ramshackle room to Pedro's apartment. She didn't want to oppress the girl's wilderness, though. She needed that for her statue, not just the fear.

She knelt down by the girl and whispered: "We are both women. Why do you feel ashamed?"

The girl closed her eyes but kept scratching her arms. She smelt of rancid sweat and oily hair – Carmen should remind Josefa, the maid, to wash her more often. She grabbed the girl's chin.

"Look at me, no tengas vergüenza."

The girl closed her eyes more tightly. Fresh blood ran down her arms. Carmen clicked her tongue.

"Very well."

She stood in front of the girl, unbuttoning her own blouse and her brown skirt. She didn't wear any lingerie when she was at home: she always found it annoying, like dressing in another person's skin. She looked at her own breasts, crowned with pink, hairy nipples. The purple stretch marks on them were tentacles under the flesh. A collection of sharp bones protruded from her body: hips, hands, wrists, knees, ankles. Blades struggling to open the dry skin. She hated that old leather colour and the unfamiliar smell. And, of course, the horror. That bloated abdomen, adorned with a trail of pink stitches starting below her navel and hiding under the black hair of her sex. The scar was six months old, but still felt tender. Carmen scrubbed it as if she could erase it. She cringed, enjoying the pain. She lifted her eyes and discovered the girl staring at the scar.

"Do you like it?" she said, taking the girl's hand and making her feel the stitches. "They took everything out."

The girl's cold fingers on her belly were light as flies.

"You know what a woman is? A woman is a vessel containing two fallopian tubes, two ovaries, and the most important thing: a womb. Well, I don't have any of that any more. What am I then?"

The girl hadn't stopped looking at her for a second.

Carmen felt exultant.

Lesson 4: ¿Tienes hambre? ¿Tienes hambre? ¿Tienes hambre?

By March, Carmen couldn't stand the girl's silence any more. Yes, the girl knew how to pose. She could stay immobile for hours in the studio, even naked now. And that was all.

Carmen knew she had tried hard. Josefa took the girl to the lavatory every morning, afternoon and evening, but Carmen was the one bathing the girl on Sundays. She would fill up the tub with almost boiling water. Brush in hand, and limb by limb, she made sure the girl's skin was bright as the moon, although sometimes the hot water, or the scars, filling with fresh blood, ruined the result. Carmen wanted to enjoy it – the cleansing of the body as an attempt to see through the girl's soul – but it was more like emptying the cat's tray when Josefa was not around.

Carmen was also the one feeding the girl. She knew food had to be important – that was how babies bonded with their mothers, by the tit. She sat next to the girl, holding spoons full of chorizo and lentil soup to her lips. When pushed, the girl would open her mouth and chew, faintly. And that was all.

One day Carmen thought that, if the girl starved, she would end up speaking or calling for attention in some other way.

"Don't give her even a colín, Josefa, you hear me?" She ordered the maid.

"But Señora, the poor creature is already thin as a baby bird."

Since the Republic, it seemed that everyone had the right to be opinionated. That's why servants such as Josefa had begun to argue with their employers. Dios, the other day she even asked Carmen what she thought of women gaining the right to divorce, and why she didn't go to church with Pedro.

"Josefa, I told you. Don't go behind my back, you hear me?"

"Sí Señora. No food for the girl," the servant replied, the tone of her voice showing how little she approved of Carmen keeping a foreign girl in her house – a girl mature enough to get married and birth babies – when she didn't have children of her own.

"¿Tienes hambre? You're hungry, aren't you?" Carmen asked the girl during second day. The girl seemed paler, but it may have been because of the early morning light.

"¿Tienes hambre?" Carmen kept asking her. "Comida." She picked up a chocolate from the box she was holding and chewed it noisily. It was slightly mouldy – it had been there since Christmas. Nothing. She opened her mouth to show the girl. Nothing. She licked her finger and drew a chocolate line on the girl's lips. Nothing.

"Very well. Sketching time, then."

In the studio, Carmen tried to concentrate on the girl's thighs and the way they led into the elegant sphere of her kneecaps.

"I'm done with you." Carmen slammed down her notepad. "Why don't you even try? You're not making any effort, you idiot."

Carmen threw the charcoal at her. It hit the girl in the chest, leaving a black mark. The girl twisted her head towards the balcony.

"I'm so tired of you."

Carmen left the studio and went to her room to dress up: a light elegant coat and a scarf over the old blue dress she wore for painting. She walked down the street, cursing and smoking. Once she arrived at El Mercado de San Miguel, she bought everything she could think of: fresh tomatoes, pomegranate, anchovies in vinegar, mussels in tomato sauce, figs, goat cheese, olive paté, three loaves of bread, ham, sugar-coated cherries, garlic, fine herb salami, chorizo, and lemon cream. Returning home up the street was hard work. Sweat poured from everywhere; her coat was heavy on her shoulders, and her scar pulled her skin as though a wild animal was biting her. She drank a glass of Tempranillo as soon as she reached her kitchen. Then she organised the food in dishes and bowls. She opened the living room curtains. They only used that space when Pedro's mother and sister visited, the first Sunday of every month – a dreadful event, in which Pedro's mother would systematically condemn the newest laws passed by the Republican government, while Pedro avoided her gaze, like a good son, too polite to contradict her. Carmen unfolded the velvet tablecloth they only used at Christmas. She brought the vase of withered red carnations from her bedside table to decorate the room.

Carmen sat the girl at the table. She used her silk scarf to tie her hands to the chair, so she couldn't grab anything. Feeling generous, she decided to ask for the last time.

"¿Tienes hambre?"

The girl didn't react.

All the different smells combined in her nostrils, and Carmen felt both hunger and repugnance at the feast. Since the surgery, food and sex were all the same to her: a rather boring activity one had to perform more or less frequently in order to be considered healthy. She started licking the sugar-coated cherries, hoping their sweetness would trigger her appetite. Next were the sour anchovies, accompanied by goat cheese and chorizo. Éboli jumped on the table and started chewing the fish, fat drops of oil hanging from her whiskers. Carmen already felt quite full, so she licked at the lemon cream to help her swallow the salami and the garlic. She looked at the girl while sucking the fat from the ham. She *had* to be hungry. Carmen bit into the fresh tomatoes, pretending she was not already full. The girl hadn't eaten in two days. Hunger controlled everyone, animals and humans alike. The girl couldn't be any different, but there she was, sitting, looking her right in the eye. Carmen drank more wine, feeling slightly sick. She finished the lemon cream and chewed on the figs and the chocolate truffles. She opened and sucked the pomegranate's insides. The food was heavy on her stomach, piling up and reaching her throat. She unbuttoned her dress: her forehead was sweaty and her cheeks burnt.

"¿No. Tienes. Hambre?" Talking was difficult. She forced a slice of bread, covered with olive paté, into her mouth.

The girl didn't blink.

With her stomach beating in painful spasms, Carmen tried to get up, but she couldn't move.

Lesson 5: La niña es buena. La niña aprende español. ¿Cómo te llamas, niña?

Carmen decided to take the girl out for the first time in April. They went to La Institución on a Sunday. Carmen had spent too many hours speaking in Spanish to the girl, writing down the simplest sentences. Sometimes the girl would look at the page, but she never made any effort to take the pen, and when she finally did, she used it to poke the wounds in her arms. However, she knew how to hold it, which meant that, at some point, she had also gone to school.

"She just doesn't want to, damn her," Carmen said to Pedro. "Have you seen her arms? She won't stop scratching until the bone shows. No fleas, nothing: just for the sake of it. She did the same with food before, when she refused to eat properly, remember? But I made her grow out of it, oh yes, I did."

"I told you to wrap her hands in bandages so she can't scratch. And call the doctor."

"Fuck doctors. They pulled me all apart for no reason."

"They saved your life." Pedro put on his jacket before heading to church. When he kissed her, Carmen felt his despair. He thought she was ungrateful.

She tried to get the girl dressed, but all her own clothes were too small and too tight. She took one of Pedro's shirts, then put a coat over the girl and covered her hair with a handkerchief. She considered covering the girl's eyes too, as she used to do with Éboli when she needed to bring her out onto the streets, caged inside a bamboo basket. Like the cat, the girl might panic, or run.

Carmen squeezed the girl's hand all the way to La Institución, but the girl didn't seem distressed by the crowds or the noise. She was familiar with large cities. They entered La Institución through the back doors. Being a Sunday, there was no one on the premises, apart from Mauro, the gardener, tending to the pink oleanders.

In the corridors, the racket of the students had been substituted by the murmur of acacia leaves. The sun created golden pools on the floor. Instead of teenage sweat, Carmen smelt lavender from the garden. It was in those moments that she realised how much she hated people. Loneliness improved every experience. That's why she liked statues. Their beauty required silent worship. No stupid chatting, no foolish demands.

They entered Carmen's workshop. The scent of clay and wood powder lingered in the air.

"Siéntate, sit down." Carmen led her to the first row of benches. Then she wrote on the blackboard:

LA NIÑA ES BUENA.

LA NIÑA APRENDE ESPAÑOL.

¿CÓMO TE LLAMAS, NIÑA?

"Ven, ven y escribe. Come and write for me." She copied the first sentence deliberately slowly.

"Here." She gave the girl a piece of chalk and, for a change, the girl held it.

"And now, you write." Carmen lit up a cigarette and sat on a bench at the back. The girl rolled the chalk in her fingers and then brought it to the blackboard. She pressed too much and the chalk broke. Dios, sometimes she seemed retarded.

"I'll bring you some books. Wait here."

Carmen left the room. The garden was still awakening on that late April day. Lavender, pomegranate and lilac trees, ivy and yellow jasmine, all bloomed in the sunshine. She sat on a stone bench under the sun and lit another cigarette. She loved that garden. She didn't know what to do to reach the girl, though. Taking her to the doctor was the only thing left, but there was the risk that they would want to do something weird to her, lock her up in an asylum. Compared to that, the girl was better off with that crew of gypsies from which Carmen had rescued her.

Carmen got up, went to the small children's classroom and picked *Cuentos de Perrault* and *El Mundo Maravilloso*. After the surgery, she thought she'd never be interested in such things again. When she retraced her footsteps, the door to the workshop was open. Carmen's heart jumped to her mouth at the thought that the girl had gone away – forever.

She found her in the garden, beside a young orange tree. Someone knelt in front of her, like a shepherd worshipping a saint.

It was Mauro, the gardener, looking under the girl's coat. "What the hell are you doing?"

The gardener turned and stood up, but he didn't seem ashamed. "Sorry, Señora, I found this girl in the garden. Must be a beggar." Carmen realised he didn't know they were together.

"Take your filthy hands off her, you bastard. I'm going to tell the principal about this."

"What? She's just a beggar! I was just trying to ask

her..." Mauro said.

"Go away," Carmen threw one of the books at him. "Go away, go away," she kept shouting.

"I did nothing, Señora!"

"Go away."

The gardener left.

The girl pulled a tiny green orange from the tree.

Lesson 6: Mujer, hombre, pechos, vagina

Her moan was unexpected, water spouting out from sterile rocks. "Are you…?" Pedro gasped.

Carmen untangled her body from his. Cold air rushed through her lungs and relieved the burning between her thighs. She let her body expand, free, on the mattress. Her stomach growled. No matter how hungry she felt, thinking about food nauseated her. Painful echoes in her belly reminded her of how empty she was, below. Nothing could fill the space. The dense fog of tobacco smoke did the trick, though. She wanted to turn into a ghost: beyond flesh and body. Like the girl. She sensed the girl was in the room with them, too. Somewhere. That moan she'd heard a minute ago – it had to be the girl.

"You alright?" Pedro murmured.

"Don't touch me." Carmen sat on the bed, cross-legged. She didn't mind being naked in front of the girl. After the long evenings posing in the studio, nudity was what they shared. But in front of Pedro, she felt disgust for her withered skin, her dry sex. She shouldn't have taken Pedro's hand earlier that night to place it on her lap. She couldn't stop thinking about Mauro kneeling in front of the girl, peeking under her skirt. She thought she needed to be touched again, but the need was all gone. Like the memories from childhood, sex was something she knew had been agreeable once, but now seemed unreal.

"Carmen, I wanted to do this. You wanted to, too," Pedro said.

"I…it's disgusting, everything is…dead. Wrong."

"You're beautiful," he whispered, kissing her naked shoulder. Carmen smelt his onion-soaked sweat.

"Today I took her out." Carmen said.

"You mean…?"

"Yes."

"No way."

Carmen reached for her mother of pearl box under the pillow. She wondered where the girl was hiding. The wardrobe?

"Not now." he complained. She lit one of the cigarettes.

"Dios, Carmen, did anyone else see her? La señora de Rabadán? You promised me we'd take her to the nuns after you're done with the statue." As always, Pedro cared only about appearances.

"I brought her to La Institución." Carmen sucked her cigarette to quiet her stomach.

"Did Yebra…?"

"It's Sunday. Your dear friend, Yebra, was not there."

Don Alonso Yebra ran La Institución. His expertise lay in Philosophy and Latin, nothing to do with Pedro's meteorological science. He said that Yebra was like a father, but they behaved more like a pair of annoying teenagers.

"There was this gardener, Mauro, you know him, right? He tried to touch her, in a nasty way. Dios, that's the first thing mothers teach their daughters. The woods, the bad wolf…Snow White, right? Wait, was it Little Red Riding Hood?"

"She's not your daughter. We don't know who she is, or where she comes from."

"I know, I know." Perhaps the girl was behind the door. How or when she had got there, Carmen had no idea.

"She needs a doctor," Pedro stated.

Carmen sighed.

"I want you to take her."

She didn't reply.

Pedro slung his gown over his shoulders and walked out of the room.

Carmen waited until she heard the door to Pedro's room closing. Then, she checked under the bed. The girl was there.

"You don't need to be scared."

The girl climbed onto the bed and curled in a corner, just like Éboli, who was at her feet.

"I know you've also been thinking about the gardener," Carmen whispered in her ear. "And now we've scared you. But you're a mujer, cariño. You need to know about these things."

Carmen put her hands on the girl's breasts. They were like small apples under the flannel. The girl was docile as a piece of clay between her hands.

"Pechos." Carmen reached between the girl's legs. "And you also have a vagina." After the illness, her vagina had turned into a piece of fabric stitched to her body. It didn't even have a smell of its own any more.

The girl started munching on her hands, wrapped in cotton strips.

"It's okay, it's okay, cariño." Carmen held the girl's warm body closer. Cheek to cheek. Legs interlaced. Having Pedro inside her had felt painful and wrong. The girl's skin smelt like rain, and it was softer than his.

Lesson 7: Para, sobrino

The following Monday morning, Carmen woke to find the house in silence. Pedro was taking water samples from the river Manzanares with his students, and Josefa had a free day. The sun coming from the kitchen window gave Carmen a headache. She forced a glass of water down her throat whilst looking at the last sketches of the girl. Something was missing, and until she found it, she couldn't start making the first clay models. It was a very hot spring: another dry year, which didn't exactly support Pedro's theory that the future held a torrent of never-ending rains.

When she came back to the room, the girl was standing on the bed, looking at the wooden crucifix hanging on the wall. Her fingers caressed the carved edges and the beautiful thighs of the agonised Jesus.

"Do you like it?" Carmen opened the doors to the balcony. "The only thing I brought from Menorca. It was my mother's. I thought I could sell it. She treated it like it was made of gold, but his face reminds me of all the shit I left behind." Carmen put on a red flowered kimono and sat at her dressing table. She watched the girl in the mirror. "Para. You're going to drop it." She threw a hairbrush at the girl.

Carmen frowned at the yellowish patches on her own face. The peach-coloured freckle on her temple seemed to be turning into a wart and, without her painted eyebrows, her eyes resembled two dirty holes. Three thick hairs grew on her chin. Purple veins covered her nose. She raised a hand and touched the lump of flesh hanging loosely on her neck.

A soft meow. Éboli had entered the room. Carmen picked her up and sniffed her odourless fur.

The girl approached them, studying the toiletries spread out on the table. Carmen had never been that interested in make-up, but now she had to make sure she looked like a woman. The sun entering from the balcony bleached the girl's skin whiter, and her blond hair glowed as if she wore a saint's halo. The girl opened a jar of scarlet lip paint and dug her index finger into it.

"You don't need that." Carmen swept the bottles and jars to the floor. The aroma of lavender drifted up to poison the air. Éboli jumped off her lap.

"Being a mujer is a hassle, cariño. And dangerous."

Yes, they said things were changing fast, and women would be able to vote in the next municipal elections, at the end of the month. Yet, if Carmen could have chosen, she would have been a man. No void to fill inside. No waiting for freedom and privileges.

She opened Pedro's side of the wardrobe and took out one of his suits and a white shirt. She searched through the drawers to find a belt and braces. The girl arranged the clothes on the bed to make a human shape.

"That's it. You can be whoever you want to be, can't you? Sit here, on the corner, and put on the shirt."

The girl took the sleeveless shirt and passed it around her neck over her nightgown.

"No, no. Come, let me."

Carmen unbuttoned the dress. The girl's ribs were no longer visible. She had peach nipples and a line of black fur down her stomach. She was an exotic creature. Her waist was wide, so the trousers didn't look bad on her, once Carmen adjusted the belt.

The girl scratched the satin on the waistcoat and licked the buttons on the jacket's sleeve. She was tall enough to be a young man. The white skin and the absence of thick facial hair had an easy explanation: he was a foreigner from the North.

"Aren't you the prettiest thing?" Carmen said, taking the girl's face in her hands. The girl's cheeks blushed apple red. The broken nose added some roughness, like the thick trail of blond hairs on her virgin lips. Carme tried to remember if, when Pedro was younger, his skin had ever been that fresh. She had felt a similar vigour when they kissed, under the old apple tree in the garden of La Institución.

"I'm going to call you Ciarán. Like the Irish saint."

The girl played with the belt's buckle. "Ciarán, Ciarán…" She started imagining ways of giving the girl a past. "You're my sobrino, the only son of my older sister who…" Carmen sat on her dresser stool and picked up a jar from the floor. She needed to find a way of explaining this story that couldn't be questioned. "Who went away, to Ireland, and married there, but now she's ill." Yes, Ireland was far away enough for everyone to accept the story and also the girl's distinctive appearance. "She's dead in fact, what a pity." With a sister out of the picture she'd become a generous, compassionate relative. "That's why I brought Ciarán to live with me." Carmen finished, satisfied with a story that had only taken her a few moments to devise. The girl dug her pinkie into the ivory foundation and licked it. "You're still too young, too innocent. You need me, don't you?"

Ciarán smiled and moved to caress Éboli on the arm-chair.

Lesson 8: El Jardín de las Delicias, tranquilo, ¿qué te pasa?

Carmen walked down El Paseo del Prado holding Ciarán's arm. The sun filtering in through the poplars and acacia trees made her sneeze. She shook the yellow acacia seeds from her dress. Summer was a messy explosion. Pigeons crowding in the fountains along the Paseo, children chasing the pigeons, mothers chasing the children, pushing trolleys that scratched the cobblestones. Artists sold watercolours of this scene, which smelt of apples, pigeon droppings, sweet Moscatel wine, and the stagnant water of nearby ponds. Carmen needed a quiet, wintry place. She headed towards the Museo del Prado, stopping to let Ciarán admire the cleanliness of the Doric pillars and marbled portico at the entrance.

"You know who the man sitting there is?" Carmen pointed to a sculpture on a high pedestal. Ciarán held a hand above his eyes.

"It's Velázquez, he was the king's painter. Come."

Inside, the chilly air tasted of dust and ancient oils. They rushed through an empty corridor. People preferred sitting on the Jerónimos hill outside, where their apples and Moscatel wine attracted wasps and red ants. Ciarán jumped to step only on the black tiles. Carmen laughed and pushed him.

They entered a domed room on the ground floor. Nine Classical Greek statues stood in a circle. Some of them had no head, and many had lost their delicate hands. The creases in their light tunics were still perfect, though. Carmen caressed a delightful kneecap. Ciarán remained on the threshold. He looked at the amputated figures with apprehension, as if they were patients from a hospital room.

"Want to see something colourful?"

Ciarán's eyes said yes. Since Carmen had named him, communication was easier. With a backstory connecting them – he was Ciarán, her nephew – she felt closer to him. He was still getting used to Madrid and the Spanish language, but that was something she could relate to. Carmen had arrived in the capital at nineteen, after having spent all her life on the remote Mediterranean island of Menorca speaking Menorquín. She found the metropolis artificial, aggressive, predatory. At first, she had wandered through El Retiro Park, hoping to find some relief in nature, but the pickpockets and perverts hiding behind the bushes scared her. Museo del Prado had been her refuge. There she had discovered a picture that mirrored everything she felt inside, a piece of art that screamed chaos and life.

She and Ciarán stood in front of *The Garden of Earthly Delights*, the only painting on the yellowish wall. Carmen wanted to explain to him that the triptych depicted the journey of humanity through Paradise, Earth, and Hell.

"El Jardín de las Delicias," she said.

Ciarán let her hand go and approached the central image in the canvas. At first, his face was calm as a pond, eyes slightly absent, but soon, waves of emotion wrinkled his skin. He narrowed his eyes, drew his blond eyebrows together and pursed his lips so hard they turned whiter than his skin. His body shrank, he started trembling. He pressed both hands to his mouth. His scars were almost healed, but Carmen could hear him biting at the scabs. His face turned red and his eyes were like two overfilled glasses.

"What…?" She rushed to hold him, certain he was about to fall into pieces. Luckily no one was around. "Tranquilo, tranquilo. ¿Qué te pasa? ¿Qué te pasa?"

Ciarán started moaning and his cries bounced off the walls. Someone was going to come and ask them to leave.

"Tranquilo…" Carmen pressed a hand against his mouth as hard as she could. "Tranquilo."

While holding the boy, she tried to work out what disturbed him. It was something in the middle part of the triptych, the scene that depicted a carnivalesque parade running along a pond. Naked people rode on all sort of animals, from deer to dromedaries. The fearsome thing was among them, in the centre, huddled down. Pink.

The bull.

"We'll go now, we'll go." Carmen couldn't even remember the animal being in El Bosco's piece. Ciarán had stopped trembling. She let him breathe. His cheeks glittered with tears but his eyes were not a tempest at sea any more. He returned to the painting and touched the pink bull with his raw fingertips.

"El Toro está aquí," he said.

St. Ciarán of the Blessed Bull
1934-1935

A Glossary of Words

Carmen says I have the stupid Spanish of a child. To improve, I'm going to learn a difficult word from the dictionary every day and then, when I'm all done, I'll show her.

Araña

This is an insect of eight legs and a body that, sometimes, has the form of a pear. Other times the body is a dot and the legs thin and long, like the filaments of a tiny flower. Here, spiders are so small. When I see them in the corners, I let them be. If Carmen sees them, though, she squashes them with the heel of her shoe and says bicho asqueroso, which means disgusting bug.

But an araña can also be an enormous lamp. I know this because yesterday Carmen took me to La Institución's great hall to see the play her students have been preparing for months. There were other professors sitting next to us in the red velvet chairs. Some of them looked excited but Carmen whispered, "This play is pure nonsense, I hate it." And then, "I taught the girls how to do masks from papier-mâché, but they are so ugly."

The play began. A woman with hair in a silver bun had given me a flier. The title of the play was *Eresictión de Tesalia y su hija*. The girls appeared on a stage that was poorly lit. Some of them wore the ugly masks. Others were dressed as trees, and then someone was cutting all these trees. I didn't understand anything. Carmen got bored after a while.

"Do you know the only beautiful thing here?" She pointed up to the ceiling, where there was an immense lamp made of thousands of tiny glasses hanging from a golden skeleton. "The araña. Is it not sublime? And they didn't even bother to switch it on."

I looked at the araña again and I imagined that its golden arms were spider's legs and the glasses were rain-drops.

Botarate

This is what Carmen says to her schoolgirls when she's marking their sketches, or going around the sawdust-covered worktops. It means that the person in front of her could have done much better.

Carmen brings me to her class and wraps me in a white cloth that has a lot of creases – because creases are difficult, that's what she said while showing me one of the most famous statues ever, the *Pietà* by Michelangelo. I stay still. I'm very good at leaving my body and looking at it from the outside. Her students have an hour to sketch me. Sometimes I wink an eye at the girls and they giggle. They think I'm pretty. Once I heard them saying I was guapo, which means beautiful boy. But when Carmen goes down the platform, the schoolgirls stop whispering, and they look down with tightened shoulders. This is what Carmen says to them:

"Does this look human to you? Surely you've seen enough humans during your life to know what I mean."

"This has no depth. How are you going to carve it?"

She allows the best students to experiment with clay, but the results horrify her.

"Even a three year old can do better with mud from the garden. How can I let you use stone?"

"Do you think that carving marble allows any mistake? None of you deserve stone. At all."

I know she's secretly happy none of the schoolgirls can make me right. I pose for her alone in the evenings, no clothes on. She has lots of clay figurines of me, and has carved some on alabaster, too. She will start the real statue when they send the marble. It's coming from Carrara. That's in Italy.

She smiles at me while she breathes deeply, finishing the piece. "Now, this is it. You're not easy, cariño, but this is it."

She's no botarate.

Cielo

Cielo is above us and has a vivid blue colour every day. Sometimes there are clouds, but they are very white because sunlight soaks everything here. I can see the cielo from the library window. When I want to sleep alone, I come back to the library. I look at the distant blue mountains, trying to remember what life was like before Carmen and before Madrid, but nothing comes. This makes me sad. The library smells of dust and dried leaves. I pick up books. Before, I used to look just for pictures, because even when I understood the small letters, reading was like untangling a messy ball of yarn. Now, I never get bored. I don't think Carmen is going to like this. I was supposed to complete all the Spanish exercises, but instead I'm writing all these things that have nothing to do with cielo any more.

Churro

On Saturdays we go to drink hot chocolate with churros at San Ginés. Churros are sticks of dough fried in olive oil and coated with sugar.

"You'll sleep in on Sunday," Carmen says, as she drags me out of her bed. (Pedro didn't like me sleeping here but Carmen shouted at him and now I can be here whenever I want). I don't even have time to wipe the sleep from my eyes because soon we're on empty streets bathed in warm sun. Carmen dresses nicely – a skirt, a pink blouse, a hat, and her brown high heels, the ones which go click-clack when she walks. I wear a blue jacket and matching trousers, and Pedro's old fedora hat. He doesn't wear it because he doesn't like the colour. Too bright, he says. Carmen takes my arm and when we arrive at La Plaza Mayor she stops to buy a newspaper, and lights her first cigarette of the day. In San Ginés, she orders two hot chocolates and two portions of churros. She hands me new Spanish exercises or lets me work on this dictionary. I drink my chocolate while it's still piping hot and eat the churros quickly, but she takes her time. There is this little jar with a tiny dune of sugar inside. She leaves it while she decides she doesn't want churros anyway – so I can have extra – and drinks her chocolate in noisy sips. Sometimes she cuts one page off the news-paper and hands it to me:

"Read this and learn about Spain," she says. Today's article was all about Juanita Rico Hernández, the girl that was killed in a shooting because she was a socialist.

When she's done with the newspaper, she takes the little jar and pours the sugar down her throat, as if it was liquid. She closes her eyes like a gecko enjoying an August evening.

De rechupete

Pedro's mother said that once. I didn't know what she meant. I asked Carmen but she said "later, later." She doesn't enjoy Pedro's mother and sister coming here for lunch. This happens the first Sunday of the month. Carmen complains when she has to spend her Sunday morning in the kitchen. "It's your family, you should cook!" she shouts at Pedro, who is behind her, tidying all her mess and doing most of the cooking anyway. "You know, before the hospital I might have cared about your mother expecting me to cook for you all, but now I don't give a shit."

"You shouldn't have got rid of Josefa," he complains. "We need a maid." (I know why Josefa left. Carmen didn't like the way she looked at me.)

Pedro's mother and sister always dress in black, because Pedro's father died ten years ago and that's the rule. As soon as they enter, I have to be there, grabbing their shawls and coats, or Pedro's mother would start moaning about me being ungrateful, considering they took me into their home just because I'm Carmen's nephew.

So we were at the table eating cocido with soup and chickpeas, and Carmen was drinking Tempranillo wine and complaining about La Institución, and Pedro was explaining how the world will sink in two hundred years, and then Pedro's mother burped.

"Está de rechupete," she said.

This means that something is so delicious that you would lick the plate, and possibly your fingers too.

Embeber

I thought this meant to drink because it's similar to beber. We bebemos a lot of coffee during the day. Carmen bebe Tempranillo when she arrives home from La Institución.

"I needed that," she says after the first sip.

She keeps the glass close when she studies the stone.

"See this?" she told me the day they brought the block of marble. "You're inside this rock and I'm going to find you."

Pedro, on the other hand, prefers Jerez liquor. It has the colour of caramel and tastes sweeter. He drinks it at night, while he reads the Bible. Today I asked Carmen if I could embeber Jerez too. She laughed and said there was another bottle in the pantry but that embeber meant something different.

"It's when you're very focused on something, like when you're writing the dictionary and I call you and you don't even hear me because you're focused on filling the page. You're embebido."

Inside the pantry, I poured Jerez into a coffee mug and tasted the burning liquid. Liquor helps me sleep. It feels wrong sometimes, though, as if in a past life someone had warned me about the dangers of alcohol. There were women dressed in black and white. I used to live with them, I think.

I have tried to remember. Sometimes, when I'm about to fall asleep, I hear the waves, and the bed moves up and down, like a boat. And there is this strong smell: rotten eggs, shit, and wet straw. El Toro is waiting for me behind the bedroom door. Cold sweat drips down the nape of my neck. I cannot move.

Last night I went to the bed but Carmen was not there. These days she spends nights at the studio. The block of stone has no human shape yet: she's just carving bits here and there. She usually wears her dressing gown open, so I can see her big breasts oscillate when she leans on the marble.

Her skin is the colour of baked clay. Her body is soft and smells of rosehip syrup. Her hips are wide and welcoming. Her hands and feet are small, but with such minuscule details: knuckles, pink nails. I want to kiss her knee pits.

She puts olive oil in her hair, so it's bright and softer than silk.

Finflón

I was walking down Calle Preciados with Carmen. I had my new suit on despite the heat – it is black with thin white stripes – sweat running down my cheeks, like tears.

"Finflón!" a group of school children shouted at me. Kids with loose teeth and black, bruised knees.

"Finflón, finflón!"

"Fuera de aquí, carajo!" Carmen cursed at them.

I asked her if finflón was something bad and she just chuckled.

"Come, mira." She took me to El Corte Inglés, the small tailor shop where I got my black suit, so I could see my own reflection in the store window.

"See?" Carmen said. "You're all blond and red, your face is like a warm loaf of bread. That's finflón." She laughed.

Here, everyone has black eyes and dark hair, and their skin is not the colour of lumpy milk like mine, but a vivid flesh hue. Carmen says it's because I came from an island very far away. She says it's called Irlanda.

Gentileza

This means that someone paid you money to do something you like anyway.

"It's only for the money that I'm teaching all these dumbasses." Carmen complains about her job at La Institución almost every day. "Working, what do you know about it, huh? You haven't worked your whole fucking life. Why would you? You have me here, providing for you."

But then she regrets screaming at me and hugs me, kisses me.

"You're too young to work. You're too naïve for the world. You're just mine."

The other day Reme came from Barcelona. Reme is a painter and Carmen's friend from the San Fernando Royal Academy of Fine Arts. Her eyes are like hot coals and her voice resounds all over the apartment like a storm.

"Ciarán, is Carmen treating you well?" She winked at me and offered me a cigarette. Her hair was long and thick and smelt of chamomile.

"Can I see your sketchbook?" I asked her.

She smiled. "A sketchbook is very private. But I'll share it with you later."

Whenever Reme is around, the house fills up with laughter and Carmen doesn't curse as much. Even Pedro stops reading his Bible and his science books and we all go to the river Manzanares for a picnic.

Yesterday Carmen and Reme sat on the studio balcony, a cloud of blue smoke above their heads, chatting. They passed me their cigarettes now and again but mostly they ignored me. Reme had Éboli on her lap and a pad on top of her. She was drawing without looking. She was sketching us (Carmen and me) sitting in front of her.

"Where is Irlanda?" I asked them.

"Look it up in the atlas," Carmen replied.

"It's up north, in the Atlantic Ocean. They call it the Emerald Isle," Reme said. "Have you ever been there?" I asked.

"No, but I have been to Paris."

"Go look it up in the atlas, Ciarán," Carmen said. "What do you think?" She asked Reme about the stone.

"Is it true that this is for gentileza of the Irish College at Salamanca?"

"Yes, they're paying quite a bit. Pedro is friends with Unamuno, you know, so I was recommended. It has to be done next year, but I told them I'll probably take longer. Unless the angels come to work for me, that is."

"Funny they want to give the commission to the biggest atheist in Madrid."

"Reme, please. This is not about religion."

"When was the last time someone dragged you to mass? Before you had teeth to bite back?"

"No, you don't get me," Carmen said, laughing. "Do you think about religion when you see Bernini's *Ecstasy of Saint Teresa*?"

Reme stopped sketching and drew on her cigarette, blowing out a draft of smoke.

"It's the most brilliant representation of the female orgasm, don't you think?" Carmen added.

Holganza

Carmen says it is holganza, which means that we'll have

fun, but I don't believe her. I don't want to go. She's angry at me because I'm afraid of El Toro. It follows me everywhere I go, lurking from every dark corner. That monster! If I drink Jerez liquor before I go to sleep it stays away, but its smell never leaves me. Carmen wants to bring me closer to El Toro. It's all because of the sculpture. She wants to carve me riding El Toro. That's why she's bringing me to a bullfighting ring.

I don't want to go. I don't want to. I don't want to.

Last night I shouted at Carmen but she shouted back and she said she's dragging me all the way to La Plaza de Manzanares if need be. Even Pedro came out of his room and I thought he was going to save me.

"Can you both keep the noise down? I'm reading," he said.

"I won't go," I said.

"Carmen?" He pointed at her with his book. "You said just until the commission is done."

"I need a bull to finish the statue."

"Ciarán is terrified," Pedro said.

"So what? He needs to get over it. And it's for the statue."

"Until the commission is done, you hear me? Then all this nonsense is over."

Pedro went back to his room and slammed the door. He didn't even look at me or speak to me. He never does. I'm less than a shadow to him.

I don't want to go.

Carmen keeps saying, "It's for your own good, cariño. You'll thank me later."

I've taken the cross-necklace that hangs from Carmen's bed frame.

I don't want to go. I don't want to go. I don't want to

go. I don't want to go.

Invertido

I have to write this. I don't care if Carmen reads it afterwards but I have to write this.

The bullfighting happened at La Plaza de Manzanares on the eleventh of August. Beasts and burning sun. The venue was crowded. Burnt oil, caramel-coated almonds and Moscatel wine. Carmen got me some almonds but I couldn't even open my mouth. Sitting next to her on the terrace, I closed my eyes, trying to forget who I was or where I was. I could pretend I was asleep until everything was done. I imagined the moments afterwards, the sun with all its flames away behind the mountains. The healing night, and me back at home. I felt the cross-necklace stabbing my palm. It made me feel better. Something to hold onto. It reminded me of home, before Madrid.

"Hombre, Carmen."

"Bergamín, how are you?" Carmen's voice.

"Excited for the evening. You and the old men from the Institución? And the husband? Wait, who's this boy?"

I opened one eye. In front of us, there was a young man: pelican face, glossy hair parted on the right.

"Pedro is at home; you know what he thinks of bullfighting. And this is Ciarán, my nephew."

"Look at those golden locks! Didn't know you had such an exotic −"

"My older sister. She passed away, in Ireland, very sad." Carmen waved her fan. Her makeup was starting to melt. "It's his first time. Thanks for the tickets."

"Then he's a lucky boy. Don Ignacio is the bullfighter today, never thought he would be back in the arena, and yet he's been making history this season. I had tickets for Federico but he's still up north with La Barraca, theatre stuff, you know how it is."

A woman dressed in white passed by us.

"Pardon me," she mumbled, looking at me with dark, bulging eyes. She gave me a quick smile.

Carmen and José Bergamín went silent as the dead.

"I heard Federico cannot stand being in the same place as Encarna," Carmen whispered, and I could see she was looking down the lower tiers, where the woman in white was sitting.

"Yeah, well, Don Ignacio is a real Spanish gentleman, but it's getting a bit expensive for him to keep both the wife and Encarna. And talking about Encarnita, she's driving everyone crazy, not just Federico."

"Who is Federico?" I asked.

"Ha. Didn't you tell your Irish nephew about Spain's finest poet?"

"Hush, José. Ciarán doesn't need to get involved with that bunch."

"Wait, am I not one of that bunch? You offend me."

"You are another real Spanish gentleman, José." Carmen smiled. Then she turned to me. "You need to stay away from Federico, hear me?"

I was feeling a bit sick. The heat and the fear.

"He's an invertido."

"What?"

"He likes other men. In a loving way, I mean."

Jolgorio

The library, where I'm writing now, is quiet, but I can still hear the enormous jolgorio in the arena when the show started. Jolgorio includes screams, drunk songs, people hitting the floor with their feet, and women shouting that they sell cider. The bullfighting started. I didn't want to watch.

"Don't close your eyes." Carmen sank her nails into my arm. It hurt, but not as much as my heart, threatening to explode inside my chest.

"Yeah, you don't want to miss anything, chico, I'm telling you, there's no bullfighter like Don Ignacio," José added.

First, some lancers came out, sitting on the horses straight as sticks. Then, a group of men wearing golden suits of light, the matadores, came, carrying their red capes folded over their arms. Just one of them was dressed in glittering blue.

"Don Ignacio, there he goes." José clapped when the blue matador walked to the side. "What an artist."

People shouted at them, asking for challenges, blood, danger. El Toro appeared.

I started crying so hard that I couldn't breathe. The smell came back again. Boiling tarmac. Half-digested beef. I was so afraid my body would switch off. That it'd go numb, and my mind would get lost in an endless limbo all over again. Yes, I know what limbo is. It's the place where thousands of babies wait. Unbaptised babies. And children. And all sorts of crying creatures.

"Take it easy! What's the matter?" Carmen said. "Look, it's very far away, don't you see? Look, look at that horseman, he's going to stab the bull, so it won't be too fierce, see? It's okay, the bull can die, it's not a monster, it's…"

But I couldn't possibly look. I swear.

Kiosko

"Chico, why are you so scared?" José asked.

"Go and get some Moscatel, por Dios. It'll do you good," Carmen ordered, putting the money in my hand. The jolgorio followed me until the closest kiosko – the portable shop where they sell wine and sweets. There was a woman inside, with a Manila shawl on her shoulders despite the heat. Rotten apples and green pulp were everywhere in the stand. She sold cider. The apple scent was somehow familiar and it calmed my sickness. Cattle eat apples during the winter months, I remembered. Horses neighed behind my back and the crowd screamed.

"¡OLÉ!"

I came back to Carmen and José with my eyes fixed on the ground and tears pouring down into the glass of cider.

Lauréola

"¡OLÉ!"

The crowd screamed again. El Toro could barely move, pink stakes hanging from his flesh. Pools of blood all over the arena. Don Ignacio shown him the red cape one more time. El Toro charged but in the last moment he stumbled. Don Ignacio twisted and sank a silver sword into El Toro's neck.

"¡OLÉ!"

The crowd applauded.

"¡Olé Don Ignacio!" José stood up.

I couldn't take my eyes off the scene. El Toro was still standing, muzzle dripping red. A dark and cursed beast.

He was the horror, yes, but not the origin of that horror. He was nothing but a mirror, a reflection of the crowd, the smiles and the cheers and the screams and the joy of those who watch pain and are amused by it.

El Toro stood, his horns like crescent moons.

"OLÉ!"

Don Ignacio approached a second time, a new sword in his hand.

El Toro's legs trembled, his body glittering in sweat and blood. He charged one more time. Don Ignacio aimed at El Toro's chest.

El Toro fell to the ground, the first sword sticking out of his body.

He dragged the matador down with him. Dust and shiny clothes.

Don Ignacio threw the sword away and tried to get up. El Toro sank his horn in the matador's thigh.

Blood rained out.

Hanging onto the horns, the matador shivered like a scarecrow. People howled.

Blades in hand, the riders and the other matadores came running, poking El Toro until he let go.

And fell.

"¡OLÉ!"

I could feel thousands of cold metal teeth biting inside my guts. People leapt to their feet and applauded the matadores.

"OLÉ!"

White-clothed nurses ran into the ring carrying a stretcher. El Toro lay in a puddle of blood.

And then, I saw it.

Bright. Clear.

A rush of fresh air cutting out the poisoned atmosphere. Lauréola, a soft light that lingered around El Toro for just a few seconds, then dissipated.

I knew it.

I got up and ran down the grades, my hand clenching round the cider glass. No one saw me.

Not even Carmen.

Down in the arena, I ran towards El Toro.

"Chico, chico! What are you doing?" One of the matadores followed me. I knelt down next to the monster.

"Chico, go away, it's…"

El Toro's eyes were still open, framed by thick lashes.

AO come here, bring your golden cattle, bring the sun, the moon, and all the beautiful things you have created. Strange words poured into my lips, spoken in mysterious tongues, like an incantation.

I opened his sticky muzzle with my fingers and poured the cider down. His sudden breath felt like fire on my hands.

Lloradera

Carmen is still crying today. I have never seen her like that, howling, saying she thought I was going to die. Yet I want to remember everything that happened, and I don't care who reads this.

As soon as I poured the cider inside El Toro's muzzle, he growled and got up on his four legs, shaking. His wounds kept bleeding and his left horn was garnet, but the rage was gone. A matador dragged me back.

"Chico, ¿estás loco? It'll kill you!"

They took me to the narrow infirmary of the bullring, where the doctors were trying to stitch up Don Ignacio, the wounded matador. It smelt of raw fish in there. I looked at Don Ignacio.

The same silver eyes of El Toro.

I still had some drops of cider. I offered him the cup.

He shook his head and turned his grey-skinned face the other way. He also knew it.

El Toro was alive, so he had to die.

Carmen keeps crying. She has been crying so much that the colour has washed away from her face and her features are about to disappear. She's like a wooden statue that has been way too long in a cellar, devoured by mould and termites. I don't recognise her. It doesn't make sense. What a lloradera, a storm of tears. Just a moment ago, I had to take her in my arms, my cheek on her cheek, to calm her. Carmen is becoming small and weak.

She also told me that they didn't dare kill El Toro again. They took him back to his ranch in Ayala and let him graze, still covered in blood.

Red drops hanging on the olive trees, and a scent of carrion under the violet twilight.

Mujer

Mujer means woman, but it's a word that I don't like. It confuses me. What is a mujer?

I scrutinise my body when I am alone in the bathtub. I can hide my breasts in my hands. My belly is soft. I have dark curly hair growing all over my thighs and my hips and if I comb them with my fingers I can feel the warm, purple labia. The same dark hair grows under my armpits, but it smells different there, like moss.

What is a mujer? Is it the opposite of man? Carmen is a mujer.

But she says, "I'm not a mujer."

Or, "There is nothing left inside. No mujer, either."

Carmen has big breasts with sweet pink nipples. Her body is warm when she sleeps by my side and I like to rest my head in the gap between her neck and shoulders. It smells like home, a bit like baked bread, but more subtle. When Carmen leaves her used lingerie in the room, I sniff it. Women smell nicer than men, they say.

But Carmen is not a mujer, because she smells of cigarettes and speaks over Pedro all the time.

"Show some respect to your husband!" Pedro's mother said to Carmen once. She said this whispering, but her eyes were bright with angry sparks.

Instead of answering, Carmen smirked.

Pedro's mother hit the table with her spoon. She wanted to smack Carmen in the face. Men hit their women when they don't behave, Carmen told me. For instance, Señora de Rabadán, our neighbour downstairs, the one with nine children, she always has fresh bruises on her face.

"If Pedro ever raised his hand against me, like that Rabadán bastard, I would get the kitchen knife and kill him in his sleep," Carmen told me.

But I know Pedro would never hit Carmen.

Is Pedro a man?

Sometimes, while she smokes, Carmen places her hand on her belly, like pregnant women do. But Carmen doesn't have a baby inside, just a knotty scar on the outside that goes from the belly button to her vagina.

She says they took everything out and now she's soulless. I was soulless, too.

I'm remembering now, bit by bit. I remember the women in black and white who taught me about Dios and the world. That must have been back in Ireland, the Emerald Island. I know they were nuns, and I was, too.

But now, I can be anything I want.

Nequicia

I have been thinking about this so much. Am I able to do any nequicia? Something bad, wrong. Against Carmen.

Am I able to hurt her?

Carmen is everything to me. She's transferring my soul to her piece of marble. She says she's making me immortal. But she doesn't look at me anymore. She doesn't speak to me. She just has eyes for the stone and everything else annoys her.

I can't betray her.

Ñiquiñaque

"It's not just a ñiquiñaque, you know."

There was a man with glossy hair and smart rat eyes sitting in Carmen's office when I went there to change the white cloth for my white suit. I had been posing for Carmen's third year students for two hours and now I had some spare time.

Ñiquiñaque means something stupid, insubstantial.

"Who are you?" I put the striped jacket over my shoulders and walked towards the man, cornering him against the door.

"Federico. I'm sure Carmen told you about me."

"Yes."

I remembered her warnings.

"I'm here to talk to you. I came all the way from Santander. For Ignacio."

"Who?"

"Ignacio Sánchez Mejías. The matador. He died last week." His voice sounded dry, like an oak tree broken after a storm.

"I don't know him. Go away."

"How sweet. I bet Carmen told you very nice things about me."

"She'll be back soon."

"Are you scared?"

"No, but Carmen will get anno–"

"They told me you didn't seem scared when you went down there and revived the bull."

I pushed him towards the door. He smelt of leather.

"The bull killed my friend," he said.

I stopped. In his silver rat eyes, there was something real.

"They don't call it murder, they say it's a miracle," Federico continued.

"Miracles aren't real," I said.

Silence.

"Carmen told you that? She's carving a statue of St. Ciarán, isn't she?"

"I'm Ciarán," I replied.

He smirked. He had purple circles under his eyes and his face was thin. Grief made him older.

"St. Ciarán now. You just performed a miracle. What kind of saint are you?"

I didn't know what to answer.

"I'm composing a poem for Ignacio," he continued. "I need details."

"Check the newspapers."

"I need the truth."

I left him in the room and went away. Carmen said

he's dangerous.

Obduración

Federico and I are friends now. We've met so many times. He kept coming to La Institución and wouldn't leave me alone until I spoke to him. Then we bumped into each other in the street. He asked me why I'm always carrying this notebook. I said it was to do Spanish exercises to improve my vocabulary. He asked to see it and, in the end I let him. He read some pages with extreme care.

"Ciarán, you're a writer," he said.

Now we meet in La Ballena Alegre to drink coffee whilst we talk, talk, talk. We talked about El Toro and Ignacio.

"What do you remember?" he asked.

"Silence. When El Toro attacked Ignacio, the jolgorio went dead."

"And what else?"

"The smell. It was like smoke, and inside the infirmary, iodine…"

"And what else?"

"Ignacio looked so frail. Like a dove."

It was so strange going back to that moment. It's like I have the memory but I can't see myself in it. I don't know what made me come so close to El Toro. Giving life back to him. I am still afraid of El Toro. But now, I feel closer to him, because he can die, too. And I can decide to save him or not. El Toro is mortal but I have Dios by my side. Dios is what protected me and what brought me down to the bullfighting ring. Dios is what I remember from before. Dios is in the cross-necklace I wore. Dios is what Pedro talks about, sometimes. A higher intelligence, he says. The only being that can make sense of all this chaos: elections, slaughters, famine, anger…Dios made me feed apple cider to El Toro.

I remember the smell of apples.

"You know what bullfighting is?" Federico asked me on another day. "It's a death ritual. Ignacio knew it. That's why he was there, that day. Death is coming closer. I can see it. El Toro lives and the bullfighter dies. Times are changing."

And just today, Federico asked me to join his theatre company, La Barraca, but I said no. And now he tells me that it's obduración, what I have. No less. This means I'm trying to resist what's good for me. He is wrong.

Carmen doesn't know anything. She's too busy with her stone – but Federico stabs my eyes with his eyes every time he speaks.

The block of marble now holds something that could be – barely – recognised as a human shape. Carmen works on it every day, and takes hours to clean out each tiny incision. She is sweating all the time, and pale. She has stopped eating. Every time she goes into the studio, Pedro rolls his eyes. I know he hates me.

Obduración. Not doing what's good for oneself.

Federico insisted on so much.

"They tell me you are with Carmen all the time, like her shadow. That's not good. Artists need solitude. I'm an artist too, I know what I'm saying. Leave Carmen alone and then she'll create."

I looked down.

"You care about her. Do you want to help her?"

Federico thinks I don't want to leave Carmen because I want her happy and her statue finished. But the truth is, I hate Carmen. I'm hating all the evenings when she contemplates the marble, instead of looking at me. I want to turn that stone into dust. I don't care about muses or creation. I want to leave Carmen alone, so her heart craves me and her skin howls for me.

Federico took my hands between his. He has a funny walk and he's short, but he has beautiful pianist hands.

"Ciarán, you are an artist too. You need to create. I know you feel it. Back then, when you saved El Toro…I bet you saw how all the pieces connected. Everything made sense, at that moment. Right?"

"Yes."

"I'll bring you out. I'll bring you out to the world. You'll perform more miracles. I know you will. You're St. Ciarán of the Blessed Bull."

Prístino

Federico brought me today to meet the people from La Barraca. The theatre company that has been going all over the "hidden and dirty Spain no one but us wants to see" for three years now. The members are tired, though. With all the strikes, there is no money coming from the government. Now the actors have to pay for the petrol, the clothing, the staging…

La Barraca was disappointed and sad. It's difficult to bring creative energy to the desolate Spanish villages when the actors are starving. They all wore blue: men had overalls and women dresses with white collars and buttons on the side. And the symbol of La Barraca pinned to their chest. A theatre mask on a wheel.

"We artists are like bulls," Federico talked to them with me at his side. "We are born in what we believe is an Eden, thinking we are the children of Dios. We believe nothing can touch us but the truth is, our destiny is already decided. We are flesh for the rich and the ignorant. Yes, they admire the beauty we create, but in the end, beauty is just another monster, and they kill the monsters like they kill bulls in the arena. We are like bulls and our lives have no other purpose than death, while wealth and ignorance cheer and stay alive."

"Yeah, I'm tired of illiterate peasants spitting at us. All the work for nothing, why do we even bother to go on the road?" a bulky man with sad eyes said.

"When the Republic gives money, then we go. We already work for free; do we have to pay for travel expenses too? And what else?" a young man with glasses and a jet-black moustache added.

"Federico, for you it's easy. Your plays are famous all over the world and you have money," a woman said. "But we need to feed ourselves and our families, pay rent…"

"Money? Who is talking about money now?" Federico replied. "Spain is a diseased body, there are convulsions everywhere. The Republic started to kill the old country, and the wages and the landowners telling us what to do, and when. And La Barraca is about a world without wages, without class, without money. It's all about sharing, and knowledge, and looking into every human being. You look into someone else's eyes and you see their soul, and you don't think about money, or violence, or rejection. Art is the answer. For women, for invertidos, artists, immigrants, peasants, students, travellers, thinkers, for the ones who believe in Dios but hate the fat bishops. Art is the only answer now, before death comes calling. Nothing is going to get easier. Did you think this would be a summer holiday, acting and having fun? Art is the only thing that matters now, art is all that will matter in the end."

Silence.

"We can't stop touring now, just because some say the Republic is doomed. We need to keep doing it, village by village, just like before. They need our stories, not the other ones, the horrors and the lies from the politicians. They need to be enlightened, these people, or they'll never be more than animals, cows and calves, and beautiful bulls, yes, but their lives will be carnage. Like all of us. We are treated like cattle. But St. Ciarán is with us. He saved El Toro."

"A saint?"

"Yes, but a real one. Spain is crumbling, and the poor claim flesh, and the rich claim blood, and we have new saints. Not the saints made from wood and wax, covered in blood and the wounds of martyrdom. Real ones. Ciarán can weep for us. He has real tears and has been blessed. He's come to look out for the underdogs, the forgotten ones. We have to believe in him."

"Is he going to turn our water into wine?"

"Or give us thousands of fish to eat?" Some laughed, but Federico hushed them. One of the women walked towards me.

"You are Ciarán?" She had the blackest hair, parted in the middle and combed into an unruly low bun. Her eyes were sweet liquorice.

"Yes," I said.

"Are you a saint, then?"

"I don't bleed. I'm not like your Jesucristo," I answered. I held her small, cold hands. She trembled.

"Isabel," Federico said. "I know it."

Then, he looked at La Barraca.

"The end is close. Shall we do this one last time? For art's sake."

He called me a prístino saint. I thought prístino meant clean (all the old statues of saints are mouldy and covered in dust) but prístino means 'primitive' or "original". Real.

Quitamotas

Federico has given me a big dictionary where I can look up new words. I remembered quitamotas. Carmen shouted that at me when I told her I wanted to go on tour with Federico and La Barraca. Federico promised me that he's going to teach me how to write stories. I want to learn. I love words. I love them and I need them. In exchange, I just have to act for him in his new play, *The Beautiful Beast*, which is all about me giving life back to the bull while Ignacio dies, all over again.

"He's a quitamotas," Carmen said. "You don't believe him for a second, do you? Acting? You? Don't make me laugh. You're my model and I taught you for years before you could be any good even at that. I was patient with you, so patient. I gave you life."

Quitamotas means someone who tells other people fake words and praises them so they can get what they want. A flatterer. But I don't think Federico is tricking me. I want to write and he's going to teach me.

Rahez

This was the last word Carmen told me when she got so, so angry at me. It's because now she knows about the play Federico just launched in Madrid. It's called *Yerma*, and it's about a woman who can't have any children. I know this because Federico let me read some of it. Carmen screamed, "how dare he." She thought he wrote of a childless, perverse woman to mock her and that I helped him. So she didn't want to see me, or listen to me. She locked me up in the library at home and swore to Dios and La Vírgen María she wouldn't allow me to come out until I returned to my senses.

"Young flesh is what you are, but you're rotting inside, you fucking monster," she howled, banging the door. "Fuck you, fuck you, fuck you!"

"I'm not an animal, stop treating me like one," I screamed back.

"You were a fucking feral creature when I found you."

And she called what I do to her rahez, which is the most evil thing one can do to another person.

In the middle of the night, the door opened. It was Pedro. He said nothing, but guided me through the house in darkness. He gave me a packed bag and his own coat before he put me in the street.

"I'm sorry," he said. "I thought you would help her get better."

I didn't answer. I knew he was giving me away to Federico, so he wouldn't have to see me anymore.

"Please, don't come back," he said.

He was freeing me from Carmen.

Sol

This is my favourite word, ever.

Sol is in the sky, always present, always warm. When I lived at Carmen's house, it used to project changing pictures onto the shelves and onto the white sheets of my bed. It tickled my eyelids in the mornings until I woke.

The morning sol appeared first in the library. It licked the oranges on the balcony and then spread through the living room, and the kitchen, and Carmen's bedroom, and Pedro's bedroom. The sol always disappeared in Carmen's studio, dying red beyond the tile roofs I could see from the window.

We're heading to Granada. My skin doesn't like the sol. It gets red and itchy. La Barraca people laugh at me and make me wear my new blue overalls and a hat even if it's so hot that I feel sweat running down my back, my upper lip and behind my ears.

Támara

We arrived at Colmenar today and we are in a támara, which is an orchard of palm trees. I never imagined that palm trees could be this tall and this greenish golden colour. They are like very thin people with long manes of messy hair. La Barraca wagons stopped under their shadow a few hours ago and we all rested and drank sangría and sang because we're very close to the sea – I can smell the salt.

I was sitting under a palm tree, writing, when someone came. An old man with a big nose and eyes that pierced me like bullets.

"This is my friend, Pablo Picasso," Federico said. "Pablo, this is Ciarán. He wants to be a writer."

"I heard about your miracles in Paris. I came all the way from there to meet you. And you want to be a writer?" He laughed. "You know about bulls, everyone tells me."

"I've met El Toro, yes."

"I've met El Toro too," he answered.

Federico went back to the actors, but Pablo sat in front of me and took a pad from his pocket. He started sketching with a red pencil in one hand, holding a cigar in the other.

After a while, I approached him to look. There were different sketches of a boy sitting under the palm tree, but his body was all wrong, as if the scene were reflected by a broken mirror. And a dark, horned ghost, lurked from the night sky.

"Why is the picture broken?" I asked.

Pablo – the painter – didn't answer, but gave me one page to keep.

Uñidura

Federico is teaching me how to write beautiful words. Today he taught me uñidura, which means the perfect and harmonious union between two different things.

"Music and words, for example, are two essences that come together in poetry, like lovers," he said.

I thought about that for a long, long time. There are these words I write in Spanish, that sometimes come slowly. And then, there are the other ones, that come in a different language: *AOcomeherebringyourgoldencattlebringthesunthemoonandallthebeautifulthingsyouhavecreated…*

I whispered these words once to Federico and his eyes got brighter.

"You're speaking English!" And then he said, in that other language, "*I speak English, too. Do you understand me?*"

"*Yes, I think so…*" My legs started trembling. "Why English? They told me I come from Irlanda."

"*They speak English in Ireland, too. And in America. That's where I learnt.*"

"*Why do I have* two languages inside my head?"

"*It's not a bad thing.* Why don't you write something in English, too? Do you remember enough?"

Uñidura.

Each evening, on the stage, Federico directs us as if we were his orchestra. We have already passed by Antequera, Mollina, and La Puebla. At night, he reads his poems aloud and the images dance in my soul like flames in the fireplace. Sometimes, Isabel liquorice-eyes comes to me when everything is quiet. We have to keep things secret because she's Federico's little sister.

"I'm already a woman," she told me the first night. It's true. Her belly is full of warm silk.

"Oh my..." she said the first time we braided our naked bodies. "You're a true inexplicable being. A saint. A mystery."

Uñidura.

I'm thinking about Carmen. I haven't seen her in such a long time. A long, long time ago, we were like one being. I remember the silence, and how she fed me the words. She was my voice when I couldn't speak, she was my body when I was just pieces. I miss her dark eyes; I miss her rough voice and the bony feel of her body.

Uñidura.

I've started writing this story – about El Toro y La Niña.

Vahaje

We just left Sevilla. I like to get up in the afternoons, like now. The ground is melting but we're close to the sea. When Vahaje blows (the sweetest wind of all) I can actually move my fingers – they are not swollen by the heat – and write. Sitting by my side, Federico writes too. He also likes silence to create. We're converting what we can only see inside our minds into something tangible.

Whiski (I couldn't find any other word starting with 'w')

We are heading to Cádiz. Yesterday we acted in a village close to Rota, and after the show, when everyone was lighting candles and the alcohol melted in the air, Federico came to me.

"Someone wants to see you," he said. "But you don't have to go."

"Who?"

He pointed out to the beach. I saw a man drinking from a bottle and gazing out to sea. He didn't seem to notice that the salty waves were licking his shoes. I recognised his sharp profile. I approached him.

"So here you are." Pedro drank more from his bottle of whiski, this liquor that smells as strong as petrol.

"You never spoke to me before. Never looked at me."

"I hated you. You destroyed everything. And they called you a saint." He laughed.

I looked at the sea. The image of a smiling skull came to my mind. A pearly laugh. "She's dying without you. She needs you. You have to come back."

He threw the bottle into the waters and grabbed my shoulders.

"Get off," I told him. "If she needs me…" I didn't dare to say her name. "She should come for me."

"She doesn't know where you are. I'd be mad if I told her you're with Federico. You know how things are. She doesn't want to get away from the sculpture, which is more of you anyway."

"You helped me escape."

"I thought I could get rid of you but I've realised that's not how it works." Pedro tried to grab my arm but I moved back. "She needs you."

"I'm not coming back. I like it here."

"You owe her, at least until she finishes the statue."

"I don't know."

I started walking away.

"I saw the painting of you in Madrid," Pedro screamed, over the sea sound. "Picasso, no less. The Saint and The Bull. It's great. But her statue will be better."

Xenoglosia

Xenoglosia is the blessing of being able to speak different languages. There are two languages living in my head and now I can't decide which one to use to write my story – *The Three Baptisms of La Niña de Irlanda* was Federico's suggested title when he read the first draft. He says once it's done, he'll give it to his friend José Bergamín and he'll publish it. All the different words and meanings are giving me a dreadful headache. I'm lying on the floor of the van and the other actors talk in whispers and Isabel is caressing my hair.

Writing the story is like tracing a path back home.

Yubarta

We were driving by the sea this morning when Eduardo stopped the lorry. "Yubarta, yubarta…" I heard them screaming.

I went out. The sun was rising. A splash in the distant sea. A whirlwind that broke the reflection of the sun into thousands of golden drops. "What's that?"

They told me they were whales, coming from colder waters. These kind of whales – yubartas – need the Mediterranean. Their bodies were enormous but graceful, and they moved as if the sea was the air that carried them away. They celebrated their uñidura with the vast, threatening sea. They were not scared.

I remember the sea, and the boat. I should write about them in my story.

Zubia

I was standing on the zubia, the wet field, when the sea approached me. White foam playing around my ankles, warm and delicious.

I am a yubarta.

I'm not scared of the immensity of the ocean.

I came here to enjoy its strength and the power of its embrace.

To kiss young Spanish girls from unknown villages and sleep with them in the barn.

To be alone with Federico. He undressed me and he smiled, because by contemplating me he understood.

"Another miracle," he said.

To hear the astonishment in the peasants' faces. To see the claps of our sad crowds.

To write what I couldn't remember. I've done all that already, and now I'll return to Carmen, and the statue will be finished.

Untitled

Attributed to
Ciarán de la Cierva*

* Original text written by hand in a booklet found with the personal notes and correspondence of Spanish sculptor Carmen de la Cierva, Ciarán's aunt and his supporter, with whom he lived in Madrid between 1931 and 1936.

I.

Once upon a time, there was a sunless island that smelt of wet grass and muddy rivers. Its sky was always dull, like eyes that can't cry.

And it was infinite.

Winds screamed over the woods all day.

And the trees never stopped dancing.

It rained every single hour.

And the fields were always satisfied.

On this sunless island there was a farm. There lived a milkmaid who was sick of the short days and the long nights. Misfortune had turned her golden braids to silver while her skin was still smooth. She had spent all her life digging out the mud and stones that covered her fields so her twelve cows could have some pasture. Her neighbours pitied her as she had recently become a widow. How could a single woman endure so much? And after all her efforts, she barely produced flavourless grass for the cattle and sour cow milk for herself and the baby inside her belly. She had tried to grow almost everything else: heather, corn, fern, birches and apple trees, but none of them took root. This woman longed for a sun whose warmth would caress the ground and encourage the seeds to pierce the ground, to bloom thicker and faster.

But her luck was about to change faster than the weathercock on her roof.

One night, the Widow with Silver Braids had the strangest dream. She was in the fields, but the cotton grass was high to her waist and there were apple trees full of ripe fruits. The wind was warm and carried the scent of silky petals unfurling. Bog orchids, heather and rosemary spread their scent. The woman's heart swelled in contentment. The sun was shining! The sky was clear blue with glowing clouds. She put her hand on her forehead and looked into the horizon. In the purple fields ahead, her piebald cows grazed happily. An unfamiliar black figure was among them: El Toro, a strong bull with horns as bright as two crescent moons. The Widow with Silver Braids was very surprised, as she never had enough money to buy a bull.

A deep, rough voice spoke to her. El Toro was very far away – just a tiny shape – but the woman knew the voice belonged to him.

"Do you want the sun?"

She felt the softness of the bog orchid's petals on her fingertips. They were as white and delicate as the baby she would hold in her arms in a few days.

"Yes," she said, feeling she'd never wanted anything as much. "Yes."

A fresh zephyr made the heather murmur. The woman turned back. Around her, the garden kept on growing: the leaves multiplied, the flowers opened, and the branches of the trees sagged and collapsed under the burden of their fruits. Her farm was nowhere to be seen. The wretched walls, the dirty windows, the flaking paint…everything was gone.

"You have to give me what you value the most, and I'll bring you the sun."

"My farm?" The woman asked.

"No." El Toro's silhouette was fixed on the horizon as a constellation in the sky. "Your daughter. I want to marry her."

The mother looked down to her belly, where the baby was enclosed, breathing quietly in its dreams. She didn't know if she carried a boy or a girl.

"She won't be unhappy because I'll give her everything she desires under the sun. Is this not what every mother wants? A wealthy suitor for her daughter?"

The Widow with Silver Braids picked a twilight-coloured apple from the ground. It smelt of abundance and merriment. She tried to be a sensible woman, but she had spent far too many cold nights alone. Rain had soaked all her dreams, and her only companions were bony cows with sad eyes. She didn't want her child to experience all those things.

The Widow bit into the crunchy skin of the apple, smiling as the sweetness filled her mouth. Under the sun everything looked better: even a bull seemed an appropriate suitor.

"Yes, if you bring me the sun, you can marry my daughter, I promise."

From that day on, the sun shone over the Widow with Silver Braids' fields while the rest of the country drowned under the crying sky. Her baby was born. The little girl, so young she was nameless, gave her first steps under the shade of apple trees, ran among heather moors and wore rosemary crowns on her wheat-coloured hair. The Widow and her daughter lived comfortably for many years until El Toro was a blurred image that rarely appeared in the Widow's nightmares.

II.

The bare branches of the trees scratched the sky when the Widow's daughter turned twelve and her first blood came, and that is how she gained the first of many names: the Girl with Apple Cheeks.

She sat by the window, counting the raindrops running across the glass. The blue clouds darkened the morning. Her cheeks were red and plump as the apples she was chopping into pieces. The apron on her lap was drenched, a tangy smell floating upwards like the promise of the storm outside. On the fireplace, her mother watched a pot full of apples bubbling. Cooking for the cattle meant that the pastures and the garden were dead. The winter was not too far away.

The Girl with Apple Cheeks took the pieces from her apron and threw them into the large bucket before the fireplace. She collected more fresh apples before coming back to the window. When she looked outside, the raindrops had turned to dust, tarnishing the glass. The sky opened and the sun shone again, weakly at first, like a child that has just woken up. The flattened grey grass unbent, turning green, then yellow. The mud dried, forming a path that led from the farm door to the fields ahead. Drops hung on the branches as diamonds, or were they newborn buds?

A dark figure strode towards the house, leaving a trail of velvety dust. The Girl with Apple Cheeks wanted to see who it was. A bolt of pain burnt into her palm. The apple flesh was drenched in crimson and she threw the treacherous knife away. The figure got closer.

The man had an enormous head, wide shoulders and a thick torso supported by thin legs on tiny feet, which bent the wrong way. He wore a three-piece navy-blue suit with a carnation on the lapel, red as the leather gloves on his hands. An orange tweed overcoat was hanging on his right arm. His Oxford shoes were black and white, and despite the dust covering them, it was obvious they were brand new. His face was hidden under a fedora hat.

Knock,

knock.

The Girl with Apple Cheeks found herself in front of the door. The sunlight added to the warmth from the fireplace making the house stifling. She needed to get out.

Knock,

knock,

knock.

"Mother," The Girl with Apple Cheeks called for her urgently, as though she was burning with some strange fever. She didn't understand that the sun was poisonous.

"Stay there." The Widow with Silver Braids brought her to the only corner of the room covered by shadows.

Knock,

knock,

knock,

knock.

"Who's this?" The Widow asked.

A deep, rough voice answered her. "Good day, madam."

The Widow gasped.

"Don't you remember me?" The voice continued.

"Such beautiful fields you have. These trees were full of sweet apples during the summer. I can hear the ground munching the autumn's leftovers, preparing for a new spring of abundance. Are you sure you don't you remember me?"

"No." The Widow kept blocking the entrance, her fear spilling through the hinges.

"Bring her out, would you?"

"Who? I'm alone here. Just me and the cows in the barn."

"Your daughter. I want to see her under the sunlight."

The Girl with Apple Cheeks pushed her mother aside and twisted the door handle to open the door. She was too curious to stay inside.

"Stay back." The Widow with Silver Braids tried to protect her daughter, but the Girl had grown up enjoying short winters and generous summers, so she was naturally fearless. She wanted to feel the sun in the garden.

"Hello, sir," The Girl with Apple Cheeks said. It was strangely warm outside, considering it was almost winter. The sun blinded her for a moment, but it didn't cover the smell. It was a mix of smoke and rotten eggs at first, which became the acid odour of excrement on wet straw before turning into a sickly-sweet scent of roses that tried to camouflage it all. Nausea climbed up the Girl's throat.

"Look how big you are. Last time I saw you, you were still in your mother's belly," El Toro said.

The Girl with Apple Cheeks stared at the two horns, sharp as crescent moons, coming out from the fedora hat. How could have she thought that *it* was a man?

"Come here, my dear, let me see you." El Toro tried to pull her closer using his right hoof. He had done it on purpose, so he could show her the thick golden watch hanging on it. "I'll buy you one like this. And expensive clothes. Who put you in these smelly rags?"

The Girl with Apple Cheeks clutched her dress, which had belonged to her mother.

"That's no way to treat my future wife," El Toro shouted at the Widow.

"What?" The Girl with Apple Cheeks rubbed her eyes, itching with the drops of sweat from her forehead.

"You're my betrothed, didn't your mother tell you?" When he leaned towards her, the black hairs of his chest came through the buttons of the waistcoat. "You are already a woman, you should know." El Toro sniffed the air with his pink nostrils as if he could smell the fresh blood between the girl's legs.

"No, no." The Girl with Apple Cheeks stepped back. "That's not true." She looked into her mother's eyes for reassurance but found them red with tears.

"What's the problem, dear? I'll take you to a mansion. I'll buy you jewels. I brought a piece of sun for your mother, but I can give you the whole damn burning star if that's what you want."

"You scare me." The Girl with Apple Cheeks covered her nose and mouth.

"Me? Don't you like my expensive suit? Or the perfume?"

"No, you're disgusting."

El Toro bellowed. His chest grew bigger, silks unstitched and the golden watch chain exploded. His muzzle became covered with yellow foam, and boiling saliva splattered on the floor. On his head, the two crescent moons shone. The animal battered the ground with his four legs and growled one more time.

The Girl with Apple Cheeks and her mother ran

into the house and closed the door, dragging the chest of drawers to it to keep it blocked. The Widow threw a bucket of water over the fireplace so the room became darker and cooler and they could finally hug each other and cry.

III.

After El Toro's visit, the Widow with Silver Braids made yet another promise upon the one she had already broken: she would never allow her beloved daughter to marry the beast. She pledged to give her to the Sisters of Cow instead.

The Sisters of Cow dwelt in the heart of the island, in a place called Tower and Four Crosses. Aeons ago, on this site, a Silver Snake emerged from her egg in the guts of the Earth and slithered around the bogs. The Silver Snake devoured everyone, including the bog monsters that dwelt in the dank pools and mud dunes. Eventually, a saint named Ciarán came riding a cow and killed the Silver Snake. Upon her nest, he built a doorless tower, surrounded by four stone crosses positioned to watch the four sides of the world. When St. Ciarán died from the plague, the Sisters of Cow erected a sanctuary on his grave.

On her arrival, the Girl with Apple Cheeks was horrified by the tower, the crosses and the sanctuary. They were all rain-rotten and covered in moss scabs. Stone ghosts. The Girl with Apple Cheeks screamed and begged, but her mother left before her child could see the tears in her eyes. In Tower and Four Crosses, only daughters were allowed.

The Sisters of Cow had one rule: silence. So, they didn't acknowledge The Girl with Apple Cheeks' complaints when they took off her clothes and cut her long wheaten braids from her head. She received a white tunic to cover her body, and a veil to cover her hair. They also took her voice away and kept it inside a small wooden cross that the Girl wore around her neck, like all the other Sisters of Cow. She understood she had to protect that cross with her life because the vows that came with it were for eternity. She was given her own mattress in a large room with a never-ending fire. At dinner time in the refectory, the Sisters of Cow made the Girl look at the pictures from a heavy codex that narrated the adventures of a dark-haired man. For an hour during the night, the Sisters of Cow gathered in the sanctuary to celebrate their silence. Instead of looking at the hundred candles that twinkled indoors, they gazed at the distant stars through the cracks in the ceiling. The Girl with Apple Cheeks couldn't take her eyes away from the skull placed on a purple velvety pillow on the altar. According to the inscriptions right below, that the Girl couldn't read, it belonged to St. Ciarán. Its smile revealed a perfect row of pearly teeth, poised as though it would burst out laughing at any moment.

The Sisters of Cow taught the Girl how to listen to books and educated her fingers so they could speak with black ink. That is how she discovered that the dark-haired man from the codex she was told to read at dinner time was St. Ciarán. On wet nights, when she was sent to get water from the sacred well, she often saw a silver spark among the bare trees: St. Ciarán's soul floating above the dense blue clouds that sometimes kissed the earth. Apart from reading, the Girl's favourite activity was the work she did in the garden. At first, because she was used to bog orchids and apple trees, the black grass seemed dull. There was no sun to warm the earth, and the only nutrients came from under the stone graves scattered here and there. But as the seasons changed, the Girl with Apple Cheeks learnt to love the rain because it blessed the ground, where she nurtured potatoes, carrots, leeks and all those vegetables that sleep in mud.

One autumn day, when the fields had turned to pools, the Widow with Silver Braids returned to the Tower and Four Crosses. She had shrunk like a raisin, and her dress smelt of stagnant water. With her, she brought a piece of dark chocolate wrapped in golden paper, just for her daughter. The Girl with Apple Cheeks licked the cocoa while her mother spoke to her:

"The apple trees, the heather, the rosemary, the wheat, the cotton grass…" The Widow with Silver Braids started coughing and pressed a filthy handkerchief to her mouth. The Girl spotted drops of blood all over it, as red as the lost apples from her mother's garden. "El Toro ate them all, and he tried to eat me too, but I ran faster."

The Girl with Apple Cheeks hugged her shivering mother and offered her warm carrot soup.

"El Toro will find you here. We have to go somewhere else," the Widow with Silver braids told her daughter during the night.

The next day, before the light rose over the tower, the sanctuary and the four crosses, the Girl with Apple Cheeks and her mother left and walked.

And walked.
And walked.
And walked.
And walked.
And walked.

Until the land ended and the grey sea stretched further than their eyes could reach.
So they took a ship.
And sailed.

IV.

The ship was as big as a whale, but because the Girl with Apple Cheeks and her mother were penniless, they travelled with the cattle. They spent their days sitting on rotten straw, moving the cattle droppings aside. Under the trembling floor, the turbines roared day and night, and the walls poured steam: they were so hot that they wore only their shifts. The Widow with Silver Braids sang her secret lullabies to calm the cows' cries, but when the smell of over-boiled beef came through the ventilation tubes, all of them were sick.

Yet the Girl with Apple Cheeks and her mother were happy. They could hold each other. They had a little gas lamp that reflected a patch of yellow on the walls. The Girl used her fingers to create shadows that told stories about St. Ciarán and the Sisters of Cow to her mother.

Until El Toro found them.

He had been in that same ship all along, camouflaged amongst the cattle, looking for the perfect moment to punish his betrothed and the treacherous widow.

It was dark.

The Girl was on the other side of the room, peeing in the bucket.

It was silent.

The cattle and her mother dreamt, nursed by a wave of sickness.

Iron hooves scratched the floor.

The Girl shivered.

A dragging tail.

The Girl stood up.

Tar.

His enormous shape appeared, covered by a pitch-like substance. He dragged himself towards them with violent contortions, leaving a trail behind. No legs were visible, only the horns like crescent moons. El Toro approached the corner of the room where the Widow with Silver Braids lay asleep.

The Girl wanted to scream, but her voice was still inside the wooden cross necklace. She ran towards her mother but El Toro stood in her way, dripping hot tar. His eyes were lost in the wrinkles of his changing skin. His mouth had doubled in size and when he opened it, it shown his brown, thick teeth. There were small pieces of flesh trapped between them, and hairs, very long hairs.

"Will you marry me?" El Toro asked the Girl. His breath reeked of half-digested beef and acid saliva.

The Girl with Apple Cheeks mouthed a second scream. She wanted to push the monster away, but her hands got burnt by the boiling tar.

"I gave you the sun and a never-ending garden," El Toro said. "I offered you gold. And yet you think you're too good for me. Too pure. All things darken when I chew them. All things darken, and wrinkle, and die."

The Girl didn't have time to lick her burnt fingertips, because El Toro was already savaging her mother. The Widow with Silver Braids opened her eyes. It was too late. Just before she was swallowed, her eyes turned white and she let one last scream out.

"Run," she said to her daughter.

El Toro swallowed the Widow with Silver Braids.

The Girl was already scrambling among the cows. Cowbells clanged, louder than the ocean waves. El Toro chased her, but now he had to drag his swollen, growling stomach. The Girl climbed up the metal stairs and her anguish gave her the strength to open the hatch. Outside, hail stabbed the ship and the sky glittered. It was the same colour as the sea: she couldn't distinguish them.

A wave smashed over the deck. The Girl's eyes drowned in water. She couldn't see, but the wind was taking her where she wanted to be: far from the smell of tar, and closer to the railing.

She had to escape.

She had to leave.

El Toro jumped on her and bit her wooden cross necklace off.

The Girl raised her head to the skies and caught a glimpse of a silver spark breaking the clouds. A seagull that didn't seem afraid of being swallowed by the storm and ending up in the bottomless waters.

The Girl with Apple Cheeks saw her cross sinking into the black waves. There it was, her voice and soul, sinking into the sea as fast as the seagull's wings flapped.

That was the last thing she saw.

Her body collapsed on the deck. Seventeen summers had blessed her body but now the apple cheeks were the colour of sea foam, her eyes had the glare of the storm and her pupils were empty.

The Miracle of Monte Toro
1935

Madrid, 15th April, 1935

Querida Carmen:

It was good to receive your letter. It's almost a month since you left. Glad to know you're enjoying Menorca.

You asked about La Institución – do you have time to think about it? I can't believe you actually miss it! Your students don't miss you. The girls are all delighted with Don Manuel, who is covering your class, as they are allowed to play with clay and coloured pencils.

Yebra asked for you and wishes you a good recovery. He told me that going back to your family was the best thing to do, and I agree, if only I could meet your family too, cariño, but I didn't say anything to Yebra, so don't worry.

My experiment is going well. Gonzalo and I are trying to get an article published. Yebra – bless him – still thinks it's a bit too radical to be in La Institución's magazine. Things are not going that well here after the Asturias disaster and everyone fearing the Communists and the Jews, so Yebra assured me people don't need to know that the world is ending in two centuries because our climate is going to change, on top of all that. But I told him that if nobody acknowledges this, how are we going to work towards a solution?

Éboli misses you. She scratches the studio door and when I open it, she wanders around looking for you. I miss the sound of your chisel, but not your food, sorry.

Un beso,
Pedro

Madrid, 29th April, 1935

Querida Carmen:

How are things going at your parents'? Do they let you work? You never mentioned how they make a living, by the way. What about your siblings? I think I recall you talking about an older sister. It's strange. We've never discussed your family situation. You never mentioned it when we met and then, after we married, I didn't ask you because I understood those memories triggered sour feelings. I wanted to respect you, so I didn't force you to turn your thoughts back to your past. But now I'm so afraid you just saw it as indifference.

Please send my regards to your mother and father. I hope your statue is coming along well. I received a letter from the Irish College at Salamanca, they want it as soon as possible. You should have seen the envelope. It had golden borders and a purple seal like in the Middle Ages. I kept it so we can laugh at it together.

Take some rest from carving.

Un beso,

Pedro

Madrid, 21st May, 1935

Querida Carmen:

Why are you not writing anymore? Every day I look into our pigeonhole but it's always empty. La señora de Rabadán, your favourite neighbour, came by the house the other day and asked if you were at the hospital again. Such an annoying woman! I bet she was thinking you were dying. So I told her you were visiting your family on the island. What island, she asked, and I told her, Menorca, and she seemed very surprised. I bet you're going to be very angry at me for telling la Señora de Rabadán something about you.

Is the carving going well? Don't forget to eat.

Un beso,

Pedro

Madrid, 19th June, 1935

Querida Carmen:

Enough, don't you think? This is the third letter I've written to you. Why are you not responding? Have I done something to upset you? Are you too busy working? So am I, but is it that hard to scribble a few words on a piece of paper and send it to me? I'm sure your parents can do it if you don't have the time.

I'm done. Is this your way of showing you don't care? What else do I have to do? Is this because I let the girl run away? What's with the girl? Yes, she's a girl, no matter how many times you insist on the opposite, and she's not our daughter, our son, or nephew, she's not even yours. She always gave me the creeps. She has brought nothing but trouble, can't you see it? A saint, ha. Your friend Federico told everyone about "St. Ciarán's miracles." Federico is such a fool, but that's hardly news, is it? He just wanted to make you angry by taking the girl, because he knows your statues are a thousand times better than his stupid plays.

I didn't want to hurt you or to spoil your art in any form. I respect that. I want you back, cariño.

Didn't I bring you the girl back?

If it's that fucking girl I'm going to…fuck, Carmen, please, just write.

Pedro

Madrid, 3rd July, 1935

Querida Carmen:

I talked to Yebra yesterday. I told him the truth: that you have left me.

He's given me a month of leave so I can go to Menorca to see if you're still alive. Thinking that you're there but you simply don't care is too cruel.

Pedro

Ciutadella, 13th July, 1935

Querida Carmen:

I'm in Menorca now, and writing this letter that I will take to the post office first thing in the morning. I just arrived at this tasca and I'm so damn exhausted. The boat trip was a pain. First, I had to go to Barcelona by train and the heat was worse than hell. Then, the boat from Barcelona caught a storm – a storm, in the Mediterranean! When we arrived at Ciutadella, I swear I knelt down to kiss the ground. I hate the water so much. What a horrible world this is going to be when oceans cover everything.

I have been eating fried calamari – after hours with an empty stomach – and now I'm dry and full of food in bed. We may meet tomorrow – so this letter is quite useless. You never told me where your parents live, though.

You just said "in the countryside" but that can be anything between Ciutadella and Mahón on the other side
of the island.

Un beso,
Pedro

Ciutadella, 14th July, 1935

Querida Carmen:

I can't believe this. I don't give a fuck if you don't read
these letters but I need to write this.

Fucking hell.

I went to the post office asking for the de la Cierva
family and nobody knew anything about them. I thought
I hadn't made myself clear, because the islanders speak
this language of theirs, or because of my accent. Yes,
I still didn't see the obvious. So I spoke calmly to the
postal worker saying that surely there had to be a mistake
because my wife is called Carmen de la Cierva and her
family lives on the island, which is not exactly big, so for
fuck's sake, can someone just tell me where this family
lives? Surely they know them. But the man, dressed in a
cheap suit, kept shaking his head.

"Ho sento, senyor, there's no de la Cierva here."

I kept insisting until everyone in the post office was
looking at me and I thought they would escort me out,
like a crazy man. Me! Finally, I had a brilliant idea and
I pulled out your photo from my wallet, and shown it to
them. She's my wife, I told them, she sent me one letter
from this office. Don't you know her? You must have seen
her around. Is she not coming here to collect my letters?

Yes, the letters. That's when someone came with a

box full of my letters, the envelopes still glued.

Yes.

My mouth dried out. People's attitude changed; they weren't annoyed any more but pitying.

They understood.

One of the postal workers suggested I went back to town and show your photo around, if you're on the island someone must have seen you, since you arrived four months ago.

Another postal worker asked the terrible question; was I sure you are on the island?

But I know you're here. I still don't understand why you would lie to me about your family's surname. There are no de la Cierva here, but I know this is where you come from. You're an islander, you always were. When I first set foot in this strange place of arid hills and carob trees, I knew this is where you came from. It couldn't be otherwise.

I'm going to find you.

Pedro

Ciutadella, 15th July, 1935

Querida Carmen:

First day looking for you around Ciutadella. Now I understand when you talked about the terrible Menorca wind, la tramontana. It gets inside my head and makes me feel like a shivering tree. The city is small but bright, the light here is different − I remember you mentioned that too. I wandered around the houses; they have a certain Italian air, large shuttered windows − but all shut down as if no one was really living there. A couple of forgotten Renaissance palaces and a mastodontic cathedral trapped in the hidden streets. A few islanders walk here and there, all wearing abarcas. They say these shoes, made with car tyres, are the only ones sturdy enough to walk around the island, but I still have my leather boots on, thank you. I asked some old women sitting at the sun in front of the lonja, the old market, and then I asked at the tasca, and I asked at the little shops that sell pearls and ceramics for the tourists, but nobody knew you. These islanders seem to have no interest at all in tourists unless they can sell them a few trinkets.

I've been fearing you have changed too much. The photo I keep was taken eight years ago, you were just twenty-four, and it was before the operation…You still have the fierce black eyes and the strong features shaped by the winds of this island, but you were alive back then. You screamed, and shouted at me, and we had sex and the way you kept me inside you, I knew you loved me. Now, you just exist for your statue.

You're turning to stone.

Pedro

Ciutadella, 17ᵗʰ July, 1935

Querida Carmen:

Today was warm. The houses in Ciutadella, close to the shore, were so white it was painful on the eyes to look at them. The sea resting in the port was silver. A head carved in the portico of the Torre Saura palace was blindfolded. It didn't seem bothered about uncertainty. Perhaps it was happy that way. I walked away from the city and the sun. I followed a path surrounded by holm oaks and grey foliage.

The path ended in a cliff. The sky was shallow.

I'm thinking about going back. There's the rest of the island to explore, but are you even here?

When I go back, I'll have to tell everyone the truth. Hopefully they won't ask too much. My mother will light candles for me at La Almudena and my sister will recite the rosary for me every night. And Yebra will get me a date with one of the young teachers from La Institución because I'm still attractive and have an excellent sense of humour.

The sea – down the cliff – had thousands of white, almost transparent spots dancing across the waves. Jellyfish.

I wanted so much to get rid of my clothes and swim. This heat. But even the sea was poisoned.

Pedro

Es Mercadal, 21st July, 1935

Querida Carmen:

I keep writing to you, I can't stop now. Last week I came back to the post office despite the shame I felt after they discovered that I am the man who lost his wife. I thought you might have passed as a native islander here, but not the girl, surely not, with her fair skin and blond hair. So, I went in again, ignoring all the pitying glances. There was this pretty woman selling tobacco. She looked at me with such genuine sadness that I decided to take advantage of that. It was not easy to confess that my wife had disappeared in the company of a handsome young man, but I kept repeating he is our nephew – you told the story so many times that I have ended up believing it.

The woman listened and finally admitted to have met such a boy who indeed came by the office to buy tobacco months ago. You cannot imagine how sweet relief tasted in my mouth; you were on the island! Too bad the pretty woman didn't know where he'd gone.

So first I went by Ferreires and then here, to Es Mercadal. It actually took me quite a long time because I kept following the wrong road signs – apparently the islanders change them to confuse tourists? Es Mercadal is so small: a handful of white houses and four lampposts on one paved street. But it's so easy to know everyone in this kind of place. So I asked an old woman. I said Bon Dia in Menorquín and then asked her about a young blond boy and a woman with dark curly hair.

It was difficult to understand the old woman, but she inserted as many Spanish words as she could in her Menorquín. I got that she was talking about another woman, called Marieta Taura, who had gone to the mainland years and years ago. She had left her family behind after her older sister died. Her parents were also dead now – and, at this point, the old woman crossed herself.

So Marieta Taura is your real name.

I said I was your husband and asked where you lived.

The Taura house, ací, ací, she pointed out the huge green mountain lurking over Es Mercadal.

I couldn't even see your house, but I walked in that direction anyway. The hillsides were sparkling green and covered in yellow vinagrellas. There were curious cows grazing here and there, and their sweet eyes followed me.

The house was perched on a slope: a skeleton under the sun, the white paint almost gone. A small pond of murky green water and a few pine trees guarded its façade. The wooden door was rotten, and the front windows had a thick layer of dust covering them. I almost thought I wouldn't find you there – and that the old woman had been hallucinating, or talking about someone else. The sun was sinking beneath the purple horizon and shadows clumped everywhere. Cowbells echoed round the valley. Then I saw them, by the window: a fresh bunch of vinagrellas in a glass.

A cat came to say hello. Grey and soft, she rubbed against my legs. She was rounded and pregnant. She was happy I was there.

Pedro

Es Mercadal, 22nd July, 1935

Querida Carmen:

I know you won't read this letter, but there are so many things I still have to tell you. However, every time I look at you, my words dry out. I can't tell you. I feel ashamed, because you're my wife. But I couldn't find you. I couldn't even touch you after the surgery – how can I even speak to you? I'd pray to Dios to show me the way but you don't want to hear about that either. "Dios" makes you cringe because you said you're broken and nothing (not even Dios) can heal you. Writing this is like praying anyway.

The sun in Menorca is pinkish. I'm sleeping a bit better now that you're around.

I found you in the garden, working on the commission. At first I thought that the statue was someone else. It's incredible how much it has grown, and changed.

The marble piece has legs, arms, a face…The bull is an impressive steed, the thick vein in his neck pulsing as if he were breathing. Your dress was covered in marble dust, your face and eyelids white.

You didn't seem surprised when you saw me. You didn't smile but your eyes did. We were separated by worlds. Finally you said, "You're here," almost annoyed, as if you were tired of waiting for me.

The girl was inside the house, wearing a straw hat, slicing some cheese for your dinner. I realised that she had been taking care of you all this time. I was so jealous thinking you had run away together but now I see you just took her because you need care when you're creating. She's a shadow to you, just as I am.

That same night you went to sleep in the room upstairs, in an iron framed bed. The windows were broken but it wasn't cold outside. The girl had a little bed on the bench next to the door. I decided to go for the worn-out armchair by the fireplace. It was dry and crisp like a nest. When I sat, it cringed and I saw spiders running out of it. I didn't dare climb the stairs to claim my place by your side. It's not the time, yet.

Pedro

Es Mercadal, 6th August, 1935

Querida Carmen:

You've been working on the statue for two weeks. I have cleaned the kitchen and used old newspapers to fix the windows.

We go to Es Mercadal and we buy creamy cheese, made from the cows that graze around the mountains.

This herd, you told me, is the property of the Sisters of Cow, an order of cloistered nuns that live up the mountain, guarding the sanctuary of La Virgen Del Toro. They make the cheese, and then the villagers sell it at the market.

The girl and I go to the sea. We catch crabs and shrimps. The fishermen in their small boats, lluts they call them, laugh at us. Vostè està fent malament, they say. Sometimes they sell us grouper.

The girl folds her trousers up to the knee and runs among the waves. When the jellyfish get trapped in the sand, she takes them back to the sea with her bare hands, even if they sting.

We've been talking. I didn't know her Spanish was so good. She's even writing a story. Sitting on the warm rocks, she works for hours. The story is about these two characters called El Toro and La Niña. She carries this huge Spanish dictionary around, *Diccionario de la Lengua Española* – Federico's gift.

The girl has also shown me the 'bull face' behind the house. It's hidden among holm oaks and sabines. Two large planks of stone, one on top of each other, forming a T. Dios knows who put them there and how old they are. Perhaps this is one of the taulas I read about.

I've been thinking about your statue. I know it's the most beautiful thing you've ever produced because I can feel it breathing. But I'm not sure people would come to worship it as you plan. It's too raw, too real for them. When they ask for idols and saints, they just want marionettes, simple ritualistic representations of something they know – perhaps subconsciously – is not real. People don't dare worship Dios in solitude because they are scared to be alone with themselves. They are scared to gaze at the darkness. Your statue will make them uncomfortable because it must be appreciated in silence and solitude. Not during Missa or an Easter procession.

I wish I could tell you…but how can you say to a mother that her own child is cursed?

Pedro

Es Mercadal, 22nd August, 1935

Querida Carmen:

You finished the statue yesterday. Or at least I thought so when you woke up in the morning but didn't go to the garden. You sat in the kitchen, looking at the vinagrellas on the windowsill, now withered. You drank water and looked at the clear sky. The seagulls cried outside.

The girl was out in Es Mercadal. The pregnant cat hasn't been around for days. The house is always so empty. I couldn't imagine a family living inside.

"Were you born here?" I asked you.

It took you a while to answer. "Yes."

"Where are your parents?"

"They're gone. They took everything away, those bastards from the village." You started chewing on a bit of hair. You didn't seem to care at all.

"It's beautiful here," I said.

"The island is carnivorous."

"What?"

"La tramontana, she will eat you."

I took your hand between mine. Your skin was parched and rough, full of tiny brown spots. Your fingers were knotty. It didn't seem like your hand any more, but a claw. You're turning into something else. That's what scared me, ever since the surgery.

"The statue is done, we can go," I told you.

"It's not done."

Your eyes were red with tears.

"Why not?" I asked.

"It needs something else, the skin, the flesh, the way we're built. Pedro, I need to know."

"What?"

"I have to be a mother."

I was shocked. "That's not –"

"I need to. A baby, the secret of life, all happens inside." You started rubbing your belly. "Don't tell me it's impossible. There is a way."

You leaned over me.

"There's a place, up there, Monte Toro," you said, pointing through the window towards the black greenish shape, the mountain that didn't allow us to look at the sea behind. It created the illusion that we were not on an island. "The old shrine of La Virgen del Toro. El Toro hides up there, you know? El Toro grants any wish. We'll go up there and ask El Toro to make me a mother." I thought you had lost it. You trembled so much. I knew your words were offending Dios but I said nothing because I didn't want you to crumble and fade away.

"Tonight there's a full moon: El Toro will be there. I'll explain to him. We'll all talk, and he'll understand. And I'll be a mother. Don't you want me with a baby? Don't you?"

For the first time I understood you were opening your soul to me, without reserve. All these years you have made it clear we were separate human beings: you were an island: you could exist perfectly well on your own. Now, for the very first time, you needed me to complete you.

And I thought we would never feel close again.

Pedro

Es Mercadal, 13th September, 1935

This wait is killing us. You don't speak to me at all. You follow Ciarán everywhere, looking for a fever, dizziness, a blush, a tremor. I can't stand this anymore and what I did, up on the mountain, it's devouring me from the inside. I need to write it down. I need confession.

Yesterday I climbed Monte Toro again. Under the burning sun, each step seemed to bring me closer to hell. I passed by the convent of the Sisters of Cow and went towards the new sanctuary. I crawled into the small prayer room that smells of sea and plaster. There is only a black wooden crucifix hanging on the wall. It must be held with fishing line because it seems to levitate on a corner. Jesucristo looking down on me, so pitifully. A young priest entered the room and his brown eyes screamed faith and forgiveness. He introduced himself as Padre Juan Huguet Cardona, and asked me about the Taura house and about you and about the boy – the girl, Ciarán, whatever. He wondered why we haven't shown up at mass and then I felt the bitterness of tears in the back of my throat. I told him I was lost. He offered me confession. I wish I could say I refused, but I went inside the confessional. And I told him that you are cheating on me with a young man who you say is your nephew but he really isn't. I told him that you found him in Madrid's streets and he was a beggar. I told him I'm ashamed because everyone knows about him and they call me a cornudo, a horned man, one who can't keep his wife faithful. And I told him that I cannot bear it any more now that you're carrying his child.

Yes, I told him.

Padre Juan listened to me, and he felt for me and guided me with wise words. It hurt even more, that, you know. Like salt burning on my lies.

This is what happened on the 22nd August, night-time:

As soon as the glowing moon climbed over Monte Toro, you called for us. We started walking as la tramontana carried the heat away and brought rosemary and chamomile to the air. Monte Toro was a menacing mass of blue grass and black rocks on the horizon. You led the way, breaking branches, stepping on the heat-dried bushes. I followed you, and the girl dragged behind.

"Hurry, hurry!" you said.

The girl was scared. I took her hand. It was the first time I touched her. From the very beginning it was clear she was another piece of you. Something I could break. Or misunderstand.

We climbed the rocks and tasted the dust before arriving at the top. There was no wilderness there but a blue building and the new sanctuary. We tiptoed pass the convent and this time la tramontana brought the Sisters of Cow's chants, and it was like hearing Dios, and my soul shivered.

You guided us towards the back of the sanctuary, where a small cave had been carved in the sterile rocks. The old shrine. Next to it there were two large planks of stone, one on top of the other, forming a T. Another bull face. The entrance to this primitive shrine was hidden between two wild olive trees. In the distance, the sea was a silver line parting the blackness.

Inside, you lit the candles you'd brought along. The wax made me feel as if I was chewing myrrh. All I could see was a minuscule altar, old as the island itself. Three figures were carved into the stone. El Toro, La Virgen and Jesús. El Toro was lying, huge horns down, like a faithful dog resting at his mistress' feet. The most miraculous mother of all held a baby with the face of an old man. And she had a pair of horns, crescent moons, on her head.

You sat on the floor and we followed. It was warm. The moon spied on us from the entrance.

You leaned on the girl and embraced her. Under the candlelight, your hands were timid dragonflies.

Suddenly the girl was naked.

I mumbled a prayer to the horned Virgen del Toro.

Your bony body came out from your dress and poured over the girl. You made her lie between your thighs, head on your scarred belly.

And the miracle happened – the second miracle, after the episode at the bull fighting ring. The girl turned into a young woman, with a fresh, tight body ready to be opened. Eyes of sea reflecting the moon. You held her shoulders and grabbed her small breasts like apples. You parted her legs, slowly, offering her ripped sex to me.

I understood.

Pedro

Es Mercadal, 22nd April, 1936

Querida Carmen:

You were right. They came. The most beautiful days. We walk through the island, greeting the taulas, the ancient bull faces. We walk through the waves. Dresses are long and dance around the legs, as if la tramontana had acquired colour and texture. Blond curls, black curls. We walk on the spongy sand. Our footprints remain there a second, then are gone forever. The water is kind. There are no jellyfish but purple seaweed. We start a collection of shells. Water will be a blessing for this world. We walk, the water up to our waists, liquid sun, blessing the rounded belly. We dance, and sing, and kiss each other. Monte Toro is behind, looking on us.

Pedro

The Death of the Trees
1936

The Siege of Madrid – November 8ᵗʰ

The walls of La Institución trembled and the workshop's ceiling spat out plaster. Ciarán stopped sewing the blankets and looked up.

"Shhhh, shhhh." Carmen calmed the baby's wails.

The students kept sketching in their notepads. They were drawing a still life: three brown apple cores and a broken cup that Carmen had fixed on her desk.

Mortars exploded.

Echoes of the shooting outside.

"Ciarán," one of the second-year girls sitting in the first row called him. "Are they coming?"

"No. They got to Casa de Campo Park, but the army is fighting them there," he said. "I heard it on the radio, this morning."

"Are the fascists coming to kill us, Doña Carmen?" one boy asked.

"Ramiro, stop asking stupid questions and keep on drawing," she answered. The baby was sucking on one of her fingers. "I'm going to go around in a few minutes to check your work. The sketches have to be done, no excuses. Have I made myself clear?"

A rattle came from the corridor.

The door opened.

"The class is over," Yebra shouted as he came in, followed by a horde of men, women, and children. Ciarán recognised some of them: Emilio, the maths teacher,

Rosaura, the owner of the ultramarine shop down the road, Vicentillo, the postman's son… "Come on, all of you. Time to join the Popular Front against the fascists. Let's go, let's go now, before the bastards burn down Madrid!"

The students stared at the principal with the eyes of starving rodents. A girl in the last row stood up and started packing her bag.

"Stay," Ciarán mouthed. "Yebra, please. Do you want to take the children to the barricades or what? I know the fascists are getting closer and we're all damn scared but at least an art lesson is a distrac—"

"La Institución closed months ago, and Madrid needs soldiers," Yebra interrupted him.

"Yes, soldiers, but the children need something to do. I need something to do too. It's just a bit of paper, pencils…"

"We're doing no harm here. These children…their parents are dead, or fighting or…They've nowhere to go. They couldn't escape from Madrid in time. We're protecting them, giving them shelter!" Carmen added.

"Just let us be, Yebra, please." Ciarán hadn't seen the principal in weeks. He looked different, with a long beard and messy hair. His suit was muddy. Ciarán knew he and his crowd hadn't come into the classroom looking for a place to hide from the bombs. They *owned* the room. It was the rifles that gave them authority, and the shotguns (the kind people used to kill rabbits in Casa de Campo Park) and the knives, and the bricks, and the sticks.

"Everyone out to fight for Madrid, now, and that's an order." The rifle that Yebra carried was rusty.

"We're not going anywhere," Ciarán said. "Not today, not ever." Yebra lifted the rifle, aiming at the blackboard.

A shot.

A student screamed, and some started to cry. Pieces of slate fell on the floor. The baby howled.

Vicentillo, one of the soldier-boys accompanying Yebra, smirked. He must have thought a lot of himself for carrying a knife.

"Asshole," Ciarán whispered. "Yebra, please." He begged.

"We've warned you. Many times. Many, many times."

"Yebra…"

"Why do you keep coming here? There's a war outside. There is no time for education. And you?" Yebra shouted at Carmen over the baby's cries. "You think your stupid art will make things better?"

"Art is the only thing that is not senseless right now," Carmen replied.

"What about Spain?"

"You're not going to leave anything behind. There'll be no Spain."

"Oh, shut up and come here, Carmen. And you too, finflón, come here, right now." Yebra grabbed Ciarán's arm.

"Get off me," he shouted. "Get off me now."

"Don't hurt him!" Carmen yelled, but two men with rifles seized her. Ciarán kicked at Yebra's legs.

"Let me go!"

"Where is Pedro?" The principal slapped Ciarán.

"He's out, he's…"

"I bet he's sick of you and Carmen. Because you don't show him any respect. Fucking his wife and all. Everyone knows the baby is yours. Weirdo." Yebra spat on Ciarán's face.

Ciarán jabbed his elbow into Yebra's cheekbone,

stumbling back when one of the men slammed the stock of his rifle into his face.

"Stop, stop!" Carmen screamed in the background.

Through the curtain of pain and dripping blood, Ciarán struggled to stay on his feet. He wanted to scream, get a stick, a chair, anything.

"You can take the boys if you have to," Carmen told Yebra, "but leave the girls with us."

"Leave you the girls?" the principal sneered. "Everyone is fighting for Madrid today. Didn't you hear? The fascists are at the fucking doors. We need to build more barricades."

"Girls fight for Spain too, you dumbass," Rosi, the ultramarines' granddaughter, said. Her rags were stained with blood, but she wore shiny pearl earrings. She shoved Ciarán hard and he tripped over a chair and fell to the floor.

"Fucking foreigner." She spat on him too. The soldier-boys roared with laughter.

Carmen ran to Ciarán and crouched at his side.

"Are you alright? Are you alright?"

"Vicente, arm these soldiers," Yebra ordered. The soldier-boy brought a flour sack, opened it, and started to share bricks with everyone.

Pieces of wooden beams.

A blunderbuss that had probably been used in last century's Cuban war. A fire poker.

There wasn't enough for everyone.

"What are you doing?" Ciarán's face had gone numb. "Carmen, we can't let him. The International Brigades are arriving today. Those are your soldiers, Yebra."

"Yeah, the government said so, but the government left Madrid yesterday, didn't you hear? Gone to Valencia.

We're just the rabble that's left behind to defend everything."

"And bringing children to the barricades is the answer? Why don't you just kill them instead, right here? It's all the same. We're not leaving. We're not going anywhere," Ciarán said.

"Yes, that's right. We're not going," Carmen added. "You can burn this school down and we'll still be here, mouldering in the ashes."

"Me cago en Dios…shut up, Carmen." Yebra hit the ground with his rifle. "Boys, get them all out."

The men with the rifles dragged them to the garden. It was a cold, crisp day. Minuscule snowflakes landed hard on the frosted grass.

"You're too good to die for Spain, are you, you dirty foreigner?" A woman with a shotgun pulled Ciarán's hair. He saw how the crowd dragged Carmen behind him.

"Leave me alone!" Ciarán screamed back. The boom and racket of shooting from Casa de Campo Park was making him crazy.

"Traitors," said an old worker carrying an iron bar.

The air smelt of gunpowder. Dark smoke clouds swirled in the sky. Branches of acacia trees thrashed in the wind above their heads.

The students circled round Carmen. They feared her because she was a strict teacher, but they relied on her, too. Many of them had wet faces but they were no longer sobbing. The ones that were armed looked even more scared. They waited for Carmen's instructions.

"Stay close, here, come here." She grabbed at them with her free hand. The other one was curled around the baby.

Her pose reminded Ciarán of *Sparrows*, a film Carmen had taken him to watch way before the war. She resembled La Virgen María, mothering outcast children.

Yebra climbed onto a bench, standing above his people, who formed a ring around him. Pedro used to bring the principal home for dinner, buying Cava sparkling wine for all such occasions. Like many of the staff in La Institución, Yebra had supported the Republic, which had been generous with funding. He had always been critical of the communists and the anarchists, but Pedro was exactly the same. Was Yebra an anarchist now, though? A communist, asking the city of Madrid to stand together against fascism? Shotguns for books, bricks for Latin dictionaries, sticks for dusty translations. The principal had turned into a different person. A person who marched with the ones who carried guns and made violence.

"I'll say it once again. This. Is. Over," Yebra called from his high position. "La Institución is gone. We have to build barricades to protect Madrid."

"From whom?" Ciarán asked.

"From the fascists, the anarchists, the communists, the socialists and all the bloody enemies outside. Books are not going to get us out of this: look what is happening! Students hide in here like chickens instead of holding a rifle to fight our enemies. At least the communist boys from the university are brave. Shame on you! Yes, you, you bunch of useless academics. I think you have to fight now or you'll be dead before this is all over."

"Carrying arms is the best way to die soon," Ciarán said. Carmen grabbed his shoulder.

"Shut up, he'll use the goddamn gun," she whispered.

But he couldn't stop himself.

"What are you going to do? Kill us all?" Yebra pointed his rifle at Ciarán.

"You ungrateful shit. Didn't you join La Barraca? With Federico García Lorca?"

"What?"

"Yes, didn't he call you St. Ciarán?"

"Yeah, that's it," a woman said.

"St. Ciarán."

"Fucking nonsense."

"Where's Federico now?" Yebra asked him. "He's dead." Ciarán felt his eyelids burning.

"He was murdered by the fucking fascists, shot down like a dog. That's why we have to fight."

"This foreigner is not one of us."

"He's a German spy," a woman with a shotgun claimed.

"What are you going to do, Yebra?" Ciarán swallowed bile. "You're no better than Federico's killers if you think you can decide how we live our lives. You can take us, you can kill us, you can burn the damn building but the trees will stay here and–"

Someone threw a brick at him. Pain.

The world turned backwards, spinning round him. A red hue flooded the scene.

Ciarán realised that he was sprawled on the ground. He couldn't open his right eye. His skull was too small to contain his throbbing brain. Where had the brick come from? One of the children? Sounds rippled to his ears from under the water. He struggled, but got up.

"We need wood for the barricades," Yebra shouted.

The armed men went inside the gardener's hut and brought out the axes and every sharp object they could find. Mauro, the gardener, was with them. The boys with the bricks had already started kicking down the slender almond trees.

The women used the back of their shotguns to break the thin branches from the lilac trees.

"Are you hungry? Are you hungry, children?" Yebra's distorted voice roared.

The smell of tarmac.

On the top of Yebra's head, a glimpse of horns.

"Help me bring wood to the barricades and I'll give you so much chorizo, and jamón, and pan. Bring that wood and I swear you'll eat until you're sick," the principal laughed.

"No, no, no!" Ciarán begged, but the students were already running after Yebra's words. Carmen appeared by his side and pressed something wet against Ciarán's face.

The children went towards the olive trees, mattocks in hand.

Yebra approached the holm oak trees with an axe. Ciarán grabbed Carmen's hand.

"Stop it, stop!" Ciarán cried.

The children, and the women, and the men circled the old apple tree that towered over the building.

The tree wobbled.

Branches scratched at the windows. Branches broke off.

When the tree fell there was a strong noise, like a moan. Screams cut into his gut, sharp as knives.

Around him there was no garden. Stumps.

Some of the children held pieces of wood. Others helped carry the bigger trunks away. Yebra went towards him and pulled at his clothes.

"The only reason I'm not killing you is because of

that baby," Yebra said. The garden of La Institución had
been turned into a barren land.

Murdered.

The Siege of Madrid – November 16th

It was always the same.
First
the noise, like the sky cracking and vomiting rebel
planes, de tres en tres
(the three widows) and the flares
(the air smelt of tarmac)
BOOM.*

* Extract from a poem attributed to Ciarán de la Cierva and published in several Republican pamphlets during the Siege of Madrid in the Spanish Civil War.

Everyone was in the streets that night, just like in Verbena time. There were no screams or laughter, though: only whispers and suspicious glances.

Ciarán rushed behind Carmen and Pedro. They were arguing.

"Let's go to El Prado Museum," Carmen said.

"No, no, no. The underground is better."

"Look at this, haven't you seen it?" She held a creased flyer in front of him. "They're bombing the north tonight. Casa de Campo Park. The University. We'll be safe in El Prado. Ciarán? What do you think?"

"El Prado," he agreed, carrying the only suitcase they had left. There was not much inside: one dirty shirt, dried cheese, and half a scarf – the other half was around his head, protecting his healing wound, the one caused by the brick. At least people liked to share things with them when they saw the baby. "It's very well protected, El Prado," he added.

"Yeah, I remember." Pedro's greasy hair had white flecks stuck to it. Plaster from the underground, where they hid the day before. "Back in October. The government was very worried about preserving the art and setting up all those reinforcements. Where the fuck are they now, huh? Who's going to preserve us?"

"That's what I mean," Carmen added. "We'll be safe there. Stop now, stop. The baby's crying. She's hungry, stop."

"There's no time," Pedro looked at Ciarán.

He shook his head. There was no milk to feed the baby. He was not going to feed the baby again. The baby was Carmen's. She'd have to take care of it.

"Let's go; they'll be bombing anytime now, Carmen, please." Pedro's voice was sharp.

Inside the museum, there were so many dust motes that it was difficult to breathe. People hid behind the paintings and next to the statues. A bunch of men crouched under *Roman Charity*, a marble statue that shown a woman offering her full breasts to a starving old man. There were empty frames on the walls, and sacks filled with sawdust on the floor. Children cried. The baby cried.

"We should have gone to the underground." Pedro said. "This is going to turn into a sarcophagus."

"No, no. Look at the walls, the windows…look at those beams. Nobody is going to tear down the Prado," Carmen answered. "They wouldn't have the balls."

"*The Garden of Earthly Delights* is gone," Ciarán told

her. "I went to look for it before."

"Fucking looters." Carmen sat on the floor and unbuttoned her dress, holding the baby's face against her nipple. She sucked with pale lips. Only Ciarán knew there was nothing there, whilst his own breasts hurt. They were so swollen. It was impossible to get rid of the pain with the baby so close to him, all day.

"We should have gone to the underground." Pedro repeated.

"Wait. I need to pee. I'll be quick," Ciarán said.

Carmen grabbed his arm.

"Don't go outside. The bombs will start any moment now. Promise."

"It'll be alright," he said. Then he sprinted out of the room. Some people looked at him. Others slept. Prayed. A mother told a story to her five children. Or six. Maybe they were not even hers.

Ciarán found a dark corner. At first his heart pounded, thinking there was someone waiting for him there, but it was just another statue. A young woman, although he couldn't be sure in the dark. He opened his shirt and took one of his breasts out and started massaging it to let the white liquid out faster. It was alien and disgusting, like his body didn't belong to him anymore. The baby. Her tiny skull covered by a soft layer of pinkish skin – and her pale lips. Nobody was feeding her. But the baby wasn't his. The baby was Carmen's. He had nothing to do with the baby. When she came out, covered in blood and a thick brown substance, Carmen had taken her between her white hands. White, like milk. He hadn't touched the baby for weeks. He hadn't dared. The baby was Carmen's.

Someone was crying. Ciarán cleaned his wet fingers

on his trousers and crawled back to the light. There was a young boy sitting by an empty pedestal, with a group of people around him, although he seemed to be completely unaware. He was focused on holding his bandaged belly with black hands.

Ciarán came to him. "Are you okay?"

The boy looked up. His face was covered in dirt – or freckles, it was difficult to tell. His eyes were full of tears, but he kept his moans quiet.

"A brave one." An old woman patted the boy's head. "He won't talk. He came with the International Brigades. Brave little boy."

A wail.

The planes were approaching. The old woman screamed. "Please Dios save us."

"Virgen María, please keep us alive…" The air in the room turned sour.

"*Oh, God…*" the boy cried. He wasn't speaking in Spanish, yet Ciarán understood what he was saying.

"*Who are you?*" he asked the boy, in English.

"*I'm Michael,*" the boy answered. Under the blackened eyelids, his blue eyes recovered a bit of brightness.

"*Are you from Ireland?*"

"*Yes, yes, Roscommon. I'm from Roscommon.*"

"*I know Roscommon! Why are you here?*"

"*I'm fighting against the fucking fascists. I'm…*" The Irish boy started crying aloud, holding his belly.

"*Does it hurt?*" Ciarán asked.

"*Yes.*"

He held the dying boy in his arms. His cheeks were burning. But the boy was from Ireland. He could tell him things. He could answer questions. Ciarán reopened his shirt and offered his right breast to the Irish boy, who started sucking. The moans stopped. The boy's teeth hurt his skin but the flow was pleasant. He held him tight. The boy's copper hair was oily and thick with dirt.

"Hush, hush," Ciarán said, placing his hand on the Irish boy's forehead.

The old woman had her eyes focussed on them. She crossed herself. "Jesusito de mi alma," she said. "He's the saint."

"What?" Someone else asked.

"He's the saint."

"Who? Him?"

"I saw him before. I will never forget it. He's healing the little soldier."

"Abuela, what are you saying?"

"He's the saint!" she repeated, holding the cross on her necklace tightly between her fingers. "From the bull-fighting. He was the one who resurrected the bull. The one who resurrected the bull at Manzanares. Don't you remember?"

"St. Ciarán!"

"Are you St. Ciarán?" a young woman asked. "St. Ciarán of the Blessed Bull?"

"How did you save that bull?"

"What happened to your head? Why is it bandaged?"

"Did the fascists attack you?"

"Yes, I am Ciarán," he said.

"Is it true that you made a barren woman conceive?"

"He's feeding that boy, like La Virgen María."

"He's like La Virgen…"

The sound of fighter planes approaching.

Silence.

Everyone froze, like the statues. The roar grew louder.

"Ciarán, please, save us."

"Save us!"

"Save us…"

"Pray to La Virgen for us."

He was surrounded by a wave of blackened hands and cold bodies, all piling on top of him.

The planes were getting closer. The Irish boy bit his nipple.

The first bomb fell.

The whole building trembled, waves of anguish and screams flooding it. "Carmen," Ciarán shouted, shoving the Irish boy away. "Carmen!"

The glass in the windows exploded.

"St. Ciarán, save us!"

"Save us!"

"Carmen, Carmen…" he yelled, crawling towards the other room. A second bomb.

The doors cracked.

"Carmen!"

He could see her coat. Everyone was covered in white, and there was plaster everywhere, like snow. But the bodies moved. The bomb hadn't fallen there.

AO come here, bring your golden cattle, bring the sun, the moon, and all the beautiful things you have created…

The words spilt from Ciarán's mouth. They tasted sour, coming from somewhere deep, as hidden as his milk ducts. All the eyes in the room were on him. He saw Carmen extending her hands in his direction, and that gave him the strength to climb onto a bench and stand there despite his trembling knees.

AO, come here, look at me: I am nothing but a drop in a storm, please take me with your hands, cast your light in these dark corners from the Bán sea to the Loughmichnois.

Nobody understood a word he was saying, yet they looked at him as though they were seeing a ghost or a god. Some started mimicking his sounds between their screams.

The building vibrated like a ship in a storm. A third bomb.

AO, come here, teach me the things I ought to know, the secrets of the rain, the milk, the written words, the secret self...

A fire raged outside the building. Heat scorched his skin as the temperature rose. Flames licked into the room.

AO, come here, I shall give you my blood and flesh, I shall be the seed that will feed the world, I shall be a beam of light in your sun.

The ceiling cracked.

An object fell through the smashed window into the room. Smoke rose and soon everything was covered in powdery fog.

Ciarán spat on his hands and cleaned his eyes. The fallen object was right in front of him. It resembled a metallic fish. He approached it and took it between his hands. It was small. Like a baby. Cold. He didn't tell anyone it was a bomb. People were already running towards the doors, trying to breathe clean air.

The planes were gone for the night.

El Prado stood still, quiet except for the crackling flames.

Colegio de los Irlandeses – November 29th

Carmen, Pedro, and Ciarán travelled from Madrid to Salamanca during the night. A man called Rodrigo had offered to drive them there. It was damp inside his car, and dark – dark as it must have been inside his mother's womb, Ciarán thought. The escape was all thanks to Pedro. Someone from church got them to the fascist front. Once they were there, Pedro got in touch with Miguel de Unamuno, one of his former teachers from Salamanca, and dean of its university.

"Not a good time for Christian families," Rodrigo mumbled, before letting them into the car. He refused Pedro's money, saying that he didn't want anything for the trip.

"Are they both your children?" Rodrigo asked, after staying silent for over four hours. He had been staring at Ciarán, sitting by his side. He was obviously curious to know where the blue eyes and blond hair came from.

"Yes," Carmen said, "my—"

"They are my aunt and uncle," Ciarán interrupted her. "The baby is theirs."

"How old is he?"

"She," Ciarán corrected the driver. "Six months."

"Not a good time for having babies," Rodrigo mumbled.

"Babies are always a blessing." Carmen rocked her

daughter. The child was her daughter, nobody doubted that. Any random stranger could see immediately that Ciarán didn't belong to the family.

"That's what you need. A blessing. Are you all teachers from La Institución?" Rodrigo asked. Pedro nodded.

"Heard of that place. It was good. What a shame."

"Yeah." Ciarán caressed the scab on his forehead. The wound was almost healed.

"Some people have lost respect for everything. Churches, museums, schools…they just want blood," the driver continued. "What are you going to do in Salamanca?"

"Just passing by." Pedro peered through the window. "We're heading to the Netherlands. We have laissez-passers to leave Spain. I'm a scientist. Some colleagues live there, see."

"That's good." For the first time, Rodrigo's voice was not as rough. "That's good. What about the package? It's heavier than a corpse."

"That's my sculpture. We're to deliver it to the Irish College at Salamanca," Carmen answered.

"It's beautiful," Ciarán said.

The car stopped in front of an old building, the Irish College. Light flashed in the darkness of the street. A torch. Someone knocked on the car window. Rodrigo opened his door.

"We have to be quick. Get off." A man with glasses and a pointy white beard grabbed their only suitcase in his free hand. He dropped it on the pavement, fumbled in a pocket, and gave an envelope to Rodrigo, wishing him a safe trip back to Madrid. The driver's door slammed closed and the car was gone. The man with the pointy beard had to be Miguel de Unamuno, Pedro's teacher from Salamanca. He had supported the fascists at the beginning of the war and, as university Dean, had many connections in the city.

Outside, the rain was corrosive like acid. Soon, Ciarán was drenched.

"Miguel, so good to meet you again," Pedro shook hands with the old man before reaching for the suitcase. Miguel held onto it, and the two men fought for the suitcase handle for a few seconds. Miguel won.

"Yes, Pedro, gracias a Dios you're all here safe. No time to talk though. Come on, let's go. Hurry. They're very angry after the communists bombed the city."

"What?"

"No time, come on. I'll take you to the other car."

"No. No." Carmen refused to move. A small puddle of water was forming around her. "We're not taking the *other* car. We're going to the Irish College first. The statue. You've to take the statue. Ciarán, get the statue," she ordered.

He went to the bulk covered in dirty sheets and cardboard that Rodrigo had left on the ground.

"Carmen, I apologise to you. Pedro told me you are a sculptor, but…" Miguel said.

"Pedro, help me here," Ciarán said, trying to grab the statue. "Help me."

Carmen continued to argue with Miguel and Pedro.

"I'm delivering the statue to the Irish brothers," she said, raising her voice over the rainfall. "That's why we're here, Pedro. That's why we stopped at Salamanca. You said so."

"Miguel has friends in Bilbao, Carmen. They're taking us up to the coast, to catch the boat. To the Netherlands. We've already discussed this. Carmen, please."

"He's right," Ciarán peered at the old man, who wore round glasses that framed his owl eyes. "We're doing nothing to upset the fucking fascists. They won't even know we're here. Pedro."

"Carmen…" He grabbed her hand but she shoved him away. The baby whimpered. "You're risking your daughter's life," Pedro said.

"Yes, Carmen, let's go." Ciarán stopped trying to grab hold of the statue and walked towards them. He knew Pedro was right. It was foolish, stupid, and unnecessary. They already had the boat tickets to go to the Netherlands, far away from the war, the horror, the bombs. Stopping at the Irish College on their way north was pushing their luck. Yet, that statue was everything to Carmen.

"Do I have to remind you who paid for the boat tickets? And the safe-passage letters?" she said. "The statue is what's saving us. They've never been late, not even with one single payment, not even after the war. I owe them, Pedro. I have to deliver it to them."

Carmen ran down the street, towards the Irish College. She climbed the stone stairs to the black wooden door and banged the knocker.

"Fuck it." Pedro came back to take one end of the statue and Ciarán grabbed the other. They took it to the door.

The rain poured down on them, heavier than ever.

Ciarán couldn't see – the water irritated his eyes, blurred his vision. The baby had stopped crying, but she shouldn't have been out in the cold. Her place was inside a car on the way to Bilbao. Dry.

The door had a small grilled window that served as a peephole. Carmen tiptoed and pressed her face against it, whispering. She must have seen someone. "They want the statue inside," Carmen said.

"The monks?" Ciarán asked.

The door creaked opened. Two men hunched in dark habits waited on the other side. One of them carried a torch. Their skin was parched, like old paper, both of them withered and desiccated with age.

"Good evening, brother," Miguel greeted the monk that carried the lamp. "My good friend de la Cierva—"

"Yes, yes. Please, bring it inside."

"You're going to need help: the statue is heavy," Carmen told them.

"This is not a good idea," Pedro said. "Carmen, we need to go. Leave it here. They can deal with it."

"Just help them bring it inside," she said.

Ciarán held one end, while Pedro manoeuvred the other down the entrance. They stumbled past the cloister, following Carmen, Miguel and the monks.

The courtyard had a well in the centre. Water leaked, pouring out of the well shaft and flooding the cobbled square. It went into Ciarán's shoes, soaking his feet. His fingers slipped on the damp wrappings of the statue.

"Can we help you?"

Ciarán let a sigh of relief when two men appeared. Until he lifted his head, saw, and realised.

The green uniform.

The arrows and the yoke.

The statue wobbled – Pedro had also noticed.

"Good evening, General Márquez," he heard Miguel say.

"Good evening, Don Miguel. This bloody rain…" one of the soldiers helped them carry the statue. "Come inside."

Ciarán met Carmen's eyes. This is it, he thought, and he almost heard her saying yes, this is it.

They all followed General Márquez into the chapel.

A few candles burnt; the smell of rain mixed with the stink of wood rotting in the damp. At the end of the room, the altarpiece shone, coated in gold leaf and painted with images of angry saints. Jesucristo stood, crucified, on top, his sad face compassionate as though sorry for them. He was used to the pain, the blood, the constant suffering. Below him was an empty space where the image of the patron saint should have been. There were bullet holes all over the altarpiece.

They set the statue on the ground. There was a deep, reverberating sound when the marble collided with the stone floor. Like the start of a ritual.

Soldiers sat on the benches and stood on the balcony on the second floor, cleaning their rifles, eating from cans, chatting in small groups. Rodrigo had already told them that the glorious rebels from the Nationalist Army were protecting the churches, convents and monasteries. Terrible news came from Barcelona and the east, where the republicans were setting the sacred places on fire, raping the nuns, and killing the priests. Some of the soldiers gazed at them. Ciarán lowered his head.

"So, what is this, Don Miguel?" General Márquez cleaned the rain from its face with a handkerchief. It was embellished with blue embroidery, and Ciarán saw the letters "J" and "M".

"It's the work of my good friend, de la Cierva. A very talented sculptor, the Irish brothers commissioned her to make this piece years ago." Miguel kept a confident tone, but Ciarán could see how he held his hands behind his back to hide their trembling.

The statue was still wrapped. Rodrigo was right. It looked more like a wrecked body swaddled in a shroud. But Ciarán knew what was inside. Carmen's finest creation. A miracle. A true one, like him bringing El Toro back to life, giving Carmen her baby, or preventing the bomb from exploding in El Prado. They were going to be saved.

"Can I see?" General Márquez asked.

Many of the soldiers had come forward and were now peeking at the bulk. "Yes," Ciarán answered.

Márquez unwrapped the statue with great care. The monks came closer to examine. Ciarán tiptoed.

The block of marble was gone. In its place, a young man with soft pearly skin was revealed.

His limbs were lustrous and slender, displaying the candour of adolescence. His head was held high, gazing ahead, with features that were too extravagant to be perfect. That's why he looked so real. So alive. His weightless body was in harmony with the bull he rode. A great animal with a thick neck and terrible legs, tail up, alert. Yet, the boy held one of his horns – fearless – and smiled, because he was not taming El Toro but guiding him along. There was so much detail – from the veins on El Toro's neck to the little bones on the saint's feet; from his teeth to El Toro's balls. The soldiers and the monks spent a long time staring at the statue. This was the first time the piece had been exhibited. Ciarán could see himself in it – the broad hands, the crooked nose – yet the real St. Ciarán, the one created from the Carrara marble, had that divine halo already.

"What is this?" General Márquez asked.

"It's St. Ciarán. It's a commission paid by the Irish College that I–" Carmen said.

"He's naked."

"Yes, well, he—"

"And you say he's a saint?" the general added. "Who are you again?"

"I'm Carmen de la Cierva, a sculptor. The Irish College commissioned me to carve a statue of St. Ciarán."

"Where are you from?"

"Madrid."

"Your documents."

"They…the car…" Carmen stammered.

"Here they are." Pedro shown their passports and laissez-passers. General Márquez looked at them.

"You're teachers from La Institución."

They didn't answer.

"And the boy is your nephew? How come you're not fighting for Spain, chico? Salamanca was bombed by the communists two weeks ago. How's Madrid doing?"

Ciarán felt as if the cold muzzle of Márquez's gun was already pressing against his nape. "Bad," he answered.

"Get the baby," the soldier told him.

Ciarán took the bundle from Carmen's arms. He was not used to holding her – and she started moving and making small noises. He was scared of squeezing too hard and hurting her, but his fingers were rigid and unresponsive. It was the cold. The baby smelt of pee and rain. He started to feel sick.

"Too many academics, not enough soldiers. It's sad seeing Spain like this, don't you think?" Márquez said. "That's the most disgusting thing I've ever seen." He pulled out his automatic pistol and pointed at the statue.

"No!" Carmen tried to grab the gun.

Márquez shot at Carmen.

She dropped to the floor.

Pedro screamed and hurtled towards the general. Márquez shot him.

Blood rained all over St. Ciarán. El Toro's eyes stayed blind.

The baby howled.

"Fucking communists," Márquez said. There was blood on his face, too.

"Virgen Santa...what in the name of...?" Miguel stumbled. "This...this is murder, you..." One of the monks held him.

The baby howled.

General Márquez pointed the pistol at Ciarán. He was numb with shock. It was not supposed to be like this. Where was the miracle? The miracle had to happen. Any time now.

"Are you a fucking communist too? Are you?" The general's arm trembled. The miracle.

Márquez's finger moved to pull the trigger.

The marble bull stared back at the general. His head was up, his muzzle open. His horns were large and undulating. He was about to charge yet he remained quiet inside the stone. El Toro.

The baby howled.

"He's holding a baby, por Dios." One of the monks approached the soldier.

Ciarán realised that his hands were like claws, squeezing the little body. And the baby kept howling, and howling, and nobody would make her shut up. He let her go.

"Dios!" the monk gasped when the baby dropped to the floor. Ciarán collapsed by her side, grabbed her with immense care and started unbuttoning his shirt.

"What the fuck..." General Márquez was still pointing the pistol at his head.

"General Márquez, stop, stop now, please, this is the house of Dios…" The monk held him back.

The baby's howls felt like hard blows on Ciarán's head. There was just one way to calm her. He took her to his breast. She took her to her breast. The baby's face was red and her eyes were closed tight but she latched on to the nipple. And sucked. Ciarán started shivering. He looked at the dark blood pouring slowly on the floor; she felt the milk flowing. He opened his mouth to wail. But there was nothing left inside her.

"What on…" General Márquez lowered the gun.

"What…?" The monks bowed down.

"He's St. Ciarán…"

"St. Ciarán…"

They joined their hands in prayer.

"He's breastfeeding a baby!" a soldier said. "That's not…"

"Look, look, come!"

"Quick, quick."

The soldiers crowded around Ciarán, the baby, and the two corpses.

Don Miguel was crying.

"St. Ciarán please, forgive us…"

General Márquez, specks of blood still on his face, fell to his knees and struggled to cross himself with shaking hands.

"It's a miracle," he mumbled.

The Book of Cow*

* Original manuscript found on The Spanish Rover, a passenger ship that arrived in Amsterdam and Joined States on the 382 AF. The ship is believed to have sailed from Neo Dublin right after the annihilation of the floating city. The Book of Cow is a hand-written Irish translation adapted from a Spanish translation (also found on The Spanish Rover). The Spanish translation is an adaptation of the original Book of Cow manuscript, written in Old Irish in Clonmac-noise, Ireland, on the 6th BF. This new version of the Book of Cow was found wrapped in a piece of fabric and hidden along with other documents in a safe in the cockpit of The Spanish Rover. Among these was a Spanish book titled *The Bull's Betrothed*. The other documents were damaged by water and have proved illegible.

Loughmichnois

I.   Hear the story of Queen Eanna's treason and how Saint Chiaráin extended AO's privilege from humans to cattle.

On the eve of Beltain, Eanna, daughter of the Tuatha Dé Dannan and queen of the Uí Néill and the Land of Connachta, discovered two outsiders trying to steal her cattle. She decided to punish them by offering them as a sacrifice to Goíldeglass, the Water God who dwelt beneath the waters of Loughmichnois. The two thieves were a sister and a brother, and they were young and smelt of lavender and honey. Both had dark eyes, and black curls like snail shells. Their skin was the texture of Persian silk, the colour of oats after they have dried. They had travelled from the Land of Everlasting Sun, Iberia, which was known in Éire as the Land of the Dead because a life lived in such brightness was unthinkable. They spoke Éire's tongue, but their words dragged with a rare tune.

Queen Eanna brought her court to the lake shore: her women warriors of naked breasts and sinewy thighs, her druid Druggan whose hands were tinted with poisonous herbs, and her dogs smelling of rabbits' fear. They were all covered in gold and purple ritual paint, the colours of the Uí Néill clan.

Close to Loghmichnois' shores, mallards swam, alert. Queen Eanna called her women warriors and told them:

Tie the boy to the pole, facing south.

Bring me the girl, she is exotic and we can use her as a gift.

The siblings cried and screamed as they were dragged in front of the queen. Eanna pulled the girl's coarse hair to bring her close to her side.

— I will call you Leah.

You will be my present to Finnian and his monks in Cluain

Ioraird, so they pray for my victory as High Queen of Éire.

Your brother will be Chiaráin, Eanna said, naming the boy after the darkness of his features.

— Please, let him go, the girl cried. Punish me but let him go.

— You will pay for your theft in service to the monks, Druggan told her.

And you will wish then that your life had ended as quickly as your brother's.

At Queen Eanna's gesture, Druggan brought forth a ritual knife with a handle carved of cedar. He approached Chiaráin from behind and laid his hands on the shivering body. The knife swooped down. The hamstringing was quick, the rendering of skin, muscle and tendon a gaping mouth on Chiarán's legs. And he never walked again.

II.   Under Beltane's purple sky, the women warriors threw Chiaráin into Loughmichnois. His eyes were still open but his broken body was unable to move, and so he sank. A grey heron witnessed the sacrifice from the other side of the lake. Her wise eyes stared at Queen Eanna, sure that the leader of Uí Néill would regret her actions one day. Black-headed gulls cried, spiralling down in circles.

III.   Rain came to wash the skies while Chiaráin sank deeper and deeper into the depths of the lake. He passed by the curious reeds. A mute swan with his orange beak full of insects and mud saw him sink. He went down, past a small colony of diving water rats. He went down.

Turning.

He floated through clouds of frogspawn with vestigial tadpoles worming inside their crystalline cages. He went down.

Down.

His body brushed the bottom of Loughmichnois, a bed of softened lime rocks covered in yellow algae and sea centipedes.

The lakebed trembled.

A silver flash.

And there he was, Goíldeglass, the Water God, the Silver Snake of Loughmichnois. Goíldeeglass was hungry because he had to keep the island of Éire afloat. Describing a god is forbidden by curses and the threat of hell, yet, a few words shall be risked. Goídeglass's eyes were deep and metallic, steel blue broken by rainbows. He had two shining horns over his head and a sharp snake face that smelt like the sorrow of reeds and newts. Gods are made from a different flesh; not clay but a mixture of silver and crystal grains. Goíldeglass spiralled down, blowing lake water currents from his nostrils. The water that came from inside the god was so enchanted that if an invalid drank it, the lame one would be immediately healed. Water like this kept the fields fertile so they gave birth to apple trees, bog orchids, bird cherries, aspen trees, wild strawberries, dog roses, and elder trees.

The Water God came closer to sniff the boy: bread and olives from the Land of the Dead. Chiaráin did not believe in Éire's gods, but in Goíldeglass' eyes he saw the beginning of the universe, its end, and everything in between. He saw AO. The Silver Snake rushed away, like a fallen star ripping through the skies. Chiaráin inhaled the trail of bubbles left behind until his lungs were drenched in black blood.

IV.   Chiaráin's body returned to the surface of Lough-michnois when the sun had set and everyone was gone. The rain-washed sky was a heavy blue colour scattered with ragged clouds. The scent of apple and mushrooms lingered in the air. Chiaráin's body got tangled in the reeds, which grew thickly on the shoreline. On the other side, next to the silent heron watching for her next prey, there was a cow.

V.   A red cow, young, still a heifer. A beautiful crea-ture. Forget Loughmichnois, and the black-headed gulls' screech, and the hoverflies' buzz. Forget the heron and its prey, the doomed baby rat. Forget the last rays of sun sliding over the water. Forget Chiaráin, even if just for an instant, and look.

The heifer had almond eyes, the colour of brushed brass, full of desire for life. Eyelashes, thick and lush like a peacock's tail, covered them. Her muzzle was the pink of dewdrops on dog roses. Her velvet skin, vibrant mahogany. And those sensual hips, and her iron hooves, fit to climb mount Sinai faster than the wind. Her undu-lating horns were the colour of the freshwater pearls from Loughmichnois, and they were ethereal yet prompt to call blood and tear flesh. This heifer, bestow your eyes upon her, she was blessed by the serenity of all that is sacred. This heifer had been called by something stronger than the bellow of the bull. She had heard Chiaráin's cry.

VI.   The red cow approached the boy. She saw a human, broken, his body wrapped in blood and mud, blue skin ready to peel from his flesh, a dark mane writhing over his head like seaweed. She licked his face and felt something that reminded her of a beating heart. She pulled him to the shore with her horns and lay close to him all night, shielding him from the cold and from the evil spirits hiding behind the reeds.

VII.   The next morning came with silver dust rain. Loughmichnois and the sky melted into each other and the sun did not dare to come out. Chiaráin's fingers moved under the rain. They were garnet, and gelid at the tips. The heifer warmed them with honey-sweet saliva, awakening the blue blood that had frozen in his veins. He sensed her warmth and followed it, like a newborn calf guided by the only thing he knows: the rhythm of his mother's heart. Chiaráin's fingers, thin as the reeds, clutched at the smoothest flesh, the breast charged with life and the sacred cream. For the heifer had lived through a single spring and she had not known a bull yet, but despite this, AO called the white gush to come down her milk ducts, to pour through her snowdrop-coloured teats. The heifer exhaled at the pleasure of nurturing her first calf. She gave the boy the blessed milk, like the cow gave milk to Noah and his family when they travelled the world imprisoned in a wooden ark. Warmth bathed Chiaráin, reminding him of the sun from his long-lost Land of the Dead.

And the heifer lowed:

— I wish for trees and their protective
  shadow, like a mother's tongue on my
  spine.
  We shall go, before Queen Eanna's warriors
  follow, like carrion crows.

Chiaráin understood what she had said, word by word.

— I cannot move, he cried. Please, take me to
  Cluain Ioraird.

And he spoke Cow.

Cluain Ioraird

VIII.   Many days passed. Skies came and went, bringing heavy clouds and winds that smelt of rivers, and
black-headed gulls' screams. The red cow named herself Rua. She walked, and walked, and walked, carrying
Chiaráin on her back. She passed by Cenél Fiachach,
through oceans of grass and waving poplars. She turned
east through Fir Tulach, under the canopy of chestnut
woods. She crossed Cairbre, and Lagore's flatland, and
then veered north to Loegaire, and then west until she
smelt wood burning. She had arrived at Cluain Ioraird.

There were hovels made of stone and crowned with
straw. Fires lit the dark fields. On top of a small hill, an
oak grew. Under this tree sat a man with hair white like
clouds. His name was Finnian, wise like an old lynx, and
founder of Cluain Ioraird. As soon as he saw the red
heifer carrying the boy, he ran to meet them. His disciples followed. They came from many places: former
druids, warriors, herders, princes, bards, peasants. They
all craved knowledge as starving eaglets crave mice.

Finnian took Chiaráin in his arms and carried him
to the oak on the summit of the hill. There was a gap
inside the large tree trunk and that was where Finnian
lived. He lowered Chiaráin to rest on his pallet. The
other monks clustered behind their master. And they all
washed Chiaráin with clear water from their holy well,
taking turns to enter the oak. Afterwards, Finnian him-

self washed Rua and polished her horns and cleaned her hooves with his own hands. He had never seen such lustrous skin.

IX.   Chiaráin woke up under Finnian's care. He was fed hot nettle soup.

— Where am I? That was the first thing he asked.
— Cluain Ioraird, Rua lowed. She had squeezed inside the tree to keep him warm.
— Where is my sister? he asked the monks.
    She is dark-haired like me, and young with onyx eyes.
    Where do you keep her?
Nobody answered.
— My sister is in Cluain Ioraird, I know it.
    She was sent here by an evil queen.
    Chiaráin tried to get up from the pallet, but Finnian made him lie again.
    She is here, in these grey fields.
    Where do you have her?
The monks dressed in black ragged habits, and their skin was a blueish white. They all had toad-eyes and hollow cheeks, and hair shaved from the forehead to the crown. The odour of chalk and fish rose from the black cloth on their bodies.
— Where is she? Chiaráin cried.
— Look at their mouths, Rua said.
    They cannot answer you.
The monks' lips were brown, and tightly closed. They were stitched together. Because the Cluain Ioraird monks had made a vow of silence and abstinence. They did not talk, or sing, or eat anything other than the thin nettle soup, which could be filtered through the small

gaps between the flesh and the thread.

— Where is my sister? Tell me where she is, tell me.

Chiaráin grabbed Finnian, but the monks circled around him like crows and held him down. Chiaráin cried and screamed until Finnian decided to write the answer on a loose piece of parchment. He wrote: "Gaillimh." But Chiaráin did not know how to read. He went on screaming and crying.

— AO, why are you doing this?

Why do you keep testing me?

Do not leave me alone on this island.

— Ask them to teach you, Rua suggested.

And this is how Chiaráin became a servant for the monks in Cluain Ioraird.

X.   Summer came. During Lughnasadh celebrations, men from the nearby village brought a pregnant cow and five newborn calves, in exchange for prayers and AO's blessing on their crops. The monks kept the animals tied to poles at the back of their settlement. Soon, the cries of calves asking for their mothers poisoned the air. The women came too, the ones who wished to get pregnant, and they stayed four nights alone in Finnian's church. When they returned to their husbands, in time for harvest season, their wombs swelled with fruit.

Chiaráin could not walk, but he dragged his dead legs with his hands and elbows to look for roots in the fields. He collected nettles, dandelions, and burdock. During the night, however, his body burnt with nettle rash, and his whimpers saddened Rua. After that, the heifer carried him on her back so his hands could reach for elderberries and apples. And from then on, the boy was always seen riding his cow, like the Dagda and Tuatha Dé Dannan had done after stealing cattle from the Fir Bolg.

Among the monks were three who were fine and virtuous, known as the three beauties of Cluain Ioraird. They were brother Cainnech, brother Laisrén and brother Ninnidh. Cainnech had been a bard, Laisrén a peasant and Ninnidh the son of an immortal warrior, Aonghus. They did not approve of Finnian allowing Chiaráin to join their community. One night, they were alone in the church, working on the Book of Cluain Ioraird, and wrote these words in the margins:

Cainnech: Chiaráin is dark. He is an enemy of Queen Eanna.
The rage of AO will fall upon us.
Laisrén: He did not come here looking for salvation, but to follow his own selfish desires.
Ninnidh: He speaks Cow.
Cainnech: That is why Finnian took him in.
He saw the splendid skin of the red cow.
He has in mind binding a book with her skin.
Laisrén: We have to test Chiaráin.
See if he is fit to serve AO.
He is weak like a leafless tree.
Ninnidh: He will not survive the winter.

XI.   When the leaves of the oak tree turned gold, Cainnech, Laisrén and Ninnidh came to test Chiaráin. They led him on Rua, to the calves and the pregnant cow and made him understand he could free them and take them to the woods. Thus, Chiaráin sang the Cow lullabies Rua had taught him, to lure the animals into the green. The calves and the cow followed him. And when the boy and the three monks were under the shadow of an ancient apple tree, Ninnidh took a semi-lunar knife and severed the calves' throats.

— Stop, Chiaráin begged.

But the monk did not listen, and when he finished, he killed the cow too, opening her belly to take out the unborn calf. There was no ritual, no sacrifice, just grass soaking up the blood, and the smell of iron impregnating the monks' habits. Cainnech, Laisrén, and Ninnidh skinned the babies in front of Chiaráin, taking special care with the foetus, as its pure skin would be used to create the illuminated pages of the Book of Cluain Ioraird. Once they were finished, they left the bodies behind for the flies and the rooks.

— Murderers, Chiaráin wept that night.
  Those calves cried for their mothers.
  Now they will never see them.
  Will I see my sister again?
— Those who pay the price of another's life,
  in exchange for knowledge, shall die cursed.
  Learn to read and write, Rua lowed, and you will
  find your sister.

Chiaráin swallowed salty tears. That same night, he dragged himself to the church. Between its narrow walls there was a fire. The monks crowded together inside, passing the Cluain Ioraird book between them. Chiaráin waited behind Cainnech, Laisrén, and Ninnidh, and he held it in his turn, looking through its parchment pages, written in Latin with black ink. The volume was still very thin. Chiaráin stared at the letters he could not yet understand, and his heart was pressed sore.

XII.   Samhain was close and with it came the white-silent winter. The monks washed the calfskins with fresh water, scraping off the hairs. A sulphurous smell of spoilt eggs remained behind. Cainnech, Laisrén, and Ninnidh agreed it was time to test Chiaráin again. They put the skins in stone vats outside the church, filled the vats with beer and quicklime, and ordered Chiaráin to stir them, day and night. The first time Chiaráin sank his fingers into the brown water, he felt as if he had touched a thousand nettles. Quicklime ate the flesh from his fingertips and left blisters like pearls. Even his tears were acidic. He tried to use a branch to stir, but within a few hours the water had eaten it. The boy whispered to the rain and the darkness:

— AO, if I do not serve the Cluain Ioraird brothers
they will take me to the woods to die.
AO, you took me from my land and my sister
you saw me become a cripple, now.
Yet I am still on your path so
please help me.

And Rua heard his words, and she bent her head and used her horns to stir the poisonous waters. She spent eight days and eight nights stirring. The acid vapours of lime and beer burnt Chiaráin's eyes and fogged his breath, but he never left Rua's back. When the three beauties of Cluain Ioraird returned, they were surprised to find that Chiaráin was still alive, that the cold had not killed him. After those days, Chiaráin's skin became thicker than oak bark, able to endure frost and rain.

XIII.   The monks washed the cattle skins with clean water again, and scraped their surfaces with the semi-lunar knife until a pink, elastic layer was the only thing that remained. After this, Chiaráin came to the church in the mornings too. While the monks collected roots in the fields, he stared at the book until the different letters started making sense. He stood with his back to the wall. The sun descended until it shone from behind the altar cross, which was carved in stone and placed in the middle of the church's only window. When the red glare blinded him, Chiaráin knew the night was about to come. One night he said to Rua:

— I never thought words could be trapped,
  yet here they are inside this parchment.
  Can knowledge be kept like this instead of dying
  with the masters?
— Knowledge can be stored, Rua answered.
  And it will be found by those who seek.
— When I learn to read, I will find my sister.
  And I will write down everything I have seen.
— You will do so, prophesied the cow.
  And your name shall be known in the four cor-
  ners of Éire.

Chiaráin did not make sense of much that Rua said, but he curled himself against her and fell asleep breathing her warmth.

XIV.   After Imbolc, the winter retired and the monks dried the cow skins by stretching them on frames. Lais-rén sent Chiaráin away to find white rounded pebbles. Chiaráin dragged his body through briars and thistle, until his tunic was torn and his forearms covered in blood. He found a vixen feeding on a grasshopper. The animal's golden eyes scanned Chiaráin and she licked her fangs. The boy covered his head thinking she wanted to hunt him. The vixen sniffed him, curious.

— Please, help me, Chiaráin whispered to the vixen,
  showing her the few white pebbles he had gathered.

And the vixen hunted around, and brought him as many pebbles as she could take in her mouth. She did this many times.

Chiaráin came back to the church with three hundred and thirty-three perfect pebbles. The three beauties of Cluain Ioraird were shocked by his determination, as they had thought he would slide down the mud, fall into the river, and drown.

The monks used the pebbles to fold the skins and tie them to a wooden frame. Then Ninnidh boiled water and made Chiaráin ride Rua to scoop it over the skins to keep them wet. Chiaráin did so during forty days and nights, and he did not sleep or eat.

When this was finished, Chiaráin was as thin as a skeleton, but he did not think about apples, wild strawberries or nettle soup any more. He came back to the church and spent day and night studying the book. This time Finnian himself assisted him and taught him Latin, showing him how to hold the goose feather to write.

XV. Beltane came again, and the skins dried and the monks scraped them with the semi-lunar knife until they were the purest white, softer than a baby's breath. Chiaráin helped produce black ink by boiling old nails in the cauldron until the water turned dark. They folded the skins into pages, which they added to the Book of Cluain Ioraird. Then Chiaráin started writing, and his first words were for Finnian. This is what they wrote to each other:

Chiaráin: Where is my sister?
Finnian: Where do you come from?

Chiaráin: From the Land of the Everlasting Sun, Iberia, The Land of the Dead, as it is called by the druids in Éire.

Finnian: And why did you come?

Chiaráin: My sister and I heard from the three-horned bull, a god, that gives all knowledge to whoever sees him. So we crossed the warm sea and climbed mountains, crossed the Bán Sea and arrived here

We learnt Éire's tongue and exchanged stories for food.

Hunger drove us mad when we found no more villages,

Queen Eanna saw us trying to take her cattle and punished us.

She sent my sister to you, as a gift.

Where do you have her?

Finnian: Blessed be AO, I sent my best disciple, Bran, to the Land of the Dead.

He has not returned yet, perhaps AO called him already.

Queen Eanna is the bravest warrior in the four corners of Éire.

We pray for her victories every night, and for the angels to sing her name.

But she did not gift us any girl.

Chiaráin: Where is my sister?

Do not lie to me, I know she was here.

Finnian: You are right. A girl came, but she was
             gone before you arrived.
             She was not a gift, and she was taken by
             others.
             We do not know what happened to her.
Chiaráin: Who took her? And where?
Finnian: You are my best scholar, Chiaráin.
             You learnt Latin as though you were
             Pádraig.
             Why do you want to go? You are a monk
             now, AO's son.
             Forget your previous life, and everything
             that came with it.
             Forget the three-horned bull: I will give
             you knowledge.
             Stay with us and write the Book of Cluain
             Ioraid.
Chiaráin: I crave knowledge and the stories told by
             silent ink.
             Yet I need to find my sister first.
Finnian: You impose your will on AO, and that shall
             cost you many dear things.
             Give us your cow, and we shall tell you
             where to go next.
Chiaráin: I cannot gift the cow, she is not mine, she
             is like my sister and stays with me under
             her own will.
Finnian: Then stay the winter with us and help us
             survive it, when Beltane's fires come again
             I will tell you where your sister went.

XVI. On Samhain's eve, Finnian gave Chiaráin the
black habit of the monks, shaved his head and stitched

his lips together. Afterwards, Chiaráin prayed with the monks four times a day and was granted permission to write the Book of Cluain Ioraird with them. In the evenings, the boy left roots outside his hut so the vixen would have something to eat. During the dark nights, he communicated with Cainnech, Laisrén and Ninnidh. Here is what they scribbled on the margins:

Cainnech: All humans are equal under the eyes of
              AO.
Laisrén: This world is an illusion.
              The real world awaits us beyond the
              bridge of death.
Ninnidh: Beyond desire and gluttony and other
              animal impulses, we will reach AO's par-
              adise.
Chiaráin: Animals have also been made by AO.
              And they are not slaves of the mind.
Ninnidh: Animals are prisoners of their impulses.
              Beasts were made to serve humans.
Chiaráin: If we were like animals, we would listen to
              AO instead of being caged by our desires.

Finnian came across and saw what everyone had written. Instead of getting angry at them for not doing their work, he wrote this:

Finnian: Chiaráin, you speak like a wise man.

XVII. After he won Finnian's approval, Cainnech, Laisrén and Ninnidh hated Chiaráin and wished him dead more than ever. Winter that year came strong as a wild boar and it was as though Imbolc would never arrive. The weather was cold, hollow as an empty stomach. The monks in Cluain Ioraird starved. Wild deer ate all the roots. The monks cut the edges from the pages of their book, adding them to the cauldron to give the boiled water some flavour. They spent the dark days hunched around the small blue fires. They prayed to AO, holding stones warmed up by the embers.

XVIII.   One night, the three beauties of Cluain Ioraird came out from their shelter to dig the ground, looking for something to boil. They saw Rua. She was licking the snow. As soon as she saw them, she felt the roots of fear coiling up her legs. She smelt the iron on Ninnidh's semi-lunar knife. The calves' flesh still clung to the blade. She smelt the saliva filling their mouths and the foul odour of stomachs full of acid. She fled. Ice fell from the dark sky. Tree branches were frozen, so that when the wind hit them, they broke like brittle bones. Cainnech, Laisrén and Ninnidh chased Rua with blue fingers and the pale smile of Death.

Rua galloped past the willows. Her hooves splashed through the freezing slush. The monks followed her. Rua wanted to hide in the naked woods or in the darkness that pooled in the hollows. The frozen swamp broke under her weight and she sank into the icy waters. The monks approached. They grabbed Rua by her horns and dragged her out with hands like claws. They poked her with sticks and tied her muzzle with rope, and took her back to Cluain Ioraird.

Snow continued to fall and the last fires were lost. The monks helped Cainnech and Ninnidh hold the cow while Laisrén sharpened the semi-lunar knife. Finnian was nowhere to be seen and the monks cried from hunger. They all stamped on the ground and, under that sound,

Laisrén raised his knife over Rua.

— Stop, Chiaráin shouted at them.

Laisrén was so shocked by the sound of human words that he did as he was told.

Chiaráin came to him, dragging himself through the dirt and the snow. His lips were bleeding because he had ripped the stitches from his mouth to speak. He had broken the vow of silence. Everyone waited for AO's rage to fall upon him.

Chiaráin said to Rua:

— Come to me.

The animal tugged at the rope with renewed energy.

— Who are the demons you listen to? Chiaráin
    asked the monks.
    Despite the hunger pangs of winter
    do not dare to kill.
    Break the stitches from your mouths.
    Eat the mud, the bark from trees, eat
    the snow. Do not call yourselves the sons of AO.
    You are murderers.
    Queen Eanna sacrificed her cattle to the Water
    God but you are mere butchers.

Saying this, he went for Laisrén's legs. AO gave Chiaráin strength and Laisrén fell into the snow. He let the rope go, and Rua kicked and ran away.

— You want to survive? Chiaráin said.
    You want a sacrifice so this winter ends? Take
    me, I am young and a cripple, but I have
    strength.
    Take me, eat my flesh, use my skin to make your
    book.
    Ninnidh had been following the cow's escape
    with his eyes, but she was gone. He looked at

Chiaráin.

— I did not steal the cow from you, Chiaráin said,
swallowing blood.

She was never yours.

But you can eat me instead.

And Chiaráin took the semi-lunar knife from the mud
and he sank it into his numb thigh and cut a lump of flesh.
Eat my body, drink my blood.

Cainnech, Laisrén and Ninnidh and the rest of the
monks stared at Chiaráin. They were horrified, frozen by
the cold that invaded their joints.

— Eat me, what are you scared of?

We kill each other in battles,

why do not we feed on each other too?

Eat me now, he cried.

And the starving monks grabbed the lump the boy
offered and drank the blood, still warm, and many
opened a few stitches to eat the flesh. They passed it
round and fed on it, for they all thought that Chiaráin's
sacrifice was their salvation.

Finnian came running down his oak. He tore his own
habit to bandage Chiaráin's leg. His disciples surrounded
him, trembling like trees under a storm. Their habits
flapped in the wind, black doves fallen from their nest.

Finnian howled a low tune, a prayer without words.
And his monks all put their hands together and knelt
facing the snow and the wind. Their lament resonated
in their empty stomachs. Chiaráin was the only one who
could chant some words, so he recited the prayer Rua
had taught him:

— AO, come here,

bring your golden cattle

bring the sun, the moon, and all the beautiful

things
you have created.
AO, come here
look at me, I am nothing but a drop
in a storm, please take me with your hands
cast your light in these dark corners
from the Bán sea to Loughmichnois.
AO, come here,
I shall give you my blood and flesh
I shall be the seed that feeds the world
I shall be a beam of light in your sun.

They prayed until dawn came, frost melted, and the
fields turned to greyish blue.

XIX.   The next morning, Chiaráin went to Finnian and said:

—	I must go
Finnian wrote:	Where?
—	To find my sister.
	You promised me you would tell me at the end of
	winter. Look at your oak. It has buds.
Finnian:	AO sent you here.
	You are one of us now.
—	Yes, AO brought me here.
	But now AO is asking me to leave and find my sister.
Finnian:	If you leave now, you will die young.
	Adventures are for warriors.
	What we seek is knowledge and all the invisible things.
—	I came from a faraway land.
	I cannot stop now, so tell me.

Finnian: I will make you a scholar.
You are my best student, and soon you
will surpass us all.
—   No. Tell me.

But Finnian refused to keep writing, and left.

XX.   That night, Cainnech, Laisrén and Ninnidh tiptoed into Chiaráin's hut. They found the boy sleeping, and left a piece of parchment next to his head. The word on it said: "Gaillimh." Later, still in the dark hours, Chiaráin read it and whispered for Rua. She emerged from the woods fast as the wind and he rode her out of Cluain Ioraird.

Once you hear the path calling, go, Rua said, when they were in the woods.

Chiaráin looked back. He could not see Finnian's oak anymore. The pipeworts growing in the land whispered to him to carry on.

Gaillimh

XXI. Chiaráin and Rua travelled through Fir Tulach and Cenél Fiachach. They headed west to the fields of Delbna and Uí Maine. They passed cattle and herds-women. They passed warriors in dirty armour. They passed hunting dogs. They travelled through Uí Fia-chrach and Aidne. The skies were infinite. And one day, when they had left Corca Mruad far behind, they arrived at the mountains that loomed over the land, proud and fierce, holding up the blue. And beyond them stretched the Bán Sea. Between the mountains and the water, a pile of houses huddled under the shadow of a fort. Chiaráin and Rua had arrived at Gaillimh.

XXII. With its stone buildings and wooden bridges, Gaillimh was the largest town Chiaráin and Rua had ever seen. The boy and the cow brought with them the grey from the paths. They sniffed the air and smelt fish entrail soup and bitter beer. It was evening time. The clouds broke over the mountains and a golden light leaked across the houses, flooding them with an orange glow.

— This reminds me of home, Chiaráin said to Rua. Sun and pale skies. I miss the warmth.

I wish I had come to Gaillimh when I sailed from Iberia.

I wish my sister was still with me.

Chiaráin stopped as many people as he could find.

— Have you seen my sister?

She is a young girl, dark like me.

— No, brother.

— No, brother.

I am sorry.

People saw his monk's clothes and gave him pieces of dried eel and a fish head, but nobody could answer his questions.

Nets hung from the windows of the houses along with fish cages covered in clams.

Rua smelt dirty steel, mixed with purple and gold tribal paint.

— Look there, she lowed.

Chiaráin looked and saw one of Queen Eanna's soldiers lurking, like a salmon waiting to ambush herring. Rua carried Chiaráin out of the town and to the beach. The sea was calm and licked the pier and the fishing boats. Black columns of stone traced a path among the waves to show the boats how to avoid the treacherous rocks.

— I know where the dark girl is, a voice said behind them.

A small boy had followed them. He wore rags, and the left side of his face was swollen, the colour of ripened apples. His left eye was but a line, yet the boy's teeth were white as the full moon that was taking shape in the sky.

— The dark girl was nice to me.

She gave me an apple.

She went to the Fir Bolg women of Inis Mór, the secret island of the Bán Sea.

Chiaráin listened to the boy eagerly and asked him who could take them there.

— People do not want to go.
They are scared of the Fir Bolg.
But I do not mind them.
I bring them eggs, and dried eel, and ground
elder roots.
You can come along with me if you wish.
— Thank you, Chiaráin replied.
Are you sailing tonight with the full moon?
The boy nodded.
— What do you want in return?
— You are a monk, said the boy.
— I am a scholar.
— Pray for me.
— Do you want to be healed?
— No, the boy replied.
People feed me because of my face.
But I have heard that God can give you a beauti-
ful afterlife,
So good that you do not want to go back into
another body any more.
Pray, so I can get that.
Chiaráin said his prayer. Then he and Rua went to the
boy's raft and sailed under the vigilant face of the full
moon.

Inis Mór

XXIII.   Rua stood on the boat, staring into the Bán Sea. The little boy rowed, and Chiaráin clung to the stern, watching Gaillimh become smaller as it receded into the distance. The boat left a trail of waves behind, like a horse's tail. Sparkling mist covered the waters, and the cold was as sharp as the semi-lunar knife. With the coming of a new day, gannets cut the air, plunging into the waters, screaming when they caught salmon between their claws. Steel-coloured dolphins accompanied the boat. The Bán Sea smelt of yellow seaweed gardens, and fish scales.

The red sun shone over the three islands: Inis Mór, Inis Meadhoín, and Inis Thiar. These islands were part of the carcass of Ekwos, the ancient Horse God who crashed into the Bán sea many aeons ago. Once the boat reached the shore of Inis Mór, the Gaillimh boy jumped out. He brought with him a basket filled with eggs, bread, and ground elder roots. He placed it on a rock shaped like a horse head and left with his boat.

XXIV.   Chiaráin rode Rua to the rocky shore and waited.

He said to Rua:

— Hunger has slimmed your limbs.
  Your red skin is like woodlands at the beginning of Autumn.

When we find my sister,
will I recognise her?

The coastline smelt of withered seaweed and broken
seashells. Beyond the shore, hills of grass and limestone
rocks rose to peaks. Seals rested on the beach, white sunlight caressing their plump, sensual bodies. Salt dried
their skins to black and silver. They beat the sand with
their fish tails to scare away the crabs. These Inis Mór
seals were larger than humans, their mouths stained with
hake blood. Rua walked down the beach, peeking at their
fangs. The seals exchanged barks, their voices wrapped
in the noise of the waves.

XXV.   Rua took Chiaráin through a sterile land
of rock and grey grass. There were no other humans to
be seen.

— I smell cattle, Rua lowed.

When the clouds gulped down the last beam of sun,
they arrived at a large rounded hut made from limestone
rocks piled on top of each other and crowned with dried
straw. One door faced south and one door faced north.
Chiaráin slid off Rua to crawl inside, and the heifer followed. Outside, rain began to lick the straw on the roof.
There was nothing in the hut but a small hole in the
straw ceiling. A single ray of light shone through it, creating a white reflection on the ground.

— What is this? Chiaráin asked.

— AO, Rua said.

There were no trees on the island.

XXVI.   Chiaráin lived in Inis Mór for many
moons, and in this time, he did not find the Fir Bolg
women the Gaillimh boy had told him about. When

there was light outside, he emerged from the hut to seek his sister. When darkness fell upon the island, he returned to the hut with Rua and no one else. At night, the wind howled and brought rain and hail to the island. Sometimes, they heard chants coming from the hills.

Chiaráin survived by eating roots and grass. The Gaillimh boy returned every full moon to leave his gifts on the horse-rock. Apples. Eggs wrapped in sheepskin. Sometimes Chiaráin found small presents left on the doorstep of his hut. Juicy yellow flowers. A carved piece of wood, which he could use as a drinking bowl. Red berries. A sharp stone knife.

Rua took Chiaráin to the hills where the high grass tasted spicy. Limestone rocks hurt her tender hooves, but from there they could see the Bán Sea surrounding them. The waters reflected the mood of the sky.

On the western and eastern sides of the island, two dark forts crouched amongst the rocks: Dún Dúchatair and Dún Aonghasa. Chiaráin approached them once. They were so tall he thought that only giants could have built them. Unnatural and ferocious, they smelt of rain and charred bones.

— Rua, we shall go back, Chiaráin whispered.
We are not allowed to be here.
Nothing good can wait beyond these doorless walls.

Ever after that moment, the black mastodontic walls of Dún Dúchatair and Dún Aonghasa appeared in Chiaráin's dreams, poisoning his sleep, and filling it with screeches and sharp claws.

XXVII.   One windy day, Chiaráin and Rua saw a woman high on the hill. She wore a bull mask and a dress made of black bull's hair. Her flesh was blue, covered in an ointment made from seal fat to protect her from the rain.

— That is my sister, Chiaráin screamed.

Rua ran towards her, as fast as the sea wind, but when they reached the top of the hill, she was gone. Her scent remained. Seal fat, myrrh, and olives.

— Seeing her now and then not seeing her,

it is like having my soul crushed a second time.

I will die here if I have to

but I will meet her again, Chiaráin promised.

He stayed, looking around the hill until the night descended. He remained there for three full days, but no one appeared.

XXVIII.   Moons passed by, and Chiaráin harvested the spicy high grass with the stone knife, and dried it at night by pressing its leaves between two limestone rocks. He did this for several nights until he had a dry sheet similar to parchment. He used ashes to create black ink, and produced his first words on his grass parchment. He wrote: "Inis Mór, graveyard of gods."

And then he stopped.

XXIX.   One night, Chiaráin slept in the hut, Rua's body shielding him from the icy currents of air and water. Outside, thunder made the ground tremble and crack open. The waves crashed on the shore, splitting the rocks. Rain forced itself into the hut through the straw and the spaces between the stones. A small, black waterfall poured through the hole that gave them AO's light during the daytime. The ground turned to mud and the straw roof dissolved. Lightning erased colour. The stench of burnt grass and seaweed filled the air. Drums pounded in the distance. Seagulls screamed. A powerful bellow followed. Rua stood up. She had smelt silver skin and lush white hair.

— The bull is close, Rua whispered.

She came out of the flooding hut and Chiaráin climbed up her back. Poisonous rain fell like knives, and wind and water blinded Chiaráin. Rua moved fast, untangling the grass around her legs. Chiaráin buried his face in the cow's warm fur:

— AO, please, do not let the black sky fall upon us,
I am nothing but a drop in your furious rain-
rage.
Please show us the way.

Fleeing from the waters, they climbed the hill. The wind changed direction and thousands of cold hands, as if from dead children, propelled them up the slope. Clouds flew over them, black, purple, grey, screaming thunder. A bellow echoed. Clouds broke into rags, and there she was: the moon. The full moon, whole and white, like Balor's eye. Mist sucked at their skin and the sound of crashing waves grew louder, but the sea was nowhere to be seen.

XXX.   After the storm the land turned into black mud, and the grass rotted. A fever came upon Chiaráin: his blood boiled, his skin turned grey, and his eyelids purple.

— Rua, he begged, bring me to the shore.
The Gaillimh boy is to come,
he will help me.

Rua did as he asked. Then she went back to the hills to look for roots and berries to feed Chiaráin, but the rain had murdered everything. The cow and the boy turned into sacks of sharp bones. Even the seals were gone. On the horizon, black smoke clouds formed over the fishing town, and at night they could see the glow of a thousand fires burning. War had come to the mainland. The Gaillimh boy did not come back to Inis Mór.

XXXI.   Consumed by fever, Chiaráin had a dream, and in his dream he was Rua, and this is what happened:

The air carried many scents: sweet almonds, liquid honey, melting sap, fresh leaves, ripening grass. And there he was. A bull, white like a frozen lake, with silver eyes, a thick neck, and slender legs. Rua felt the heat in her hips and called to him. The bull had pearl-coloured horns and the water from the storm glittered like diamonds on his skin. A third horn grew between his eyes. He shook his head and approached Rua. She lifted her tail. He bellowed and scuffed the ground. They bucked and chased each others' tails, forming a white-red whirlwind, until they were covered by stars.

XXXII.   Chiaráin slept for a full moon cycle and when he woke up these were his first words:

— I do not hear the waves.

A tanned woman with a dark curly mane was applying a blue ointment to his skin to awaken his body after the fever. She was Leah, his long-lost sister, but he did not recognise her at first, for his mind was still weak from the fever.

— You are safe, she said.

— Where is Rua?

— She is here with us, Leah said, pointing at the

cow, who sat behind Chiaráin to keep him warm.
Chiaráin looked at his sister again and finally he
recognised her.

— AO,
    frost is melting and seeds swell.
    Beyond the snow, storm and the
    waves,
    you are here.

And the two siblings entangled their arms like two
trees growing together. And they laughed and cried and
spoke in their foreign tongue.

— Where have you been, tell me.
— I knew you were alive, she replied.
    But I had to run away from the black monks of
    Cluan Ioraird.
    Their lips were stitched, but their free hands
    hurt.
    I escaped with a tribe of roaming traders head-
    ing to Gaillimh,
    and went into the Bán Sea.
    I listened to Fir Bolg's call,
    I am one of them now.
    I saw you arriving and I wanted you by my side
    but the Fir Bolg did not trust you.
    I told them our souls are one.
    I told them we both are children of the Bull
    God.
— We shall leave.
    We shall return home.
— Chiaráin, here we can find all we have always
    looked for.
    The three-horned bull and all the mysteries.
    Éire has already cast her cruel mark upon us:

we will thrive in this land of darkness.

And that is how Chiaráin stayed in Inis Mór and called it home.

XXXIII.　　　Leah had brought Chiaráin to the door-less black fort in the east, Dún Dúchatair. A herd of bulls grazed inside. There were black bulls, brown bulls and grey bulls, larger than the animals from the mainland. They all had three horns. Their teeth were worn to stubs and their horns had infinite rings.

An old woman took care of the bulls. Nobody knew her real name, but she liked to be called Máthir Tarb. Her silver hair was braided, and she wore a sealskin over her shoulders and a bull mask over her head. Her skin was also painted with the blue ointment. She moved among the herd, mumbling honey-sweet words, like a mother among her children. She fed the bulls tender buds, since the grass inside Dún Dúchatair was still green and vibrant. When she saw Chiaráin sitting on Rua, her face turned sour.

— You must go, she whispered, voice dry like bark.
— Who are you? Chiaráin asked.
　Where are the Fir Bolg?
　Why is there no one else on the island?
— Go, now, Máthir Tarb ordered.
— There were more Fir Bolg women, Leah said.
　The mad bull…
— Silence, siur, Máthir Tarb scolded her.
　You shall not reveal your sisters' secrets.
　The cripple is a man, he has no place in our island.
　He must leave.
— Máthir Tarb, there is just us now,

and who will protect the sacred bulls?
Chiaráin, listen, a poisonous rain came, two
moons ago.
It infested the grass and hurt the sacred beasts.
A white bull, the eldest of all, lost his mind.
Now he roams around the island, starving.
He ate our sisters,
and will hunt us, too.
— I heard the bull, Chiaráin said, and Rua smelt
him, too.
Máthir Tarb intervened:
— Siur, curses will fall upon you for revealing our
secrets to a stranger.
— And Máthir Tarb said to Chiaráin:
— We, the Fir Bolg, followed the Bull God from
Iberia.
We are god keepers.
We are Balor's
water.
We are the seal's
sisters. We see beyond
names.
We know the secrets of the bones, and how to
call a storm.
— I want to learn. Please, Chiaráin begged.
But Máthir Tarb hissed, turned back, and disap-
peared within Dún Dúchatair's walls.

XXXIV.   Chiaráin stayed with the Fir Bolg. Leah
gave him more blue ointment for his skin, and he noticed
that with it he was free from the piercing bite of the rain.
    Leah and Máthir Tarb gathered together inside the
walls of Dún Dúchathair every nightfall to eat, shivering

each time they heard the distant bellow of the white bull. They fed on a white substance offered in wooden bowls.

— Máthir Tarb, where is the white bull? Chiaráin asked.

And later:

— Máthir Tarb, how do you make this blue ointment?

But Máthir Tarb refused to speak to Chiaráin. She only allowed Leah to share her bowl with him. It tasted like powder and cream and it was very sweet. Chiaráin found that by drinking this, his body was warm and full of energy for several days. He soon discovered that it was milk from the breast. All the Fir Bolg women, he was told, had full breasts, even the older ones, and they took turns to feed the community.

One day Chiaráin was given an empty bowl by Leah.

— Try, she said.

But Chiaráin's breasts were flat and his nipples were dry. He looked at his sister, whose hands were busy braiding a rope from the slender dry leaves of a bush that only grew inside Dún Dúchathair.

— You will be taught the blessing of milk soon, she promised.

XXXV.   The blue ointment was scarce, so Chiaráin and Leah rode Rua down to the beach. The smoke clouds lurking over Gaillimh were darker. On the dunes lay the carcass of a seal. Its ribs were cracked, and lumps of dry meat hung from them. The sand around it was still stained with blood and bile.

— The white bull, Leah whispered,
  has been hunting again.

That night, when they were all eating, Leah said:

— Máthir Tarb, the seals are gone.
The mad bull is feeding on them now.
Without seals, there will be no blue ointment for
us.
We shall perish when the next storm comes.
— So be it, Máthir Tarb grunted.
We will join our sisters at last.
— Chiaráin, Rua lowed, you can help them.
— Yes, the boy said. Sister, Máthir
Tarb, I will find the white bull.
I will talk to him, make him stop.
— Chiaráin, it is dangerous, Leah cried.
The mad bull ate his keepers.
He will be the end of you.

But Chiaráin did not listen, and that same night he went out from Dún Dúchatair riding on Rua, seeking the mad bull of Inis Mór.

XXXVI.   Chiaráin and Rua went down the beach. Under the full moon, the sands were silver and diamonds. The wind had brought ashes and the sour smell of war to Inis Mór shores, but the bull was nowhere to be seen.

They climbed the rocky hills, covered in dead grass and abandoned rabbit warrens. They circled the ponds formed by the rain. The moon reflected on the water, but the bull was nowhere to be seen.

— Let's go to the cliffs now, Chiaráin suggested.
To the ruined fort of Dún Aonghasa.

And so, there they headed, to the second Fir Bolg fort, larger than Dún Dúchatair, and empty since the Fir Bolg race had been cursed and slaughtered by the white bull.

XXXVII.   They found the creature licking the rocks,

as he tried to find some fresh grass inside Dún Aonghasa. His three horns shone like crescent moons. His muzzle was covered with fresh rabbit blood and he had shreds of flesh trapped between his teeth. As soon as the bull caught the scent of Rua, he raised his head. His eyes were white as the moon, and blind, burnt by the malignant rain. He headed towards the smell.

— Cow, cow, cow, cow, he grunted.

Then he sniffed the air with his gigantic nostrils.

— Flesh, flesh, flesh, he bellowed.

The white bull prepared to charge. He waved his tail, and his front hoof scratched the ground. The beast thundered towards Chiaráin, faster than the storm winds of Inis Mór.

— Please, stop, Chiaráin cried, please, do not eat us.

The bull halted in mid run.

— Who are you, you talking flesh? he asked.
  I am ravenous.

— I am Chiaráin, the boy said.

— I know you are hungry, but you must
  stop. You are eating everything on this
  island.

— I am hungry, the bull said, I am hungry, and it
  hurts.

— What does? Chiaráin asked. Tell me, and I shall
  heal you.

— My entrails burn, burn, burn, burn.
  My insides are an ocean of fire.
  Flesh will calm them down.

The bull bellowed and charged again. Rua flung herself to the side to avoid his sharp horns.

— You are poisoned by the rains, I was,
  too. Listen, I can save you, Chiaráin insisted.

— He is beyond cure, Rua whispered to him.
His insides were burnt by the poisonous rain.
His mind is already gone.
— It hurts, it hurts, the white bull bellowed.
Where are you, you talking flesh?
He sniffed the air again to follow their trace.
— I can help you take the pain away, Chiaráin
promised.
— No, no, no, no.
— Let's jump over the cliff together, Chiaráin sug-
gested.
AO, with the ocean's water, will cleanse us both.

And saying this, Chiaráin went from Rua's back to
the stoned ground. He dragged his body with his arms
and came to the white bull. The creature's breath was
like water boiling and reeked of rotten flesh. Chiaráin's
fingers nudged the bull's iron hooves, and the animal
felt the presence of AO so he lowered his legs. The boy
climbed up, holding onto locks of white hair, until he was
perched on the bull's back, arms around the beast's thick
neck, safe from his deadly horns.

— Go now, Chiaráin commanded, let's meet the
waves.

And under the dark skies, they went. Chiaráin did
not own the bull like Gilgamesh had owned Gugalanna,
like Hathor had owned Apis, like Minos had owned
the Minotaur, like Moses had owned the Golden Calf.
Instead of owning the bull, Chiaráin was one with him,
while both of them sank into Balor's eye.

XXXVIII.   Chiaráin and the white bull hit the black
waters of Balor's realm. AO protected them, so they did
not drown. Currents kept them afloat and safe from the

hidden rocks at the base of the cliffs. Chiaráin bobbed up and down with the sea-swell. And he saw that the bottom of the ocean was covered with the skulls and bones of humans and cattle. He swam up to the surface again, always holding the bull's horns. A falcon took flight from the cliffs. There was a flat rock, and next to it, a crack opened, giving way to a cave. The white bull climbed the rock and collapsed there. His head crashed against the rock, and his central horn broke and wobbled from his forehead.

The bull grunted:

— The pain is here, but I remember who I am,
   now, drink from my milk,
   yours is the strength.

And Chiaráin was dismayed and weak but he did not dare to disobey the bull, so his fingers tapped the creature's stomach until he found his small teats, hidden between the soft fur and his huge testicles. Chiaráin tugged on them until a few drops of grey liquid dripped into his mouth. It tasted sour but energised Chiaráin's spirit.

And the white bull said:

— Dry darkness, away from the waves.
   Take my horn and stab me between the eyes.

Chiaráin was terrified when he heard these words, but again he did not dare to disobey. The blood dripping from the bull's broken horn flowed down to the sea. The boy grabbed the horn and pulled until there was a crack. He held the horn between the bull's eyes.

The creature bellowed:

— Do it,
   death is calm
   immortality a curse.

The boy sank the horn in the bull's thick skin. There was a golden spark, and that is how Chiaráin killed his first god.

XXXIX.   Leah's heart ached for Chiaráin, so she went out looking for him. When she found Rua peering down the cliff, she did not despair but went to the cow carrying the rope she had braided for many moons and told her:

   — So Chiaráin fell down, but I know he is alive.

     Siur, let me tie this rope to your strong neck.

     I will go down and save him

     and you will pull us both up and back to life.

Leah tied one end of her rope to the cow's neck and the other to her waist. She lowered herself down the cliffs, stepping on the overhanging rocks and reaching for them with her hands. For Leah was fast as a gannet and knew Inis Mór's cliffs well. She found her brother curled next to the bull's corpse, keeping warm from the icy waves, holding the broken horn tight between his hands. Leah took him on her back, and Rua pulled them both up the cliff. The cracks smelt so intensely of seagull droppings that Chiaráin felt acid form in his throat and was about to faint, but Rua pulled strongly and brought the siblings back before sunrise. The strength of the red cow was such that, from that day onwards, she had a place in the Fir Bolg's legends, next to the Primal Ox and the Bull God.

XL.   Máthir Tarb fed Chiaráin fermented liquor made of seaweed, and that helped him recover. When she saw the horn in his hand, she knelt down and said:

   — Siur, you have become horned now.

You have drunk the bull's milk.
You are blessed by the Primal Ox.
Yours shall be the secrets hidden between the doubles
of Life and Death, Light and Dark,
Woman and Man, and the white torrent of life.

The boy did not say anything and stayed quiet for several days, as he was tired and weak after riding the bull. But from that moment on, his body acquired strength, and dark hairs grew on his face, arms and legs, for Chiaráin became both female and male, and held the power of the Primal Ox.

XLI.   Chiaráin collected the high-grass growing inside the fort and turned it into parchment. He made pens from seagulls' lost feathers, and ink from ashes. Then he went to Máthir Tarb and said:

— I want to know how you create the blue ointment that fights the rain.
I want to know the secret words to enrage the seas and wake Balor.
I want to know where the three-horned bulls come from.

Máthir Tarb did not want to reveal the Fir Bolg sacred mysteries to a stranger. Yet, Chiaráin had saved them all from the white bull, and he had drunk the creature's milk.

— Leah will show you, she muttered.
The three-horned bulls are our ancient herd
from the lands of Mesopotamia and Iberia
we brought them with us, to Éire.

And then, Chiaráin looked at Leah. Her sister's body was changing: her breasts were larger and her belly was growing. He asked Máthir Tarb.

— We need no man, the old woman answered.
Our bodies breed our daughters.
The Womb unfolds like a flower, then a fruit,
like the Primal Ox created the world from darkness
and Mary offered us her light by creating Jesus.

Chiaráin listened to all this and then he wrote it down.
Máthir Tarb complained:

— Siur, our secrets are not to be kept in
parchment so despicable eyes can steal them.
But Chiaráin replied:

— This book will keep your wisdom safe for gener-
ations
should some evil arrive to this lost island's shore.
The master can die, but Balor and AO are
immortal in these pages.

Máthir Tarb did not have anything to say to this, and she and Leah helped Chiaráin produce more high-grass parchment. He wrote the tales of the Bull God on them, and the stories of Dún Dúchatair and Dún Aonghasa too, and these scrolls survived for millennia before the sea destroyed them.

XLII.   With the white bull gone, seals returned to the beach. When the old ones died, Leah took Chiaráin and Rua to cremate the large, grey bodies. Before offering them to the flames, the girl used a stone knife to cut the skin and take the thick layer of fat that lay over the flesh. Aided by Chiaráin, she spent the whole day collecting the golden substance. They brought the seals' fat to Dún Dúchathair in wooden bowls, and there they boiled it for fifty days and fifty nights until it became hard and black in colour. While the seal fat boiled, Leah walked around the fort's walls collecting young leaves from the woad plant. She cut them into small pieces with the stone knife and left them to dry until they were the consistency of wood. After this, she added water every day until the woad fermented. In the cauldron, she mixed it with bull urine and the fat from the seals. She stirred and stirred. The smell made Chiaráin sick for the first days. It reeked of raw bowels and rotten leaves, and only the freezing winds from the sea weakened the stench.

After one hundred days, an ointment formed: bright blue in colour, oily and spicy. Leah gave it to Chiaráin to cover his naked body so he was immune to the rain. Chiaráin used it on Rua too, and her red hair sparkled in gold and blue.

XLIII.   The time came for Leah to give birth. A storm raged that night, and the winds carried the uproar of the war in Gaillimh to Inis Mór's shores.

Máthir Tarb took Chiaráin to the side and said:
— Look across the waves
   the mainland is lit by a thousand fires.
   Like stags, the clan leaders fight for Éire's
   throne. Now, tell me,
   did you see the future in the bull's entrails?
— I saw a golden spark, Chiaráin answered.
   Nothing else.
— Gold is one of the colours of the Uí Néill.
   Queen Eanna will defeat her cousin Diarmait.
— Let the world spin in its madness, Chiaráin said,
   scared at the sound of Eanna's name.
   This island shall outlive them all.
Back inside the fort, Chiaráin saw his sister in great

suffering: red and brown waters fountained between her legs, and she had a feverish face. He called Rua, who allowed Leah to lie against her body. The heifer licked the sweat off Leah's forehead to keep her fresh. The air was ripe with fish and salt. Máthir Tarb pressed Leah's belly and guided Chiaráin's hands so he could ease the new-born into the world. A breeze of fresh-cut grass wafted between the walls when the baby girl emerged. Her skin was blue and purple, covered in a sweet white molasses. Chiaráin held her tight and her tiny pink lips attached to his nipple. The baby sucked, and a thin stream of milk spurted into her mouth.

And that is how Chiaráin learnt the ways of the womb.

XLIV.   While Leah was sleeping with the new-born baby on her chest, Máthir Tarb whispered to Chiaráin:
— Take the placenta to the shores and drop it into the sea:
Balor shall be honoured after an auspicious birth.

Chiaráin did as he was ordered, and taking the dark maroon placenta, he rode Rua from the hills to the sea, not knowing that by doing so he was bringing doom to the Fir Bolg.

XLV.   Queen Eanna was greedy. She wanted to destroy her cousin Diarmait but she had heard of the three-horned bulls of Inis Mór and wanted them in her herd too. So, when the sun was at its highest point in the grey skies, she took a boat with twelve of her warriors, and they rowed to the island faster than any storm.

When they arrived on the shore, they saw Chiaráin and Rua, and they chased them like hunters chasing deer, and that is how they found the entrance to Dún Dúchathair, where Druggan the druid had told them the bulls were kept. Once inside, the soldiers set fire to the high-grass, to frighten the bulls. Máthir Tarb woke to the smell of blood, fire, and cattle's grief. When she emerged to protect her herd, Queen Eanna laughed at her, eyes tainted with the ocean's rage.

— Look at this monster, she said to her soldiers.
      The Fir Bolg are not human, but more like animals.
      They are of no use to me, hunt them if you find it amusing.
      They wear seal skins; we shall see how quick they are on the ground.

And Chiaráin took his sister and the baby, and the three of them hid with Rua between the walls. Chiaráin had in his hands the white bull's horn, but his fear of Eanna was too strong and he did not dare use it.

Máthir Tarb said to the queen:

— Eanna, the rage of the Bull God will fall upon you and your kingdom.
      Make dirty what is sacred and you shall regret it during many lives.

But Eanna answered:

— You, the Fir Bolg, come from the Fomorians, an extinct race.
      I am daughter of the Tuatha Dé Dannan,
      and do not care about your prophecies.

And with a single blow she cut off Máthir Tarb's head with her axe, while her soldiers captured the bulls with ropes and dragged them to the Queen's boat.

Leah cried to see her sister slaughtered; she let out a shriek and came out from the walls, with the baby tied to her chest. With her stone knife, she began cutting the ropes that held some of the bulls. The animals ran away, violent with fear and fury, and charged the soldiers. A few fell from the cliffs and the waves gulped down their screams. When Queen Eanna saw Leah helping the bulls, she recognised her from her sacrifice at Loughmichnois.

— I let you live once,
 but this time I will send you to the Tech Duinn
 and the Otherworld.

And saying this, the Queen buried her axe in Leah's face. The girl toppled to the ground like a falling tree, with her child in her arms. Queen Eanna kicked them and shouted:

— Goíldeglass, the Water God,
 has promised me Éire
 and everything that dwells between the water
 and the sky.

And the soldiers took the bulls that were left and brought them to the boat and they all came back to Gaillimh to keep on fighting the war.

XLVI.   Chiaráin crawled across the blood-drenched fields to his sister's body. Máthir Tarb lay dead on the burnt grass, beside Eanna's soldiers. Leah's skin had already hardened to stone. There was white and red where her face had once been. The baby was cold as the rocks under the sea. Chiaráin said:

— AO,
 I will not stop
 breathing
 until Queen Eanna's bones

are regurgitated by carrion crows.

And he took Leah's clothes and dressed in them. He threw her body and the baby's over the cliffs to Balor, and did not speak a word for one hundred and four days.

XLVII.   Chiaráin and Rua built a raft out of the pieces of wood that had been washed up on the island's shores. When they pushed their raft into the waves, only the seals watched them sail away. Chiaráin took nothing from the island but the white bull's horn. On the top of the mountains, a shadow observed their departure. Nobody knows if any of the Fir Bolg women survived, but none have been seen in Inis Mór since that grim day.

Hare Island

XLVIII.   At Gaillimh there was fire, screams, and the thunderous sound of blades clashing together. Arrows cut the air faster than the flight of terns. The place stank of dead flesh and anguish. Gold and purple banners from the Uí Néill washed over the waters. Queen Eanna fought her cousin Diarmait to decide who would hold control over the once prosperous town of Gaillimh.

Chiaráin's raft drifted on the currents to a small island in the bay. It was called Hare Island among the people of Gaillimh because thousands of hares leapt around the sterile rocks. They were exceptional swimmers and fed on fresh fish. Chiaráin guided Rua to a side of the island protected by a rock wall, on top of which grew a single elder tree. He sat next to her in silence. The screams coming from Gaillimh were like waves crashing against the cliffs of Inis Mór. Chiaráin sat for so long that his dark hair grew to cover all of him and honeysuckle tangled around his limbs.

On the thirty-second day, people began to come to Hare Island. First it was the young orphans escaping from the war. They jumped into the waters and, like the hares, they arrived swimming. Next came the fishermen who had lost their boats, because the port was in flames. Then the traders whose markets had been destroyed. Then the beggars and the scholars who could not find a scrap to put in their mouths. They were all starving, but the first thing they saw in Hare Island was not the flock of hares but Chiaráin sitting at the base of the rock. He was dressed in his cow-hair tunic and he was as fair as the Virgin Mary. By his side, everyone felt safe and protected. The elder tree growing above him flowered and gave white berries. Rua guarded Chiaráin and she licked his hands and feet every day to keep them in the warmth of life.

XLIX. People fell ill because they did not have fresh water and the berries were not enough to keep them nourished. They did not dare hunt the hares because they thought they had been blessed by the saint. Instead, on Imbolc, the sixty-seventh day, a woman suggested they took milk from the saint's cow.

This woman approached Rua. She was a fishmonger but she knew how to milk. However, before her hands could grab the red cow's teats, the animal spoke, and this time AO made everyone understand what she said:

— Woman, you shall not take milk that has not
   been gifted.
   Like your hands enslave and slaughter cattle,
   mankind enslaves and slaughters you and your
   sisters.
   You are kept for breeding,
   your fruit is abused, they eat everything you keep
   under your skin.
   Woman, praise the milk and you shall be
   respected.
   Learn the secrets of white and no man will dare
   hunt you again.

Everyone knelt when they heard the cow speak. And some of them laughed, and others cried, and the wise ones prayed to AO. The fishmonger woman brought a feverish baby to Chiaráin.

— Please, forgive me, she said.

Forgive me for offending your sacred cow.

But I need to feed my daughter, she implored.

I need her to live, to see the coming of spring.

And Chiaráin extended his arms and he took the sick little girl and let her suckle. And this time, a white torrent flowed from his breast, and the child was healed. And Chiaráin fed the child mother's too, and everyone in Hare Island. Because they had tasted the saint's milk, they were free from disease and acquired the strength of young cattle. And when some of the women went into labour, Chiaráin assisted them and brought healthy babies to their breasts. Children used white stones from the sea to build a circle around Chiaráin, and everyone on the island worshipped him and his cow. Since then, every Imbolc, Éire's people pour milk into the ground to thank the generosity of Saint Chiaráin.

L.   On the ninety-first day, Queen Eanna finally managed to break through Diarmait's defences. She set fire to Diarmait's camp and hunted his soldiers. Diarmait himself was wounded but ran to the sea. Swimming across the dark waters, salt burning his wounds, the warrior thought his end had come. But then, he remembered the stories about the hermit from Hare Island who was said to have saved everyone from the horrors of the fight and had a beautiful red cow by his side. And so Diarmait swam to Hare Island.

People panicked when they saw him arrive, his body covered in blood and sword still tied to his waist. He told them:

— Fear not, sons and daughters of Gaillimh.
   I came to worship your hermit.
   So they took him to Chiaráin.
   As soon as the warrior saw him, he fell to his
   knees.
— I visited Finnian in Cluain Ioraird
   and prayed in the Hill of Tara
   but I have never cast my eyes
   on a holy figure before.
   You are fair like the Morrigan,
   mysterious like the Water God of Loughmichnois,
   in your black eyes there is the compassion of
   Christ.

For Diarmait was feverish, and infatuated by Chiaráin in the same way he had been infatuated by women. In truth, and aside from his black beard, Chiaráin was exactly like his sister Leah, hair long like the branches of a willow tree.

The warrior said:
— My name is Diarmait, from the house of the Uí
   Néill,
   grandson of Niall Noígíallach.
   I have come to ask you
   save Gaillimh from Queen Eanna.

And after saying this he collapsed, as his body was closer to death than life. But Chiaráin had heard about the Queen, so he raised his eyes and spoke for the first time in one hundred and four days.
— I shall be Eanna's doom, he said.

LI.   The people from Gaillimh witnessed the encounter between Diarmait and Chiaráin. They saw Chiaráin

treating the warrior's wounds, nursing him during the fever, and saving his flesh from decay. Thus, many of them swam back to town and spread the news: the hermit of Hare Island had healed Diarmait. The young Uí Néill was still alive and hadn't perished with his troops. At the same time, Cabhan, one of Queen Eanna's warriors, saw a dead falcon falling out of the sky, as if struck by lightning, and thought of it as a bad omen.

As soon as Diarmait could stand on his feet again, Chiaráin prayed to AO. He whispered Balor's secret words, the ones Leah and Máthir Tarb had taught him, to invoke a storm. A silver whirlwind of clouds appeared in the sky and the full moon shone briefly before the rain arrived, mixed with hail. Lightning blinded Queen Eanna and her army, whilst darkness provided shelter for Diarmait, who devised a surprise attack.

The three-horned bulls that Eanna kept tied at her camp went wild with fury. They growled, bellowed, and rubbed their heads against the ground. Lightning struck the camp three times in a row and soon flames shot up everywhere. Fire ate at the ropes that held the bulls, set their horns burning and seared the animals' eyes white. The bulls tore themselves free and stampeded through the camp, charging and destroying everything they found. That night, they killed many of Queen Eanna's warriors.

At the same time, Diarmait battled like never before among the ruined buildings of Gaillimh. He used the smoke as a shield, and with his own sword, he defeated many other warriors before the moon had reached its highest point in the sky.

— Cursed be the storm and lightning, Queen
  Eanna said,

I see my warriors turned into meat.
They will feed the fields.
Others run to join Diarmait
saying the gods are with him tonight.
Diarmait, she yelled, come, let us meet.
I want to see your blade strike.

She found him by an oak and they fought under the full red moon. Diarmait made a deep cut on Eanna's shoulder and she buried her axe into his thigh. The two of them received many terrible wounds but never fell down, not even once. When Queen Eanna was about to knock Diarmait's head from his shoulders with her axe, a three-horned bull charged her from behind. The burning horns pierced the Queen's flesh, but she reached back blindly to slash at the bull's neck with her blade. The bull sent her flying through the rain, and she fell to the ground with her armour on fire. She rolled deep into the mud to quench the flames, and survived to limp back to her camp.

The mad bulls chased and murdered warriors all night, until they stampeded down to the sea. By sunrise, Queen Eanna's banners were scorched and she had been expelled from Gaillimh. The corpses of bulls carpeted the shores.

LII.   Diarmait celebrated his victory in Gaillimh for three days and three nights. He came to see Chiaráin, gifting him with a purple tunic made from the smoothest sheepskin, and a chalice of gold and rubies, but Chiaráin refused them.
   — I do not wish for goods and treasures, he said.
     And Diarmait was amazed at the generosity of
     Chiaráin, and because of this, he admired him

more.

LIII.   After her first defeat, Queen Eanna was furious. Despite the ulcerated wounds in her back, she rode her horse to the four corners of the island to talk to Éire's other clans and convince them to join her in a final battle against Diarmait. She demanded that it take place at Loughmichnois.

Queen Eanna's followers said:

— King Diarmait is strong like a wild boar and fast like a gannet,
And he is handsome like the golden sun during its rise.
But what can he do against an army of thousands?
He shall have the brief life of a dun butterfly.

But Diarmait's followers replied:

— AO has already chosen Éire's new High-King.
Chiaráin is by his side, like in the fires' night of Gaillimh.

And Diarmait came to Chiaráin at Hare Island one more time and begged him:

— Before AO requires you take your place by his side up in
Heaven, come with me and pray for this last battle.

Chiaráin looked at the young warrior, then at Rua, and he said:

— I remember the three-horned bull I met at the cliffs of Inis Mór.
I saw a glimpse of gold in his blood
the same colour as the gold in Diarmait's hair.

— Diarmait may be called to be a king, Rua agreed.

There is a regal brightness in his eyes.

And so Chiaráin took Diarmait's sword and kissed it with his white lips.

Loughmichnois

LIV.   Chiaráin left Hare Island and rode Rua in the footsteps of Diarmait and his army. They passed Uí Fiachrach Aidne, Uí Maine, Delbna, Cenél Fiachach, Tethba and Cairbre before arriving on the shores of Loughmichnois. Diarmait positioned his troops on the south side of the lake while he waited for Queen Eanna to arrive. The young warrior was nervous. Queen Eanna's army was several times larger than his, and the battle would take place in her land. Diarmait's druid, Jarlath, came to him at sunset and said:

— I will assure your victory tomorrow on Beltane.
I shall crown you as a king tonight in the Dagda's presence. Let Him see you are not afraid of fulfilling your destiny.

Jarlath made a crown from mistletoe and oak leaves, and sang an incantation as he set it on Diarmait's head. He lit a branch from an elder tree and spread the violet smoke around the golden warrior.

— Let's sacrifice five cows to please the Dagda, the druid said.

The soldiers brought the weeping black cows. Their udders blossomed with purple ulcers, green flies stuck to their eyes and to the gaping wounds where their horns had been severed.

Jarlath said:

— Look Diarmait, this is a present from Finnian,

the saint from Cluain Ioraird.
These cows were meant to feed his entire mon-
astery.
Now he and his monks keep abstinence
while they pray for your crowning at Tara.
— Leave them be, Chiaráin commanded the druid.
Murder would only repulse AO.
Diarmait will be the next High-King.
— What do you know of the Dagda, our gods and
rituals?
You have dark skin; you were not born in these
lands.
— What do you know of Finnian and the Book of
Cluain Ioraird?
And the secrets of the Fir Bolg?
Do you know the magic hares of Gaillimh?
Do you speak Cow?
And saying this, Chiaráin grabbed the burning stick
and tossed it to the ground where it set fire to a bird-
cherry bush.
— Look, that is the only God you will find, Chiaráin
said.
There are no others dwelling in the skies or
under the ground.
There are no ears eager to listen to your words
or hands ready to accomplish what you ask.
Take action, fight, soil the sword.
That is how Diarmait will be High King.
Now go and find yourself a weapon for tomor-
row's
battle or hide with the cowards when the sun
goes down.
Do not kill what is innocent

and use AO's name to clean your hands.
Jarlath was white as the sky and he smelt of
damp moss and burnt fabric. Diarmait said to
his druid:
— Listen to what Chiaráin says.
Do as he commands.
Chiaráin gave me Gaillimh.
Under the dark skies of Éire,
there has never been a fairer soul.

The black cows were freed, and Rua licked their
wounds. Chiaráin cleaned their ulcers with fresh water
and elderberry sap. Afterwards, he ordered that they
should be treated as though they were noble women.
They grazed all over the campsite but no one dared to
touch them, for they had become sacred.

LV.   Night fell and Chiaráin went to the woods. Diar-
mait saw this and went after him. He found the hermit
sitting on the roots of an oak, with Rua by his side.
Chiaráin said:
— Fear not, Diarmait.
Eanna is a worthy opponent but
you do not need the Dagda.
I was the one who promised you Tara.
— You spoke wise words, Diarmait answered.
Your ways are mysterious, but I do not
forget that I owe you my life
and because of you I won Gaillimh. Now,
however, we are at Loughmichnois.
And in the four corners of Éire, it is known
Queen Eanna is the favourite of Goíldeglass.
The Water God will assure her victory.
But Chiaráin added:

Fear not, Diarmait.

You will be crowned in Tara.

That night Chiaráin was beautiful like an angel from paradise, with lush dark curls. His scent was that of a young heifer to the nostrils of the bull.

And Diarmait said:

— Kingship begins with a ritual.

A high-priestess is always the one
who receives a vision of the next High-King
and she takes the role of the land
before the High-King is crowned.
She is the goddess that blesses him
to assure his reign shall be fruitful.

Diarmait grabbed Chiaráin's hands, and he found they were light as birds, with bones of air and glass. And he continued:

— I wished to worship you in solitude
since the first time I cast my eyes on your form.
Your features have not been eroded
yet by the winds and the rain.
Your skin is warmed by AO's sun
and you have the sweet gaze of a cow.

— I saw gold in the bull god's blood, Chiaráin
replied.
You are called for this.

And Diarmait said:

— Be the land for me.
I need your blessings.

And the hermit shown Diarmait the blue ointment he had taken from the Fir Bolg. He covered his hands with it, stroking it over Diarmait's body, strong and nimble like a young bull. And on Beltane's eve, Chiaráin knew him.

LVI.   Before the first light of the morning, Chiaráin crawled back to Rua, who was eating burdock outside Diarmait's tent.

 — I have felt warmth for the first time, he con-
   fessed,
   since my chest turned into a frosted dead tree.
   Diarmait's hands have brought the sun to my
   soul.
   When he took me, I felt blessed by the Bull God,
   the Horned God that has come to survive the
   longest night.
   I understood why all things are connected.
   Union is life, war is returning to fragments.
 — Remembering the sun is good for you, Rua
   lowed.
   Your grief burns like tar.
   But tomorrow you will see Diarmait perish and
   Queen Eanna rise.
   Gold was from her banners, not Diarmait's locks.
   I know it now.
 — Eanna will never win, Chiaráin said, and his face
   darkened. He took out the white bull's horn.
 — You do not belong to war, Rua said.
   I saved you three times:
   At Loughmichnois.
   At Cluain Ioraird.
   At Inis Mór.
   The fourth time, tomorrow, something terrible
   will happen.

But Chiaráin closed his ears to his cow and AO's words.

LVII.   On the next morning, Diarmait called his troops.

He had three hundred soldiers, seventy archers, fifty-three horses, and a black stallion beneath him. At his side, Chiaráin rode Rua. They waited for Queen Eanna by the shores of Loughmichnois. The black-headed seagulls did not dare screech out their thoughts this time, and a row of herons watched, with sharp eyes, from the other side of the lake. The water smelt of rain and mallard's droppings. Carrion crows circled the clouds.

The horizon darkened, and a tumultuous roar filled the air. Queen Eanna's army was so large that it filled the landscape. Minor clans had heard of Loughmichnois' battle and arrived to swear loyalty to the Queen, joining her in that last fight. Trained falcons flew over Eanna's warriors and her horses neighed, impatient for battle. Grass bent, herons flew away and otters hid beneath the water. The surface of Loughmichnois reflected the white sun of Beltane and its surface was calm.

— This is your last day on Éire, Diarmait, Queen
    Eanna said.

She wore leather armour with a breastplate of bronze to protect her ribcage, and a helmet on her head.

— It is my fate to be your opponent.
    Here I am: I will not ignore AO's will.
— It is your fate to be sacrificed on Beltane,
    to die young and green, like the Bull God,
    Queen Eanna laughed.
    But, before I sever your head, I will honour Goíldeglass,
    Water God from Loughmichnois.

At the Queen's gesture, Druggan appeared, leading a pair of cows to the water. They were twins; both white with black spots and the pattern that finished on one continued on the other. These cows were only a spring old. They cried:

    — Where is Mother?
    Where are our Sisters?
    We still need time,
    we have not met the bull,
    we have not grazed the high grass, escaped the
    herder's gaze.
    Where is Mother?
    Where are our Sisters?
    Druggan took flaming branches and pushed the
    cows to the waves, saying:
    — Finnian, from Cluain Ioraird, used to gift us
    golden calves,
    and the most beautiful cows.
    Now he says he does not pray for Queen Eanna
    anymore.
    Says he is waiting for Chiaráin to come and
    finish his book.
    Move, beasts, enough of that crying.
    You will be sainted in Goíldeglass' guts.

Druggan and three warriors followed the cows until the dark waters rose to their waists. The warriors held the cows by their horns while Druggan used the sacrificial knife to hamstring the animals, the same knife he had used to hamstring Chiaráin many Beltanes ago. There were bawls as the twin heifers sank beneath the dark mirror-surface of the lake.

Druggan said:

    — Blessed be, Queen Eanna of the Uí Néill
    daughter of the Tuatha Dé Dannan
    wife of no one but her blade.
    Goíldeglass protect her.
    Assure her victory one more time.

There shall be no other High Queen in Éire.

He threw gold coins to the waters and a handful of human teeth. When he was finished, the Queen said to Diarmait:

— Where is your druid?

Where are the gifts that you have brought for the Water

God? His kingdom will be our battlefield.

Show some respect, youngster.

But Jarlath was nowhere to be seen. He had left Diarmait after his fight with Chiaráin and was travelling towards Cairbre at that moment.

Druggan said of Diarmait:

— He is godless.

The outcome of this battle is already set.

Queen Eanna raised her sword, but lowered it when Chiaráin appeared from behind Diarmait. He and Rua advanced to meet Queen Eanna.

— AO is here behind Diarmait.

And he who will be High-King of Éire does not need anyone else.

The Queen looked at him. And she saw what she thought was a beautiful bearded woman with a dark curly mane of hair, and olive skin, riding on the back of a large red cow. The woman's eyes were darker than the spaces between the stars at night. Queen Eanna did not like them.

— I have killed you before, at Inis Mór.

You are the one who tried to steal my cows, the one I gifted to Cluain Ioraird, the Fir Bolg's pet.

How can you be alive?

Are you a ghost?

A creature of the Otherworld?
— I am Chiaráin, you named me, he said.
You sacrificed me to Goíldeglass
and murdered my sister.
I have come here to honour your god.
And saying this, Chiaráin directed Rua towards the lake, and the cow walked into it, dark water licking her coat of fire.
— Goíldeglass, come, show yourself to me,
Chiaráin commanded.
And he used the secret language of the Fir Bolg to call for the Water God. And down under the waves, under the reeds, the otters' dens, the fish, the water spiders, toads and seaweed, the Silver Snake opened an eye and heard Chiaráins's calling and he swam up, fast as lightning, to the surface of the lake.
This is what they all saw:
The waters, clear and smooth as a mirror, trembled and cracked. A freezing rush of air sent the bog orchids and the blue-eyed grass on a mad dance. The black-headed seagulls flew away first, screeching, and after them, a whirlwind of birds followed: gadwalls, white geese, mallards, curlews, lapwings, and mute swans. The sky was so crowded with birds that their shadows swallowed the last beam of sun. Another flurry of rain scratched the lake's surface. It stank of rotten eggs, of meat turning green, and of old silver. A huge purple wave formed in the middle of Loughmichnois.
— Move, Queen Eanna yelled to her warriors.
Goíldeglass is about to come out
and those who look at him shall turn blind
and lose all reason.
The wave blasted the shore like a mountain crum-

bling. It struck Diarmait and the Queen's troops.

Goíldeglass appeared. He had the head of a viper and four crystal fangs protruding from his gaping jaws. The transparent scales on his long-coiled body were made of bone and liquid silver and they shone with an iridescent spark. Two sets of braided horns crowned his head between his translucent eyes. A mist of blue, mossy hair extended from his forehead, along his spine, and his forelimbs resembled something between lynx paws and lizard claws. Around the trunk of his body, water boiled and turned white.

— Goíldeglass, hear me, Chiaráin called him from the shore.

Goíldeglass, why do you feed on dead bodies and the sad offerings they bring in your name? You know nothing of time and you are trapped in this

lake. You are but a prisoner of the human race.

The Water God was lured by these strange words. He remembered Chiaráin's scent of olives and warm sun, and sniffed the air searching for him. His claws flexed in the waters while his body contorted, bringing his muzzle close to Chiaráin's face. The saint brushed the divine scales of Goíldeglass but avoided his burning gaze.

Chiaráin brought forth the horn of the white bull from Inis Mór. He raised it and sank it between the Water God's eyes, where a smooth patch of flesh stretched, unprotected by the scales.

And that is how Chiaráin killed Goíldeglass and the Water Curse was released upon Éire and the rest of the world.

LVIII.   The Water God screeched and the sound

of his pain exploded eardrums and stopped hearts. Goíl-deglass's body twisted, coiling and thrashing, turning the lake's surface to foam, and finally convulsed before falling back into the depth of the waters. Chiaráin turned back, the bull's horn still in his hands, searching for Queen Eanna's gaze. He met her eyes and said:

— This is your god, go
   and pray to him now.

LIX.   When Goíldeglass's corpse hit the waters, a great wave of darkness spread. It was larger than any mountain on Éire, and it grew out of thick poisonous mud. This time, whole armies fled, screaming. When the black avalanche slammed to the ground, many were killed, including Queen Eanna, but others escaped, and amongst them was Diarmait. A deadly odour of boiled blood and fish covered the ground for three days and three nights. After that, Loughmichnois and its poisonous mud dried and disappeared, giving way to fertile land. Where Goíldeglass had fallen, a silver river appeared that would henceforth be known as Abha na Sionainne.

LX.   When Chiaráin fell into the water, the dark mud filled his nose, travelled down to his throat and into his lungs. He stopped breathing and his heartbeat slowed. Rua dived into the waters looking for him. When she found him, she grabbed his tunic with her muzzle and brought him back to the surface. And so his life was saved a fourth time, but the poisonous mud burnt the red cow's hair, and from that moment on, she was the colour of charcoal, dull and grey. Her eyes turned milky white and could not receive the light.

CLUAIN MICH NÓIS

LXI.   Word travelled all over Éire that Chiaráin had killed Goíldeglass and that Loughmichnois had disappeared, leaving strange blue fields and a silver river behind. From that moment on, people referred to Chiaráin as Saint Chiaráin and they came from all over the island to see him and contemplate his miracle. Word also spread that Diarmait would be crowned High King of Éire on the next Samhain, and no other clan leader or warrior dared to challenge him.

LXII.   Chiaráin and Rua stood on the blue fields and refused to leave what once had been the bottom of Loughmichnois. The mute swans, the mallards, and the black-headed seagulls moved to the river and other wet places. Mice came to feed on the blue-eyed grass, the bog orchids and the cherry bird trees. Stoats and shrews followed.

   Diarmait knelt next to the saint and said to him:
   — Chiaráin, your eyes are dull like stones.
   Your skin is grey, silver-powdered.
   Tell me what I can do to heal you.
   — My tongue feels like wood-ash, the saint answered.
   — Please, bring me some water.
   Diarmait rushed to the river and brought clear water in his upturned helmet. Chiaráin drank but was not sat-

isfied. Diarmait went back to the river and brought more water, and he did so many times. Every time the saint drank, his body bloated but he was never satiated. By his side, Rua lay curled up. The tips of her horns were dark, and one of them was shattered and stained with black blood.

— The whole river will not quench my thirst,
  Chiaráin cried.
  Not even the whole Bán Sea can calm me now.

Diarmait took Chiaráin in his oak-strong arms and bore him to the riverside, walking into the cold currents. The water was tainted by the gold rays of the dying sun. He submerged Chiaráin's body in the waves that smelt of pebbles and algae. After a while, Chiaráin's cracked skin started to heal.

— Hush, Diarmait whispered, rest.
  You have given me Éire and now I shall protect
  you. I will give you anything you ask for,
  between the ground and the skies.
  Saint Chiaráin, your name will outlive the Water
  God's and will be tangled with mine forever.
— I want stones, said Chiaráin, huge limestones
  from Inis Mór
  I want to build a fort, like Dún Dúchathair.
  What I learnt, the secrets I keep,
  they shall not be lost.
  The Book of Cluain Ioraird,
  the blue and white power of Inis Mór.
  What I know I shall share with everyone
  so I can save them from the Water God's curse.
— What curse? Diarmait asked.
  What are you saying?
— Goíldeglass has left, but the world, like me,

craves water.

There will be rain, and seas that will grow larger than any lake.

— Your words come from grief, you are still confused, Diarmait said.

Feel the healing water, there is no curse here.

You are a favourite of AO, you are blessed.

And I shall do as you ask and build a school.

That same night, Diarmait dug a hole in the blue fields and brought water from the river to fill it until it was like a small well. He took Chiaráin there and let him rest with his whole body under the water, except for the head. This gave the saint great relief. He rarely emerged from this healing water, and the well would be known as Saint Chiaráin's Well for centuries to come, its water bestowing miracles.

— Take care of Rua, please, I cannot move,

Chiaráin implored Diarmait.

The warrior scrubbed the cow's grey hair, but the red colour was gone forever. He washed the cow's white eyes but he could not heal them. Rua refused to move and stood silent by the well. Diarmait went down to the marsh and walked until he found a white rock soaking up the moonlight. He carried it back to Saint Chiaráin and said:

— This is the first stone of Cluain Mich Nóis.

Here we shall erect the towers of knowledge.

LXIII. During the following days, Diarmait organised the people who had come from all over Éire to Cluain Mich Nóis and together they started building a small temple, made of stones and bog-wood, around Chiaráin, Rua and the well. The saint did not eat or drink anything apart from river water. He was always thirsty and only when it rained could he breathe, relieved from the dry pain.

— I am so thirsty, Rua, he mumbled.

But the cow did not respond. Since the death of Goíl-deglass she had lost her will to speak.

After a few moons, the temple was completed. Saint Chiaráin spoke for the first time to the people:

— Listen, my time is coming.
    Before I go, I shall share with you my grass books
    and the secrets of cattle, milk, and how to
    deceive the rain.

LXIV.   One day, three monks arrived, dressed in black habits, guiding a herd of cows with calves, all of them white as clouds, and healthy.

Chiaráin saw them approaching and asked:

— Who are you, and why do you bring cattle?

The first monk shown him a piece of parchment, unable to speak because his lips were stitched closed. It was a letter from Finnian of Cluain Ioraird, and this is what it said:

Finnian: Chiaráin, blessed be.
            You have expelled the serpent from Éire like
            Pádraig promised.
            Here I send you Cainnech, Laisrén and Nin-
            nidh. They keep a sweet memory of you in
            their hearts
            from when you were a brother and inspired
            them.
            Take them with you, I am too old to travel.
            Take our cattle too,
            and make your own book.

— Cainnech, Laisrén, Ninnidh, free the animals,
   ordered Chiaráin.

Let them roam.

And Cainnech, Laisrén and Ninnidh obeyed and
did as Chiaráin commanded. And the cows ran to the
woodland in the marsh and were never seen again. Cows
without herders are beautiful wild beings, faster than any
wind and shy like deer.

— And now, Chiaráin told the three monks,
   unstitch your mouths.

I want you to speak and answer for your sins.

The monks pulled at the stitches and soon their lips
were covered in crimson. Their voices were weak and
childlike because they had not used them for many years.

— Saint Chiaráin, we heard of your miracles, Cainnech said.

— Saint Chiaráin, you have found the next High
   King of Éire, Laisrén said.

— Saint Chiaráin, you killed a god, Ninnidh said.

And then Laisrén added:

— Saint Chiaráin, we want to know why the rain
   falls,

why we live in the darkest island.

Does AO even bother to look this way for us?

We want to know the secrets of cattle.

We want to know what is to happen.

We want to know.

— I hear you, brothers, Chiaráin answered.

— Stay in Cluain Mich Nóis if you wish so.

— I shall entrust you to Rua.

Attend to her as the Virgin Mary attended to her
celestial

son. This cow has taught me more than any

human master.

If it is her will, she shall reveal the secrets to you.

And from that day on, the three monks stayed at Saint Chiaráin's temple. Before the sun rose above the horizon, they went out looking for blue-eyed grass covered in dew, and they collected tender buds to feed Rua. And they brushed the heifer's hair and cleaned her and gave her comfort.

LXV.   By Lughnasadh, the blue fields of Cluain Mich Nóis bloomed and there were cherries, blackberries, elderberries, dog roses, strawberries and apples, thriving thanks to the Silver River. A stone-worker called Ailbe came from Dal Riata to work on a high cross that was to stand facing north. She carved the story of Saint Chiaráin and his miracles, of his encounter with Diarmait and of how Cluain Mich Nóis had come to exist. She had heard the story of the saint killing Goíldeglass with a bull's horn, and knew of the saint's love for his cow, so she carved an image of Chiaráin horned, like Cerunnos.

Every night, people gathered inside Saint Chiaráin's temple and he taught them the secrets of writing, of making books from high grass, of cooking the blue ointment which protected the skin from the rain, and he taught them about the power of breast milk. Everyone listened except for Diarmait, who was becoming restless. He came to the saint when the sky was dark and said to him:

— I see you are recovering,
    building up Cluain Mich Nóis has been like
    stitching your wounds.
    You share knowledge, and through knowledge

there is hope.
Come with me in Samhain, to Tara,
where I will be crowned High-King.
Be my advisor.
We shall keep Éire together.
But Chiaráin said:
— I prayed to AO for Queen Eanna's defeat
and now look, she is forever with us here, in
Cluain Mich Nóis.
Her bones melt in the waters that feed our fruit.
My fate is set.
I shall finish my life as she did, in the water.
And Saint Chiaráin refused to be moved, and did not
follow Diarmait when he left.

LXVI.   With the coming of Samhain, Chiaráin's
skin turned grey, like the stone of the high cross, and
started to crack. His hair was silver straw and his eyes
lightened, from dark brown to an amber hue. Rua had
not moved for many days either, and her body was wrinkled like a raisin. When the sun came out, she spoke to
Saint Chiaráin for the first time in many moons. She
said:
— Chiaráin, I want you to safeguard the secrets,
you should preserve everything at Cluain Mich
Nóis.
Grass is weak and once you go, they may not
remember.
Take my skin instead,
I will be your book.
And Chiaráin said:
— Rua, my friend, I want to cry but
only dust comes to my eyes.

You brought me back to life here, where Loughmichnois once
stood, and now I have brought a curse on you all.
Creating a book from you would be like eating
my own entrails.
Rua, please, stay with me.
— Chiaráin, I want to tell the others.
I want my skin to be turned into pages
which explain where everything came from
and what to do to go back to AO.
Chiaráin, do it yourself,
cut me,
wash me,
dry me.
Through the book, you will make me immortal.
Drink from me now, and regain your strength.

Rua offered her white, virgin teats to Saint Chiaráin,
and when he drank from them, his thirst was finally
quenched, and he healed. When he finished, Rua was
cold and rigid, and her flesh smelt of withered elder
flowers.

Chiaráin said:
— I thought I was beyond grief after seeing Leah
murdered.
Now my soul is crushed a third time.
I shall come back, he promised, and find you
again, friend.

And he embraced the cow and cried. Then he called
for the monks of Cluain Ioraird and took the semi-lunar
knife from them to flay his friend. Rua's hide was soft as
silk, and did not emit any odour. Chiaráin washed it himself in lime water, without feeling any burning in his cold
hands. He stretched it under the sun and when it was dry,

he smoothed the surface with the semi-lunar knife.

LXVII.   Wild cattle came from the woods because they had smelt Rua's skin warming under the sun. Black cows led the herd, and these were the ones brought as a sacrifice for Goíldeglass by Diarmait's druid before the Loughmichnois battle. Their horns had grown back, long and smooth as crescent moons. Their limbs were strong and nimble. They all surrounded the stretched skin and licked it with their rough pink tongues. Rua's skin smoothed and turned a pearl colour. Cattle ran all around Cluain Mich Nóis, over the mud and through the blue high grass, and people looked at the animals as though witnessing a miracle, because they had never seen cattle unguarded. These cows were more beautiful than the goddess Hathor and the golden calf. People feared their sharp horns but admired the lustrous hair and the elegance of their limbs. By evening time, all the cattle rested around Chiaráin, and the saint whispered to them while he cut Rua's skin into pages and bound them together with thread and a bone needle. Then he wrote for many moons.

LXVIII.   The night he finished the book, Chiaráin called for the three beauties of Cluain Ioraird and told them to keep the manuscript safe in Cluain Mich Nóis. Then, he asked them to build for him a boat made from the wood of apple trees, and to cover it with what was left of Rua's skin. Once the boat was finished, Chiaráin coated the hull with the blue ointment from the Fir Bolg. The black cows gathered around, curious. When he stepped inside, the monks pushed the vessel into the river. Two black cows jumped into the boat with the saint, and the others ran into the waters and swam, following the slow pace of the boat.

   — Where are you going, Saint Chiaráin? the monks shouted after him.

   — I will go wherever AO carries me.

     The mountains down to the Bán Sea. My sweet Iberia.

     Some mysterious land.

The current carried the boat farther away and the cows followed it, swimming. The monks stayed on the riverbank, and prayed to AO. People who had come to Cluain Mich Nóis from all over Éire witnessed his departure. Rain fell furiously against the grass, and a pearl mist closed, like a curtain, around the river. The boat and the cows shrank into small black dots and were finally swallowed by the purple waves of twilight.

CASE FILE 477

CAMERA 556 – THE CORRIDOR


```
The  door  opens.  A  woman  in  civilian
clothes  receives  the  boy  standing  out-
side.
   "Kerry?  Ja,  hoe  gaat  het?  Thanks  for
coming."
   The  boy  enters  and  the  door  closes.
```


`<record>` **DEEL 1.** *Jesus Christ crucified on a windmill*

Hermanas, ¿do you want to know the truth? Alright, yeah, I won't lie. I'm not lying, I promise. Ja, ik ken het. I'll tell you. I'll tell you the truth.

`<...>`

Neo Dublin started sinking the day of the 333 Excommunicationes.

That night, I was at home in the barco, ready to watch them, like we did every Thursday. I switched the deskreen on. CHISS. CHAK. The buttons were all rusty, because that's what happened when you had to live on the water.

On the deskreen, the bells began to toll.

BONG.

BONG.

Nobody spoke in the *Excommunicationes,* but you heard the bells. They played them crazy.

BONG.

"Alcalá, it's starting," I called to my sis. A paperbook

flew from her cabin. It was Alcalá's way of saying she didn't care. Pfff. Well, if she wanted to miss it…

I went to sit on the hot water-filled cushion on the floor, but Ree was already there.

"Keep off, I can't see." I pushed her away. Ree was my stepsister. She was fourteen, two years younger than me, but three hundred times fatter, en serio. How she managed to be like that when everyone else was starving was a miracle.

On the deskreen, a panoramic of Neo Dublin. The New Trinity College, the most important building in the city, where the Domini celebrated Missa and the Irish lived. Black and brown because of the acid rain. The clock was like the eye on a Cyclops, marking ten to midnight.

BONG. BONG.

Attached to the NTC were millions and millions of houses, like rotting cockles refusing to leave their rock. That's where all the Irish stayed, as far away as they could from the fetid waters we lived on. Far away from the Spanish.

There were spheric drones swimming in the grey skies, two antennae on each side. The Domini called them Angeli and they were right, the things watched you closer than your Guardian Angel. They recorded everything and being watched meant you'd be caught committing sins, sooner rather than later. Everyone sins, like.

BONG.

Pass the NTC.

Black waters.

Shark reefs.

Bridges. Like mad fishing nets of greenish metal. And under them were the grey piers and hundreds of barcos.

¿Have you ever heard of North Liffey's bridge? That's where our barco was. But the cameras didn't show us because we were under the most repulsive of all bridges. The kind of place where you don't want to get lost in the dark hours, ¿get me?

The deskreen shown the old submarine yard, where El Mercado de San Miguel hid. You could buy anything there, even synthetic Vitamilk, provided you had enough cash, that is, which was every Spaniard's problem, ya ves.

Then the camera shown a small corner of Fairview, with its ships' graveyard, water bubbling in red rust. The Domini ignored the illegal bullfighting going on there. I knew it well, my mother being a bullfighter herself, a matador, we call it in Spanish.

And finally, the Crucifix Farms floating on two massive black decks.

BONG.

The camera zoomed to the Crucifix Farm on the left.

"Ree, fuck off. You shouldn't be watching this; you'll puke or something."

She didn't move.

The windmills were like crucifixes, ¿sabes? They had small figurines of Jesus Christ attached. They kept going on and on, dark hours too, pumping their energy into Neo Dublin. The Domini said that they should remind us that the world feeds on suffering and pain. There's no end to it, no end, ever.

BONG. BONG.

The procession of green-robed Domini holding the golden cross halted. They were carrying a palanquin with a steel statue of the Virgin Mary, the only one crying for the sons who had betrayed her.

Tied up to five windmills were five men. Real men.

Arms and legs tied to the blades. All these windmills had been switched off. For the moment. The men on them wore the yellow cloaks of fishermen. Fishing was banned. Only the Domini could be fishers, fishers of men, sí. Even stupid children knew that. We hadn't seen synthetic cucumbers for months, we had the shortage of Vitamilk, and the SugarHosts were expensive, which meant that ninety-nine percent of the Spanish couldn't afford them. We were so fucking hungry all the time. Illegal fish markets flourished everywhere. The smell of rotten fish gills made our stomachs roar, yet the fish were poisonous. Eat fish for three days, the fourth day you'll wake up with another hand growing on your ass. Mutations. So those days it was all about dying of hunger or cancer, pues eso. ¿Get the picture?

The camera zoomed in so we could see how the fishermen were trembling. They were probably shitting themselves too, but you couldn't see that with all the white rain.

A Dominus, with a hand ladder, started covering each of the sinners' faces with a veil.

Uno.

Dos.

¿Do you repent, my son? Tres.

Wait. I knew that fisherman. Fuck. I knew him. I knew it.

Mamá was not in the room. She never watched the Excommunicationes with us. I could hear her working down on the engine room of the barco. ¿Did she know that Da was there? (Sí, one of the fishermen was my stepfather, but I called him Da). Mamá had told him stay away from the fish. Cannot be worse than your bullfighting, he used to answer her. Fishing will kill you first, Mamá said. And there she was, damn right.

Cuatro.

Cinco.

BONG.

Ree started making ugly noises. Her lips formed an inverted "u" and her face got all red. Up until this point we thought Da was gone. He'd got involved in shady deals before with bullies from El Mercado de San Miguel and sometimes had to go hiding for weeks. But none of us wanted to think he'd been caught by the Domini this time.

Ree was crying. Fucking Irish. They think nothing can touch them. Ree was Da's daughter, so she was Irish, like him, even if they'd decided to live in the slums with us. ¿Did Da think that being Irish would spare him the Excommunication? For once, the Domini were treating the Spanish and the Irish equally. With his head covered, Da was just one of the sinners. About to be crucified.

BONG.

I wanted to scream at Ree: "Don't look now, don't."

But I couldn't. My tongue was stuck in my mouth like a piece of iron, and my eyelids were glued open.

BONG.

The windmills started spinning. Slow at first, the bodies contorting, as though they were made of chewy SugarHosts. So unreal it was almost funny. Then the windmills kept moving and the red spilt and you knew it. It wasn't just a nightmare. </record>

<record> **DEEL 2.** *Dad is gone pero Ree got new boots*

We didn't get any sleep that night, but next morning Mamá sent us on our way to the New Trinity College school. Absences weren't allowed. I was so numb I didn't fight her.

Turbines wailing. Half-dead UVA lampposts. No ripples on the water. FISHERMEN GO TO HELL signs.

I felt sick, and it wasn't the hunger.

The barcobús wasn't coming. Waiting on the platform at the North Liffey stop under the hard rain. Me, Alcalá, and Ree. All nauseous after what we'd watched yesterday on the deskreen. All with hatraguas, goggles, ponchos. Drenched. We didn't have enough money to buy Sunnaluz to waterproof ourselves. In front of us, a billboard.

YOU CAN'T REACH GOD'S HAND
WHEN YOU'RE MASTURBATING.

Ree was wearing her new boots. Jodidas electric blue boots. They had ultra pink laces and fluorescent yellow spots and tooth-white soles. They were massive. Ree was so fat that everyone in her class called her sunfish, but I called her vaca, so I did. That's Spanish for cow and annoyed her more. We were waiting for the barcobús. Ree bounced up and down. Mud stuck on the patches of her worn-out poncho. She didn't look at me.

Da was dead.

Da was dead.

That sentence was still trapped in my head but it didn't make sense.

I dragged Alcalá's wheelchair closer to me. Alcalá was my older sister. The upper half of her body looked like the seventeen-year-old she was, but her legs hadn't grown since she was seven. She was lucky, though. In North Liffey, kids and cripples drown all the time. You know, you can make water wings compulsory but it's not like they were of any use. Skelpers were getting larger, I'm telling you. Silver and dusty black. Fast like knives. Not even talking about the insane jumps an orca could make.

Da was dead. Probably because he went to fish skelpers to feed us. Their meat was hard and too gummy, and you had to burn it or otherwise it would give you a stomach ache. Barely digestible. But a delicacy these days when the Spanish only had SugarHosts to eat.

Da was dead.

Hermanas, I was thinking back then, that you clutched at things as hard as you could but life would just take them away. La muy puta.

"Nice boots, eh," I said.

Ree dipped her foot into the mud. "Very nice boots."

Ree kept digging up the mud with her jodidas expensive boots. The more I looked at them, the angrier I got. I was happy to be angry. At least that meant feeling something. She kept digging those flamboyant boots into the mud. Now, Hermanas, you've to understand that in North Liffey mud is toxic. Made from shit, oh yes, and the last body fluids of a thousand creatures that died in sickness.

"Stop it, you puta vaca."

Her boots were completely submerged in that mierda.

"¿Did Da buy them for you? ¿Did he?" I touched Ree's shoulder. Maybe I grabbed it. "Stop that. It's your fault Da's dead."

She froze.

"You kept asking for stuff and he had to buy you all that girly shit. Y now Da's dead," I said. "He wasn't your

Da, Kerry. He was my Da."

"Yeah, he was, and you fucked around asking for money and now he's dead. You knew he didn't have any money."

"I–"

"Yes you did. The money for the boots, did he…?"

"Kerry…"

Alcalá pulled my arm. She wore a respiradero outside because her lungs were weak, so she couldn't manage to spit out a word.

"Botas de mierda. Your Da is dead because he didn't have money to pay for these boots so he had to do that fishing thing," I said.

I wanted to kick Ree in the face. I wanted to take her hatraguas off and pull her hair until I burst her face.

"Greedy vaca, vaca avariciosa de mierda."

Alcalá's respiradero started doing a whistling sound. "Stop that," I told Alcalá, "que te vas a ahogar, tonta."

Then I turned to Ree.

"See what you're doing, ¿vaca? It's all your fault, you – ¡Argh!" Alcalá had run her wheelchair into my back. "¿What's wrong with you know?" I screamed at my sister.

There were drops on Ree's goggles. It wasn't rain. Then, Hermanas, I felt I had won. She ran along the platform and climbed up the stairs to cross Cabra bridge. ¿Where was she going? I didn't mind the least. I was too pissed off because Da was dead and I had to go to school anyways. </ record>

<record> **DEEL 3.** *The buttery angel tells me to kill Doll Face*

My classroom at the New Trinity College had to move to the sixth floor because the ones below were flooded. Waters had been rising for months. Anyhow. Sí, classrooms in the NTC are huge. Seriously. ¿Do you want me to describe them?

The walls were so thick that you couldn't hear the rain. They weren't mouldy, but corpse-cold and super white. The floor was a metallic grid, always so warm and smoky. Myrrh. They buried the Irish in some areas of the NTC and used myrrh to cover the smell of rotting flesh, because they wouldn't throw their bodies to the waters like we did, oh, no. And those days, people were dying like flies, kids and old folks, mostly. Without Vitamilk they lost their teeth and they died. Like Da, ¿you know? He had rickets, like most folks who live on the water; he'd lost all his teeth, but he had these beautiful dentures that were so pearly and perfect they were obviously fake, they screamed fake, but everyone under our bridge wanted ones like them, so they did. He got me similar dentures as well, ¿see? So I didn't have to show this gap here, or this other one at the front.

Sí, the NTC classroom, sure. Let's get back to that. The ceiling was painted. There were obese clouds, singing angels, flowers and curly calves. I've memorised the classroom ceiling so well I can tell you all about that angel on the left corner, with buttery skin, holding a double flute and a bunch of flowers.

There were about thirty desks in front of the digiboard, and I always sat at the very back, ¿why wouldn't I? They made me go to an Irish class, "they" being my father – no, I don't want to talk about the bastard yet, thank you very much. Yes, Spaniards went to different classes, and it was also boys with boys and girls with girls, it couldn't be any other way with our Domini, ¿could it? I was the wild card there, the only crossbreed in the boy's school, half Spanish half Irish, so they didn't know where to put me until my father, who was Irish and a Dominus and a Master at the NTC, got the brilliant idea of enrolling me on a fucking point-based programme to get the Irish card. That meant I got the right to be in the Irish class. ¿Did the other Irish boys like it? ¿What do you think?

The classes always started with a small prologue in Irish, before changing to one hundred percent Latin, at which point my brain literally switched off. That day Dominus Domitius started by telling us (again) about what happened After The Flood. We were never taught about Before The Flood, when there was land with tons of cities erected on it. That big, glorious chunk of land was supposed to be Europe, a place a million times worse than Sodom and Gomorrah. That's why Deus had cursed it with a second flood.

Dominus Domitius howled the usual nonsense from his seat in his scooter. No, the Domini weren't immune to rickets, no matter how much they thought they were better than the rest of us. And Dominus Domitius's legs were so deformed he couldn't walk anymore. "Deus sent the rain to punish mankind," he said.

I spent my time carving a hole in the right side of my desk, using a paper clip.

"But Deus spared the only true faithful race, the Irish, and sent them to the Iberian Peninsula to bless the only patch of land left in the once so-called Europe. And the Irish brought the Spanish, the last remainders from the cursed continent, the Truth of Deus, allowing their sinful souls to dry in the afterlife."

I looked at the ceiling, cursing the cheesy angels. After the Excommunicationes the previous night, all I wanted was to twist their wings. Poke their skin with my paper clip. Stick all those flowers up their culos, especially thorny roses.

KNOCK, KNOCK.

"Come on in," Dominus Domitius said. Someone entered the classroom.

The first thing I thought, ¡joder, es un tapón! I mean, he was so short. Like a ten-year-old. Long yellow hair with a fringe. Milky skin, but not in a bad way. What I mean is that he didn't look ill, ¿you get what I'm saying? He had blue eyes and a doll face. His uniform was super new. The classroom was warm but he was still wearing the jacket with the big NTC logo on it. The clothes sparkled because they were completely covered in Sunnaluz, like when you have so much of it on you that you can go outside without feeling a hint of humidity.

"This young fellow comes from the Vatican Boat," Dominus Domitius told us, "and will stay on land with us for the time being."

Whispers everywhere. I mean, it was the Vatican Boat. Sometimes we saw it, bright like the sun, sailing in the distance. The Pope hadn't put a foot on land for years. ¿Who would want to stay in this dump, no?

"¿What's your name, my boy?" Dominus Domitius asked the new guy.

"Sceilig."

What a stupid name, ¿right? And he said it in a perfect posh Irish accent, no me jodas.

Sceilig came to sit in between me and Sona. Of course, there was an empty desk there. Nobody wanted to sit next to me. The days when the other students waited to ambush me at the school doors when I was on my way home were over. Now I had the privilege of receiving the silent treatment.

"Dominus Domitius, ¿are we going to get Vitamilk today?" Sona asked.

"No, not today, and we won't get it tomorrow either if you keep asking. Fasting is a holy act and will bring you all closer to the Saviour," the Dominus answered.

"But we're not in Lent yet."

"¿Do you think Jesus Christ preached about fasting and purifying the soul just in Lent? And quiet now, my boy, or you'll get the power stick."

"Maybe we can eat Kerry's fat sister," Purts whispered from the fourth row.

Laughter.

"That Ree, man, is like a sunfish," Sona told Sceilig. Laughter.

"Quiet now, boys, or blood will be spilt," Dominus Domitius threatened while he typed some Latin in the digiboard.

All the classroom was looking at me, Sona and the fucking posh Irish kid, you see. Sceilig smirked.

I started shivering. If I thought about Ree, then I automatically thought about Da. If I thought about Da, then I thought about the Crucifix Farm and the Domini putting the yellow hood on him, so he stopped being Da even before they twisted his body and killed him.

"You know you have to beat him. He's laughing at you."

That was the buttery angel with the bunch of flowers and the double flute speaking. ¿Can anger make you hallucinate? I guess so.

"Beat the shit out of him. Break that pretty face into

pieces," The buttery angel said.

"Yeah," I promised the buttery angel. "Later." </
record>

<record> **DEEL 4.** *El Diablo finds a way to put a cucum-ber inside my trousers*

Y pues, I waited.

Hermanas, I waited for Sceilig in the school graveyard, where all the teachers and notable pupils were buried. There were two spiky statues hunched over by the big doors. One was the Virgin Mary of the Anguish. The Steel Maria. The other one was a rust-coloured marble St. Ciarán, riding a bull, naked. The saint's balls were like seaweed pips.

Sceilig came out too, of course; I could see everyone was leaving him alone because sí, they knew. They hadn't told him anything. We all have to learn from the blood. Even Íscar, Dominus.

Domitius's altar boy, who was supposed to keep an eye on us during break time, looked the other way. Lead-co-loured clouds rushed through the sky. It was raining so hard I could barely see.

I stepped in front of Sceilig. I want you to understand this: we couldn't be more different. I was the crossbreed mongrel with dark curly hair, goggles, and the deformed rickety arm. He was the glowing, perfectly beautiful Irish lad from the Vatican Boat.

"¿What?" Sceilig said when he saw me coming.

I punched him in the face as quick and hard as light-ening. Oh, that delicious crunch, his nose cartilage collapsing. He walked backwards. Fat drops of blood stained his sparkling Sunnaluzed jacket. Instead of holding his swelling nose, he charged at me. He hit me with clenched fists. I punched his stomach so hard it felt like I was getting inside his ribcage. He screeched like a broken flute, and fell. I kicked his shoulder. He grabbed my feet, so I fell too, and tasted the mud, Hermanas, so I did. He punched my face and grabbed my hand and bit it like a rabid sea otter. I pulled his hair until I had some yellow in my hands pero el muy jodido wouldn't stop, ah, no. My hand was throbbing with pain. I tried to suffocate him by pressing my knee on his throat, then hit his face. His forehead was red. His body was moving under mine, like. Mud splashed everywhere. The others were around us, screaming. My hand…I opened my mouth to groan, then he hit my chin and all went white. Pain in my nape. He was on me. But my hand was free, oh, finally, it felt so good, so good, but Sceilig was punching me as hard as he could with his tiny fists. I felt so hot. The others were screaming.

"Kill him Kerry, kill him Kerry…"

"Kerry loco, Kerry loco."

"Mad fucking bastard, get him there!"

I grabbed Sceilig's throat. He kept hitting but I didn't care anymore. I pressed harder and harder. His hipbones seemed to puncture my stomach whenever he curled up, trying to escape. I pressed harder.

I think I could have killed him, like the buttery angel told me to do, because I wasn't just fighting him, no: I was fighting all the fucking Domini in the green robes at the Crucifix Farms, fighting them as hard as I could so there wouldn't be any of them left to switch the windmills on.

Then, as Sceilig and I rolled into the mud, something disgusting happened. As soon as I noticed I got up and ran away. The others might have believed that I saw one of the Domini coming or something. Or that it was my natural crazy behaviour. Pero, ¿sabéis? El Diablo can take so many forms and paths, oh yes he can. And El Diablo was between my legs, making me very uncomfortable. Like having a synthetic cucumber inside my trousers. It was that white curve in Sceilig's neck. The image of it had messed me all up. Sí. I ran. </record>

<record> **DEEL 5.** *Wild Spanish girls*

I came home from school completely battered. Yes, we lived in a barco, I've seen some of you here do too, but in Neo Dublin it was different. Barcos were basically floating shacks, and only for the Spaniards, yes, who were not holy enough to share the NTC with the Irish and the Domini. Now, Mamá was pretty particular in that she actually loved living there. No, no, you don't get it. She loooooooved it. Each plank, each board, each gear from the engine. When Alcalá and I were little we rode the oceans in the barco instead of being stuck in Neo Dublin, like.

Pues I crawled inside the barco like a sticky sea worm. Mamá and Alcalá were there. Alcalá read a paperbook while Mamá fixed the barco's satellite disc.

Since Da had been taken by the Inquisitors and then killed there was always something wrong with the barco: the ventilation system, the boiler, the compostable toilet, the kitchen unit, the lights…Sí, Hermanas, that was

Mamá's way of keeping the madness at bay, I suppose. I see it now, even though I didn't then, and I used to think she just did it to mess with us all. Mamá. Yeah, she was fucking brilliant with machines, like nothing you've ever seen. She knew how to reduce a barco to pieces then put it all together, better than before. Yet the Domini never gave her a permit to work as an engineer, which is what she'd wanted all her life. Ah, no. Instead, they offered her a job cleaning toilets. A Spaniard couldn't be an engineer, no, but cleaning shit was way more fitting, yes it was.

"¿Dónde está?" Mamá asked, because she didn't care that Spanish was technically banned, and she used it to speak to us all the time, like.

I squatted in front of the deskreen next to Mamá. There were screwdrivers and gums scattered all over the floor. She was hacking the satellite dish again so we could watch Space Ducks and other sinful programmes instead of the compulsory Vigil Missa.

"¿Is there any food?" I asked, although I already knew the answer.

Without Vitamilk, there were only the rancid Sugar-Hosts we dissolved in water to make the most revolting gruel you've ever seen.

"Ree's not here. ¿Dónde está?" Mamá grabbed my shoulder. "And what on hell happened to you now?"

"Don't know, get off, you stink." I didn't want to talk about what had happened with the new boy. ¿And Ree? She hadn't taken the bus to school with us, ¿but why wasn't she at home?

Mamá's fingers were black with grease and now my uniform was dirty.

"Tú sabes dónde anda," she said. "Where's Ree?"

Hermanas, I've to admit that I started thinking about Ree then. It was this time of day that

the vagabundos started going out, looking for free ways to get Sunnaluz or a shot of V-D. Ree was a sunfish of sweet eyes. Presa fácil.

I left the barco through the back door. I put my hatraguas on, zipped up my poncho and wiped the mud off my goggles. I had to wear goggles, inside and outside, porque my eyes were weak and they turned into itchy tomatoes pretty fast. Father, I mean, my biological father, used to say that was Deus's will, but I'm telling you, it was the polluted rain.

I walked the swinging bridges up and down, Cabra, Phibsborough, King, North Bolton y Parnell, cursing, asking everyone I stumbled on.

"¿Seen my sister? Ginger hair, short, fat like a sunfish. ¿Seen her?'

I found her at the corner of a junk food store at the end of O'Conell Bridge. It said *Best Fish & Olives in town.* Yeah, sure. In these places they cooked the dead fish that came floating on the surface each morning because factories had been throwing up mierda all night long.

Ree wasn't alone, though. A bunch of Spanish teenage girls circled round her. Poking her and pulling at her poncho.

"¿A dónde vas, vaca?"

"Eh, mira, que se nos pone tímida y todo."

"¿Y esas botas? Qué chulas, ¿no? Can I have your boots?"

There were three of them, flashy holy cards pinned on their own ponchos. I think St Aidan and, of course, Jesus, were in that week.

Ree was like a baby mouse without teeth.

"Eh, largando, que es mi hermana," I told the girls. They all turned back.

"She can't be your sis, a ver, ¡no os parecéis en nada!"

"Dáselas, guarra," I said to the girl who was holding Ree's new boots.

"¿Qué?"

"Dáselas, guarra."

I punched the girl's face so hard that her upper lip exploded in blood. The others took out their iron rosaries and used them like flails. I kicked, hit, bit, but there's a limit on how many times anyone can get the holy cross smashed into his head.

Al final, Hermanas, you'd be glad to know that I got Ree out of trouble. I let the Spanish girls take the boots because they were such a jodido eyesore.

We walked past Fairview to get back home. Breathing in the rust.

"¿Does it hurt?" Ree said.

"Nah."

I wiped the blood off my face. A few scratches, nothing too awful. My right forearm had started to swell. One of the girls had stabbed it with her rosary. Bah. In North Liffey, sea-mosquito bites were way worse. Plus, it was my rickety right arm I didn't use all that much.

"You look awful."

"Shut up."

The mud felt like ice. I was walking barefoot because Ree was wearing my Sunnaluzed shoes, the expensive ones Father bought me to wear with the NTC uniform.

I was happy though.

Ree wouldn't wear those horrible electric blue boots anymore. </record>

<record> **DEEL 6.** *Infernum is at the end of Jacob's ladder*

Wow. My mouth is all dry now. Could I have something to drink, ¿alsteblieft? Sí.

<...>

Bedankt, this is good. Yeah. ¿What's this? ¿Sinaasappelsap? Si-naas-a-ppel-sap. Ja. Got it.

Hermanas, I'm thinking now about what happened three years ago, when I was a sweet little boy of thirteen. Domini said the Infernum lay beneath our feet, under dark waters and starving skelpers and hammerheads. At the NTC we were told that Infernum was that bottomless swamp right behind the NTC (that's where they threw people after their bodies had been torn into pieces during the Excommunicationes). We would sink in there forever if we didn't submit our daily online confession, or reject thoughts such as the white curve in Sceilig's neck.

The best depiction of the Infernum was in the NTC's Oratorium, in the mural that covered the circular walls and depicted a huge cavern where humanity endured never-ending rain. You could see by the size of the raindrops that they ruptured the skin. There were no hatraguas or Sunnaluzed ponchos there. Dominus Domitius assured us that the stench of thousands of humans rotting together would be so abominable that we wouldn't have time to puke because we would be ripping off our own noses instead.

¿Water? ¿Rain? Hermanas, I'm not afraid of them. When I was little, Mamá didn't buy me fancy water wings or try to keep me as far away from the waves as most parents did with their children. No. She taught me how to dive in water and y mud. I could swim so fast that skelpers didn't have time to bite me. I was basically immune to the poisoned waters. I could also hold my breath for almost eight minutes. Cool, ¿eh?

Hermanas, I'm going to tell you a secret: the Infernum is at the end of Jacob's ladder. Sí, that ladder Dominus Domitius made me climb once. He knew I was responsible for burning the Steel María's crown. I know I shouldn't have done it. But I'd bet ten harps that the steel wool crown would explode into rabid pink flames. Don't you love fire, ¿Hermanas? Whenever you have it in front of you, burning in all its glory, ¿don't you see the rest of the world under a different light?

Fire is so sun-like.

Dominus Domitius couldn't punish me officially because he didn't have any proof. Pero he hated me so much. He hated Father, too. All the Domini did, because Father had used his Papal Dispensation to marry a Spanish woman and raise mongrel children. I guess in their eyes it was as if someone had married a sea slug and bred with it. So Dominus Domitius made me go to his office and from there we went up the private corridors. Íscar, his altar boy, followed behind us, a well-trained water cockroach he was, like. Dominus Domitius had started riding a scooter then. His skin was dark brown like an old toad because of the excess of V-D. He always carried a little box in the front basket of his scooter, where (so he said) lay the uncorrupted corpse of a newborn calf. Land animals were not born in Neo Dublin any more, but you could always put one harp or two inside the calf's box to thank the Steel Maria for that miracle. The Irish had money to spare, ¿you know?

Dominus Domitius stopped in front of a narrow door.

"Go inside and get me the Book of Kells. You're going to copy so many versicles your fingers are going to burst before you finish."

I opened the door, already smiling. ¡What a stupid task! But I didn't see any room, just a metallic ladder against the wall.

My eyes itched when I started climbing. Soon I found there was no air left to breathe. My lungs folded, tight as fists. Sweat on my upper lip, nausea in my stomach. I kept going up. I couldn't look down. My legs were wobbly like a pair of sea worms. My hands were sweaty. My mouth tasted of herrumbre: I'd been biting my tongue because I didn't want to scream. The ladder contorted. A clock mechanism echoed from above. I was about to go into the NTC clock room, the highest point in the building. Joder. The treads were slippery. I couldn't look down. I couldn't move. The treads were melting. ¡I was going to fall! I shrank my body and embraced the ladder as hard as I could, closed my eyes and ears, so I did.

Someone screamed.

Maybe it was me.

How Dominus Domitius discovered my fear of heights, which I've had since I was a brat, I never knew. Perhaps Father had told him.

I stayed there, hanging on that ladder, for hours. At some point, Father climbed up to get me.

"¿Do you repent, my son?"

I couldn't utter even a word then, but I kissed the Fisherman Ring on his hand.

He covered my goggles so I didn't have to see the infernal ladder any more, and got me down. \</record>

<record> **DEEL 7.** *¡¡¡Ree tries to sink our barco, with all of us in it!!!*

The morning after I brought Ree home, Mamá summoned us all: Alcalá, Ree and me.

Everyone dropped their water wings, ponchos and hatraguas before sitting. I left the hot water-filled cushions around the table for the girls and planted my ass on our online *Lives of Saints* projector, family size. Father had bought it for us but it'd been broken for ages (I poured hot Vitamilk over it, when we still had lots to spare…) It was the only item in the barco Mamá never had the time to fix.

The barco trembled. Ree came crawling from the toilet, her index finger still bleeding after the daily confession. Sí, we had daily blood tests to check our Vitamin D levels in case we needed a larger dose of V-D during the Sunday Missa. Ree's hair was loose and messy; she smelt of dusty pillows and damp sheets. All places (including barcos) were supposed to have a private confessional space. Pero Mamá said our barco was too small and that, in any case, the toilet was already a very private place, so that's where she installed the confessor. Hermanas, I admit it was quite good to take a shit while I was recording my daily sins. I always came out of the toilet feeling truly liberated.

Mamá opened her mouth, but I interrupted her.

"Venga, danos la gran noticia."

"Yeah, Da's dead. And the money is gone."

She seemed ok when she said it. She was wearing a blue striped jumper, but she hadn't changed it for a whole week. It smelt of rotten Sunnaluz. Her curly hair hung limply over her shoulders. Mostly silver. She hadn't dyed it in months.

"Da had to go fishing because he didn't want you go to the Matadores again," I said. Mamá was involved in her own illegal stuff: corrida de toros. She said it was her only way of making decent money, but I can tell you, Hermanas, that she also loved it. So she did.

"Da took all our money to get into fishing, they caught him and now he's dead, ¿didn't you get that, pea-brain?" Alcalá said. "Y cierra la puta boca."

I wanted to remind Alcalá that Da was the one who bought her that fancy wheelchair with an attached deskreen and all. The money had come from the fishing, sí, ¿from where else?

Ree chewed the solid pieces of sugar floating in warm, desalinated water. The ends of her hair soaked in it. When she was finished, she cleaned the bowl with her finger and licked it. I wondered if she was going to do the same with her hair. She didn't look at us.

"It's ok," Alcalá said. "We can do this."

"¿Without money?" I replied.

"I have another corrida soon," Mamá said.

"Sí, sure," I answered. "¿Going to come back from this one?"

During the day, Mamá cleaned toilets in the NTC, but at night she joined a group of mechanics, the Matadores. They fixed monstrous drones called toros, sí, bulls. These drones were a mix between a race boat and a tank, like. Mamá didn't just enjoy building the drones. She also jumped in the pool and fought against them. She was a good swimmer and knew the machines so well. Pero now and again she got in trouble. She had a scar on the left side of her face (you could still see the stapler marks) and had lost her ear. Pretty revolting, that scar.

Every time she had a corrida, we all knew that could be the last time we saw her.

"I can work too."

"¿You?" I laughed at Alcalá. With her shaved hair and her dragonfly body. "Pero qué dices, gilipollas, you can't even walk."

Alcalá grabbed an empty can of Sunnaluz and threw it at my face. My first impulse was to

make her swallow it, but then, my sis is the only one I'd never raise a hand to.

"Parad ya." Mamá massaged her temples.

"¿Am I leaving?" Ree asked.

"What?" Mamá said.

"Am I leaving?"

"No, what're you talking about?"

"My Da is gone." I hated her for that my: he had been living in our barco for five years. "I don't know where my mother is…"

"Oye." Mamá tried to take her hand but changed her mind midway and left it on the table. "You're not going anywhere."

Mamá always ignored all that mierda about Irish and Spanish having to live in different places. People in North Liffey respected her, so nobody would lay a finger on little Ree anyway.

"Well, I guess it's all fixed now then, we are all a jodida happy family," I said.

Mamá hit the table.

"¿Te callas? ¿Can you just shut up? If you don't want to be here, just go."

Her voice was sharp, her eyes reddened. Alcalá shook her head and dragged herself back to her room, grabbing one of her paperbooks from the floor. Ree started ugly crying and this time Mamá caressed her hair. Ree collapsed and started soaking Mamá's shoulder in snot and tears. They were like a picture from the NTC: the Virgin Mary of the Beautiful Love (who was also North Liffey's patron, no kidding) holding an ugly fat child. The only problem was, Mamá was not a Virgin and much less a saint. I wanted to tear Ree off her.

"Venga ya, you're such a drama queen," I told my stepsister before crawling down to my cabin.

The annoying sound of a drop falling from the ceiling into a sack of toilet sawdust in the opposite corner of the room had been saying it all day, loud and clear. Hermanas, we already had enough water, we didn't need more tears to sink the barco. </record>

<record> **DEEL 8.** *Smoked orca tapas*

So, a few days afterwards, Father dragged us to this religious feast in Mater Misericordiae Lake. To see this nun with special powers, like. Back then, I thought that anything related to Deus was bullshit. The Domini spoke of mud, darkness and the wet Infernum, while standing in opulent rooms: walls covered in golden leaves and crucifixes so full of diamonds you would think Jesus died suffocated by them. When they slapped you it hurt like hailstorm, porque their fingers were loaded with sapphires and amethysts.

Father, yes, you heard that right. I'm talking about my biological father here. He was one of them, though not that rich. You see, because he had mixed himself with Spaniards once – that is, he had married Mamá – he was never promoted and remained in the lowest ranks of the NTC, wiping all the other Domini's asses. Yet, ¿you think he was less faithful to them? Hell no. Whenever we were with him we had to attend the online Missa two times a day and not sitting, ¡pero kneeling! on the floor. And floors in the NTC attached houses were made of marble.

"You have to turn El Diablo away from your soul, Kerry," he told me all the time.

Sometimes his eyes were full of tears and I wanted to puke. Hermanas, the truth is that I never saw any light in Father's eyes. No Deus, nothing.

But the thing I hated the most about Father was how irrational he got whenever he saw my crippled sister and how many stupid, expensive, useless, and painful medical treatments he made her undergo. I'm thinking now of those iron clamps they put inside her legs to stretch the bones (the clamps eventually got infected). Or when Father paid one thousand harps (all his savings, like) to a woman called Maria Inoculata, a saint, so she would personally bless my sis. ¿Do you also have cripples everywhere? I have my dumb rickety arm, ¿see? The Domini said that Deus sent the poisonous rain to punish our sinful bodies. Father said:

"Your sister's condition is my punishment for leading such an impious life when I was young." That was the worst. What a ton of mierda.

Me, Father, Alcalá and Ree weren't the only ones on the creaking bridge over Mater Misericordiae Lake. A crowd of curious folks and believers were gathering there too under the not-so-bad drizzling rain, ignoring the hazard signs saying that this bridge was too old to stand on. What a joke. Everything in North Liffey was too old and clapped-out to stand on.

I saw a few Irish people. Dominus Domitius was there, and a large queue had already formed to peek inside his calf-box, but mostly there were only Spaniards. Whenever you didn't have enough money to buy a hospital voucher, you would go to this kind of thing.

"¿Think this woman is a real saint?" Íscar asked me.

He was taking a break to munch on dry seaweed while Domitius and his box enjoyed all the attention.

I knew Íscar well. His barco had been moored next to ours for a few years now. He woke up before five in the morning every Sunday, singing 'The Irish Rover' while emptying the piss and shit tanks from every single barco in our pier. This was his duty, a sort of extra rent he had to pay to all of us. Sí, I know, Íscar was pretty unlucky. Pero that was because he was an Extraño, with hooded eyes and brown skin. That's why he couldn't live in the NTC. The Irish looked down on the Spanish and the Spanish looked down on Extraños. There was something else everyone whispered about. Íscar was all crazy in the head, because he liked fucking other men. Well, he brought men to his barco, and they stayed the night there, so obviously there had to be some fucking going on, ¿get what I'm saying? It may have all started with Dominus Domitius, Hermanas, who was a bit too nice to Íscar. You could tell 'cause Íscar was always wearing a tight black poncho sparkling with Sunnaluz and chewed on dry salty seaweed, all day, like. Fancy stuff that, for someone from North Liffey.

"It's going to be a bloody waste of time," I said.

He passed me a bit of seaweed, nodding.

"Wow, look at that," Íscar said, pointing out a boy in the crowd wearing an NTC uniform.

An NTC uniform outside the NTC, no me jodas.

¿Guess who was that? Sceilig, of course, or shall I call him Cracked Doll Face, because he still had the marks of our first encounter. There was a tall woman by his side, and I realised Íscar was actually pointing at her. Now, Hermanas, pay attention here, don't forget her. She was Sister Ciarana, although I hadn't the faintest fucking clue about that yet. I recognised her as a nun, though, because of the white scapular over the black tunic. She wore a white cornette on her head that looked like a pair of horns. She was one of the Sisters of Cow. I'd never seen one before, because they never left the Vatican boat. That's where all the real cows lived. I'm talking about the only real cows in the world. The Sisters of Cow milked them to produce Vitamilk, which was then blessed by the Pope himself. ¿A Sister of Cow walking around Neo Dublin? They were at the same level as angels. Almost. And Sceilig by her side, all made sense then. She was Sceilig's mother, I mean, her hands were nailed to his shoulders, and they looked alike. No, nuns couldn't have children, but the Sisters of Cow were the only ones who could conceive without sin. Or were fucked by the Pope himself. Whichever story you like best. No wonder Sceilig was such a freak.

Everyone screamed "¡oooooh!".

¿Deus's sign? But no, people were screaming because of these three men moving among the crowd. They had the yellow robes of fishermen, but under them they wore red habits. Yes, the red habit meant Inquisitor. They patrolled the streets, mimicking normal folks until they saw something that was not Catholic enough. They all carried harpoons on their backs and by that moment we'd all realised they were not going to make orca's tapas.

The whispering grew louder than the pissing rain.

Father stepped between the Sister of Cow and the Inquisitors.

"Deus bless you," Father said to them.

"Deus te benedicat, dominus," one Inquisitor replied. His face was not visible under the massive hatraguas. "Exeunt."

"I'm here to get my daughter cured," Father said. "If that's Deus's will."

"Exeunt," the faceless Inquisitor said. Meetings of more than three Spanish people were forbidden, ¿you know? But it was a rare thing having the Inquisitors bothering to pay us a visit in our crappy neighbourhood. Especially then, with all the starvation thing going on.

The other two Inquisitors shoved people away.

"Putos," an old man whispered.

"You're offending Deus," a woman complained.

"We're not doing anything wrong," Ree said. The faceless Inquisitor pushed her away. Ree kicked him, and the fucker smacked her across the face.

"You asshole," Alcalá said, and rammed her wheel-chair into the man. The Inquisitor raised his harpoon.

Alcalá got nervous and tried to go backwards. Ree shouted.

"¡La niña!"

Someone screamed.

BLONG.

BLONG.

Celestial bells?

It all happened in a second, Hermanas, pero the bridge over Mater Misericordiae crunched and broke, right where Alcalá's wheelchair was standing.

SPLASH.

Down she went.

We didn't even hear her scream.

"La niña,' a woman said.

Ree yelled.

"Go, go down and get her," a man said. "The girl, the girl has f–"

It all turned into chaos. I don't really remember it well, but I sort of reconstructed the facts after that. See, my sister fell into the water and sank like a stone. Everyone panicked except for one person: Sister Ciarana. She jumped into the waters to save Alcalá before the orcas gulped her down (wheelchair and all).

The nun dived down and managed to get my sister before swimming towards a barco anchored under the bridge, but things got a bit complicated. See, there were ripples in the brown water. And bubbles. Skelpers. So many bubbles.

Sister Ciarana had to swim among hordes of hungry skelpers before making it to the barco's deck. She left my sister there (who was nothing but a bundle of wet clothes) then climbed onto it. Her habit was dripping blood. Arms with open wounds.

A black triangle pointed out of the waters. An orca, sniffing the blood.

I watched all this from the bridge. One of the Inquisitors appeared by my side. "Deus will save her, my boy."

I punched his face and got his harpoon. An orca jumped out. Red gaping maw. I threw the harpoon.

I missed.

The orca swam beneath the boat. A wave hit the deck. Another came, almost immediately. I understood what the orca was trying to do: create a wave big enough to wash off the nun and shove her into the waters again. The nun crawled back on the deck holding Alcalá.

"Deus."

"Deus, help them."

"You, help them."

A woman wearing an orange poncho was pointing at the Inquisitors. The one with the red stream running out of his nose gurgled.

"Tell Deus to save them."

"Eso, salvadlas."

"Sí, we want a miracle."

"We want a miracle now."

"Right now."

"Vamos, putos."

At first people were just pulling the Inquisitors' ponchos, but soon they were grabbing them in all directions.

A scream.

Someone else hit the water.

¿Do you want to know who? The crowd had thrown one of the Inquisitors in the lake, thinking his miraculous powers would save Alcalá and the nun. Or perhaps they were all very angry, ¿no? In any case, it worked. The orca went quick as lightning for its new prey. Sí, sí, in the end all the Inquisitors turned into orca food.

In the midst of all that mess, people helped the nun, who was still holding my sister, to get up to the bridge again.

As soon as Sister Ciarana was back on the bridge, I ran towards her.

"My sister, cura a mi hermana, por favor. Cura a mi hermana. Sálvala. Tienes que salvarla, sálvala, sálvala, es mi hermana, mi hermana."

I grabbed the nun's habit.

Mud, salt, blood.

"Es mi hermana, es mi hermana, she's my sister, my

sister."

Sister Ciarana looked directly at me. Wind had pulled her cornette back, seaweed hung from her dirty gold hair. Instead of wearing a habit, it seemed she was carrying a nauseating portion of the ocean with her. It smelt of carrion, illness, and acid shit. ¿Were those things on her face freckles or drops of mud? Sister Ciarana's eyes. I looked into them just before someone grabbed me back. They were the colour of the sea under the sun. I've never seen such a thing pero, Hermanas…

I knew it. `</record>`

`<record>` **DEEL 9.** *The Steel Maria is listening (not really, pero someone's out there)*

What I'm going to tell you here is the truth. Hermanas, you might think, well, this guy has just lost it, or perhaps he wants to add some spice to his olives, you know, make things up so they seem more interesting. Pero no, I, we, all saw what happened that day porque we were there. Deus, El Diablo or the Steel Maria if you want, put us on that fucking bridge, I'm telling you.

Before that day, I used to think my life was mierda. Laughs.

Insults. Blows.

Boys screaming.

Beating.

Chasing.

Sceilig's milky skin.

I wanted to smell it. Bite it.

I couldn't.

Mamá working at the NTC. Her corridas.

Da, on the windmill.

Bueno, pues that was nothing, Hermanas, nothing.

Nothing compared to seeing Alcalá in Sister Ciarana's arms. A mess of mud and limbs and wet clothes and seaweed. She wasn't Alcalá. She wasn't. She couldn't be. I wanted to shout at the nun SHE ISN'T, pero the pain in my brain had frozen my whole body.

The nun looked back at me.

"Mi hermana…" I managed to say.

I kept looking at the nun, feeling I was going to throw up my heart. She nodded.

I knew I had made a deal. Something had listened to me, and it was the Steel Maria if you want. To be honest, I didn't care, because I had been listened to for the very first time in my life.

Sister Ciarana knelt on the bridge, holding my sister tight. People gathered closer.

I felt the light pouring all over me. My eyes ached, and my flesh burnt. Acid drops ran down my chin. It wasn't rain, it was sweat. ¿Was this real sun on my skin?

COUGH.

Alcalá was coughing.

The dirty sky glowed.

Hermanas, my goggles were filled with water. It was like opening the only window in a narrow house. PFSSSSSS. Fresh currents of air breaking in. I knew, from that day on, that there would be a price to pay, though. I had asked, I had been listened to. The deal had been closed and I'd have to give something in return.

The nun never said so but, Hermanas, I knew it. </record>

<record> **DEEL 10.** *Blessed V-D for everyone, oh yeah*

Next Sunday, you wouldn't believe it, but we went to Missa at the NTC all together. Failing to attend brought Excommunication, the fancy word for we're-going-to-tie-you-to-a-windmill. You could watch the Excomunicationes on Sunday evening on TV, live stream and all, but you didn't want to have the lead role in the next one, no.

Además, there'd always been a real good incentive to attend Missa. ¿Where else could we get a shoot of V-D? Sí, there was the illegal market, but it had its cost and these days we couldn't gather even enough to buy Sunnaluz.

I pushed Alcalá's new wheelchair. I was a bit concerned in case other boys saw me, sure. Pero I would break their jaws if they laughed. Alcalá had been in a comatose state since she fell into the waters.

"Vamos…¿you coming?"

Mamá struggled to follow us, hands covered in black bandages. Jodidos toros. She had used all the money from her last corrida to buy a new wheelchair for Alcalá. She couldn't forgive herself for what had happened (not being there when Alcalá almost died). Mamá's skin was yellowish, covered in sweat. Tonta. She didn't want to spend money on painkillers.

"Kerry, wait for her."

"Mierda."

On Rory O'More bridge we mixed with the dark mass of wet folks who were heading to the NTC. ¿Do you want me to describe it? ¿Again? Thick steel cables, tentacular, wrapped the building, perpetually keeping it from sinking into the waters. The rain-stained windows were hundreds of mouths vomiting darkness. Shiny plastic angels stood as snipers on the windowsills. The waters surrounding the NTC sparkled in gold and garnet; if you looked down you could see the crucifixes covered in diamonds. Indulgentii. Sí, the rich Irish paid for them then threw them in the water so Deus would forgive their sins. ¿Does it make any sense to you? I always felt like diving in to get one and be rich the rest of my life. Pero it was not that easy: some of the ghostly white crosses were camouflaged hammerheads.

The embarkment was at the end of Rory O'More. The ferry that came to take us wasn't bigger than a sperm whale so it didn't accommodate more than thirty people – all of them standing, squeezing together, like sinners in the Infernum. Ah, there was also this projector with images of Noah's Ark. With the sound of animals in that recording, it all seemed like a zoo. ¿Can you imagine, the sweat and flatulence mixed with rotten seaweed and children being sick? It was especially bad if some of them had been eating pepper crabs for breakfast. But that day I didn't joke with my sister about that, because she hadn't uttered a word since the accident. Before we could step out, Dominus Ahenobarbus, who had a nose like a rotten potato, made the sign of the cross on our foreheads, while we knelt and shown him our cross-necklace-ID.

"Deus te benedicat."

"Deus te benedicat."

I had to show Alcalá's because she wouldn't move.

Inside the NTC chapel, rain made the stained-glass windows cry. Moving candles on the ceiling reflected purple y yellow in hundreds of sleepy faces. On the walls, versicles winked at us in pink neon.

AND DEUS SAID, LET THERE BE RAIN. JESUS SHINES DOWN ON YOU ALL. PRAY TO DRY YOUR SOUL.

As always, there were screens featuring chapters from the Book of Kells playing all at the same time, buzzing like wasp hives. I can sense the smell even now (myrrh and electricity). We (Irish and Spanish happily together) knelt on the individual plastic mats and put the headphones on. Dominus Domitius's angry speech was so loud you felt your brains were going to commit suicide by throwing themselves out of your ears, like. There was no volume control or anything. He talked about the same old bullshit:

Infernum.

Punishment.

Sin.

We were all condemned to endure the rain porque humanity was miserable. We let the son of Deus die, ¿what can be expected from such a cruel race?

From time to time he would get so excited that one of his crutches (he never said Missa sitting on his scooter) would fall, CLASH, and someone would scream.

"¡Save me, Deus!" Or: "¡María, protect us!"

After that, the Flood Songs came. Of course, I just moved my lips and looked down, as Mamá taught me to. Ree was really into it, though: she even had tears running down her cheeks.

And finally, we all queued to receive the Communio.

I looked up when I saw Sceilig walking towards the altar. He had plasters on his nose and on his chin. ¿Had he been in another fight? Something warm poured into my hips. Even with a black eye, he was still some pretty thing. Hermanas, I felt nauseated after having that thought.

On the altar, Sceilig made the sign of the cross and mouthed:

"Sanguis Christi."

He extended his bare arm. It was thin and ivory-like. Dominus Domitius took a disposable syringe from the chalice that Íscar held and gave Sceilig an injection of V-D. The old toad seemed to enjoy it. Puto. ¿Was Sceilig feeling the frozen liquid ascending through his veins? ¿Was he feeling a cold chill and the start of nausea? He licked his lips and took a piece of cotton from the paten to press the wound.

"Amen."

He kissed Dominus Domitius's Fisherman Ring before walking away. It was disgusting. `</record>`

`<record>` **DEEL 11** Sending sinful souls all the way up to Heaven

Sí, sí, there was something even worse than being a fisherman, like Da had been. Sure, he'd done something wrong, according to the Domini, and disobeyed the rules, but if he'd repented while tied to the windmill then he'd still have had the chance to go to Heaven, because Deus is a loving father who punishes His children but wants them to be fine in the end. ¿But liking other boys? That was beyond evil, it goes against nature, against every single law Deus designed for us. It was the worst sin, the only sin for which there wasn't repentance or compassion. Liking a boy, or a girl if you were a girl, sí. ¿Why do you look at me like it's so hard to believe? I'm telling you the truth, I swear. ¿You are actually checking to see if what I'm saying is true? Ha, ha, ha. ¿Why would I lie? Look at me. Look. I have nothing. Just this story to tell. This, all this, here, in this room, this chair. I was born to be here, at this precise moment. To tell you this. And you are all here to listen.

<...>

On Thursday I decided to take Alcalá outside the barco.

She hadn't said anything since the accident. Her mouth was a straight line. Her eyeballs were two enormous onyx marbles about to fall from their sockets.

We only had SugarHosts to give her (Pope-blessed, according to the package, though).

"Don't move her," Ree said.

She hadn't left Alcalá's side since the accident. She'd been doing all sorts of stupid things: putting a stinky blanket on her legs and trying to feed her SugarHosts dissolved in warm water with a straw. I mean, ¿what? Of course Ree ended up drinking it all herself whenever Alcalá spat the straw out and turned her head.

"You're always in my way, ¡get off!" I pushed Ree aside.

She complained, but there was no one there to hear her wailing. Mamá was back with the Matadores fixing a new toro.

I took Alcalá to the pier. Her new wheelchair was made of lasered steel, Hermanas. It looked so neat. I wished my sis had been made of lasered steel too.

I tried to put the respiradero on her to see if it helped things, but she groaned.

"Venga." I forced it on her but Alcalá's face turned red and her eyes filled up with tears.

I threw the respiradero away. She went quiet. Her chest was going up and down, but she didn't suffocate, even though the air in North Liffey was the worst in all Neo Dublin. Alcalá's eyes closed and her lips dropped. Hermanas, I couldn't believe what I was seeing. She'd just fallen asleep outside, in the rain, like a baby.

¿Another miracle? ¿After she'd been brought back to life by the Sister of Cow? Hermanas, I felt relieved and scared at the same time, I can tell you now.

I decided to do something fun to keep myself distracted. I had a bunch of bangers. They were hidden inside an airtight can of Sunnaluz that I kept under the water, tied up to the pier with a rope. Smart, I know. They weren't fancy or anything. If I had the money I'd buy more Sunnaluz first, ¿okay? I'd made those bangers myself, and they may have not been fancy, but they were fucking lethal.

¿You know? The Irish had billions of these plastic figurines of saints: Noah, Saint Brendan, Jesus, Saint Patrick...They changed them every season. They gave them away for free, all over the city, along with printed prayers and stuff. So I used to cut the plastic heads off and pierce them with a nail, pass a string through them, fill them up with gunpowder and...¡BOOM!

Alcalá used to love that. Let's set the waters on fire, she'd say, ohhh yeah.

I put some bangers on her hands. She opened her eyes when she felt the warmth, but she wasn't quick enough to launch them. So I did it for her, porque I didn't want to set her on fire. I mean, c'mon.

It was so pretty. Glittery rain, PZZZZZZZ, dying in

pinkish red and green and then disappearing forever in the black waters. I laughed. Alcalá laughed. Alcalá laughed like crazy. Her voice outside sounded strange, naked without the buzzing of the respiradero.

BANG.

BANG.

Íscar came to complain about sparks falling on his deck.

"Come on now," I shouted back at him, "we're just having a bit of fun over here."

"If you set my deck on fire, I'm going to launch one of those up your ass," he threatened.

"Cierra la puta boca or I'll throw one in your face," I said.

That was when Sceilig appeared, walking towards us. He was wearing (¡once again!) his NTC uniform. The trousers were dirty with mud, though. In North Liffey, mud was so thick that no matter how much Sunnaluz you put on, you drowned in it anyway. He was looking a bit on edge and when I threw a bit of mud into the water, he jumped as if he'd seen an orca, like.

Hermanas, he was funny.

"Hey Kerry," little Sceilig said to me, taking his goggles off. His irises were the kind of blue you'd never see in those poisonous waters. Clear like the sky used to be. Maybe.

Alcalá focused her eyes on him.

"Eh, tú, ¿qué coño quieres?" Her fingers tried to push the wheelchair's buttons to move forward but she was too weak.

It was the first time she'd spoken since the accident. Sceilig looked at me.

"He's Irish. No habla español," I told Alcalá. "He's a

classmate."

"¿Whaaat…?" Alcalá bursted into laughter. She was high on SugarHosts. Great.

"Hey, ¿what the fuck are you doing here?" I asked Sceilig. There was still quite a distance between us. We were by the barco, whereas Sceilig stood next to the bridge.

"Here." He got closer to hand me a blue plastic box. Painkillers in the form of ugly cherub faces. The expensive kind. "Thought she may need them."

"We're fine," I said, but I grabbed them, so I did. Not for Alcalá, but for Mamá.

"They're cool," Sceilig said, meaning my bangers, of course. ¿What was going on?

"Look, you better get the fuck out. They don't like Irish boys around here, ¿you know?"

"I'm not Irish." Sceilig came even closer.

Alcalá looked at him and laughed a bit more. A thread of saliva hung from her lips.

"Can I take one?" Sceilig asked.

"You *are* Irish." I pushed him away from my sister and the bangers.

"The Irish are from Ireland. ¿Where is Ireland, you smartass? I'm from around here, the same as you."

I pushed him again.

"Don't call me smartass."

"Sure," he said. "Look at these."

He took something out of his pocket.

"¿What?"

"Anima Impii. I swiped some during Missa. I thought it'd be cool to light them up from this bridge. Try to bring that down."

He pointed out the old Angelus that patrolled over

our pier.

"Let me." I grabbed one. The Anima Impii were proper fancy stuff the Domini used during funeral masses and the like.

"The Domini are going to get so pissed off."

"I thought you loved the NTC."

"¿This?" He pointed at the NTC logo on his jacket. "This is just a symbol. I do whatever I want with it. Like, wipe my arse with it, ¿get what I mean?"

Alcalá laughed.

I didn't know how to react. Sceilig was there, holding the Anima Impii and suddenly my old hoodie with patches of rotten Sunnaluz felt itchy.

"¿Are we going to light these or not?" Sceilig asked.

I grabbed them from his hands without looking at him. It still made me nervous to look at that pretty face of his directly, Sí, I can say this now, but back then even the thought of it made me sick.

¿What?

¿What happens next? I don't know. I don't think I remember. I don't even know now why I was telling you this…I just…Sí. I don't know. Sí, sí, I know this is not relevant. I'll get back to the point. </record>

<record> **DEEL 12** *The jodido miracle of the crippled: ¡get up y walk! (I wish…)*

Fog season started two weeks earlier than usual. I was heading home one day and everything was covered in a cold, thick layer of cloud the tone of Vitamilk. You felt like you were walking under the sea, breathing salt and waves. I heard that clicking noise orcas make when they're hunting. I moved towards the middle of the Cabra bridge, but I may have got closer to the water.

"Kerry."

A voice filtered through the fog.

"Kerry."

A shadow appeared wearing a massive hatraguas with a front torch. I recognised Íscar's voice.

"Kerry."

"Switch that bloody light off," I said. All that flashing right in my face was electrocuting my brain.

"Tienes que ir a por tu hermana."

"¿What's wrong with my sis?"

"Alcalá's down El Mercado de San Miguel. You need to go and fetch her before she gets into trouble. Here." Íscar passed me a tube of Sunnaluz and I rubbed a bit on my goggles so I could see what I was stepping on.

¿You want to know about El Mercado de San Miguel, Hermanas? It was the only Spanish market left in Neo Dublin, hidden inside the old submarine yard. You had to go down a rickety ladder in Grangegorman Bridge. The plastic-made industrial unit reeked of piss, Rioja, and the ghost stench of submarine fuel. Yes, it was a black market, like, everyone could go down there and sell or buy anything.

Alcalá, I thought, ¿what the fuck have you done?

Oxygen was not abundant in El Mercado. Every time I went down, my lungs melted. Groups of people gathered there with trolleys of random stuff, calling out the best offers of the day.

"¡Bonito y barato! ¡Bonito y barato!"

A toddler with a respiradero played inside a box full of colourful hooks.

An old man with no legs, sitting in a wheelchair, picked a videodisc from a big pile. Beside him, a young girl (¿his daughter? ¿whore?) was selling them. If you hacked a deskreen, you could watch these instead of Life of the Saints or Noah's Ark.

Two thin sisters sold synthetic SugarHosts. They were so sweet you almost couldn't taste the plastic and they gave you a good boost anyway. A woman smelling of fried skelpers (joder, I don't get how people can eat those monsters) tried to sell me a bastardised version of a Sunnaluz can. Probably skelper gelatine.

¿Who could I ask about my sister?

There was a man who had put a tablecloth on his stand (¡a tablecloth!) to display his V-D tablets. He spat on a junkie who approached him crying for a shot, and threatened him with a half-broken harpoon.

"Vete a la mierda, yonki."

My eyes went to a heap of weapons and tools that three kids were guarding in a corner. The weapons were quite rusty but there was a harpoon gun that looked pretty cool. They had got them by diving down into the mud, where their original owners had lost them. Sí, one of the kids had a greenish rash all over his face. Wasp-seaweed.

"¿Have you seen my sister? Va en silla de ruedas, es morena…"

The girl pointed out a stand on the other side. Paperbooks. Of course.

I found Alcalá on the floor, checking out her queridos paperbooks. In that, she was like Father. I never understood what they saw in those unreadable things. Plus, ¿is there anything more useless in the rain? Alcalá's little legs lay on the ground, two sleeping animals, like. Pero her face, joder, I swear she was fucking smiling.

"¿Where is your wheelchair?" I asked.

"I like it. It has illustrations." She looked at me, holding one of the paperbooks.

"Don't tell me you've lost your wheelchair. Just don't."

"This one is called *The Bull's Betrothed,* and it's about a Spanish sculptor Before the Flood that—"

"You sold your wheelchair because you don't fucking need it any more, ¿right?"

"Hey, cool down. They gave me all this money." She shown me a bunch of notes.

"You're probably going to spend all that, and more, to get it back, 'cause ¿how the hell am I going to take you home? ¿How the hell are you moving from now on?"

"Shut up and relax." She tossed the paperbook. "We need the money and we're all making sacrifices except you, shit-sack. Now get me up and take me out. I'll get Father to buy me another wheelchair soon."

Mamá got really mad when I came in carrying Alcalá on my back and without the wheelchair she had spent so much money on. A screaming match ensued while Ree and I covered our ears and tried not to go deaf. Finally, Mamá left the barco, still shouting, and she was gone for a long while, but when she returned, we had delicious synthetic cucumbers for dinner, jellyfish sweets, and lots of fresh Sunnaluz to use in the morning. </record>

<record> **DEEL 13.** *White dolphins are not just ghosts*

Something I like about fog season is that everything disappears in soft, white foam. Cool, ¿don't you think? I swear the fog in Neo Dublin did look like foam or soft white mould, secretive, but good. It puts you in a mood, that fog, it does. At times it'd get so thick that everything came to a halt around the city. The barcos and barco-buses couldn't see where they were going, and the risk of accidents and crashes wasn't worth it. Classes got suspended too, which was my favourite part, clearly, and sí, now that I come to think of it probably also the reason why fog was always a good omen for me.

We sat on the barco's deck, Alcalá and I, letting the wet softness of the fog wrap around us. Wasting the Sunnaluz Mamá had got us to stay more or less dry, only because we both loved the strangeness of the landscape. Thick white, like Vitamilk (thinking about it made our stomachs rumble). The orange and pink smooth glow of the fog lights from other barcos nearby.

¿You know what? I'll tell you. I'll tell you why I loved the fog so much. Really. It reminded me of when I used to live on the sea, in the same barco, not permanently moored on to North Liffey, but roaming far beyond Neo Dublin, around what was known once as the Iberian Peninsula, or so the Domini tell us. That's how we grew up, Alcalá and I, with Mamá, in the waters. And fog thick like this wasn't rare then, and it lasted for weeks, but deep in the waters you could see seagulls cutting through now and again, and you could also hear whales.

"¿Remember?" I asked Alcalá. We didn't speak that much those days, not much chance, but that day we did, yes, we did.

She nodded. Being my older sister and all, she's smart, and she gets me better than anyone else.

"I just don't get why Mamá brought us back. Everything was fine when it was only us," I said.

Alcalá shook her head.

"No Domini, no bullshit rules. And we were never hungry. There was always fish, and no one to tell us we couldn't get them," I continued.

"Mamá wanted to give us a life. She wanted us to belong somewhere," she said. "On the waters we were homeless. Also, we were children, and we liked it, yes, but it wouldn't have been like that forever. We'd have wanted out of the barco eventually. That's why Mamá brought us back."

"To this shithole."

"It's where we were born."

"It's a shithole," I insisted.

"It wasn't that bad until the food started to run out."

"And we started sinking," I reminded her.

Sure, it hadn't been bad for her, because she could stay home all she wanted, reading her paperbooks and enjoying herself, and if she had to go to the NTC school, which wasn't all that often, she went to a class of Spaniards where she fit right away, no issue there.

Acalá sighed. I couldn't quite get used to watching her without her respiradero outside. But somehow her lungs had improved.

"¿What did it feel like," I asked, "when you fell into the waters?"

"Cold. Then nothing. I don't remember much."

She'd been in the water a fair bit. And Mamá said that she'd gone into shock after that, and that's why she spent days without talking to us.

"¿But you know what I saw?"

I thought she was going to talk about the orcas that almost had her for dinner.

"A white dolphin."

"¿What?" I laughed. "¿You opened your eyes under the water?"

"So I did, ¿wouldn't you?"

"White dolphins aren't real."

"But they are. What would you know, you never read anything, you peabrain."

"Okay, they are,' I said. "But they don't come to Neo Dublin. The water is too dirty."

"I saw one."

"It was a ghost then. The ghost of a dolphin."

"Oh, shut up," Alcalá smacked the back of my neck. Ouch. She was strong, fuck me.

We stayed there in silence. Even with the Sunnaluz on, my goggles started to get too wet for me to see properly.

Mamá came out on the deck whistling, which she always did when she was in a good mood. She had an apron on, stained with the sweet whale resin she used to insulate the barco. With the water going up day by day, she was getting nervous.

"Alcalá, don't stay outside for too long," she said. "Your lungs."

"I'm fine," my sis replied. Wow. A few weeks ago she wouldn't have been able to speak outside. Not enough air. I still had trouble believing this miracle.

"¿Your friend not coming today?" Mamá said to me. She was talking about Sceilig, of course. I've been waiting for him, actually, 'cause today there wasn't any class, which meant he'd be free. But there was also the fog, which meant he was probably staying put. He'd been coming a fair bit to hang out with us. He usually brought painkillers and bits of food, his mum must have got a nice special food card on account of being a Sister of Cow and all. I secretly wished he'd come though, and it wasn't only because of the painkillers, although it was nice to see Mamá doing better. This is disgustingly cheesy, yeah, but I wanted us to be friends, I guess, even though I knew that me being friends with an Irish lad was as likely as me seeing a big bunch of white dolphins jumping Neo Dublin's polluted waves. </record>

<record> **DEEL 14.** *Father eats nun-tits y he doesn't even share*

Next day, Mamá and I went to see Father at his office in the NTC. Mamá was wearing her cleaning uniform. The blue plastic apron reeked of moss. Her face was a wizened mask. And that was not only the effect of the fluorescent ceiling lights. She was getting old, Hermanas.

The corridors were empty. School time was over. The carpets were full of words, Book of Kells verses that glowed whenever you stepped on them, so the Domini could meditate while exercising their earthly bodies.

Father often made me walk all over the NTC, reading, every day after the classes. He was obsessed with me passing the final exams. He couldn't quite accept I was still in ninth grade when I should have been in eleventh. He needed me to complete twelfth grade to get the Irish Card. As if I cared.

Father's office was more like a mouldy cupboard. It barely fit the two china virgin martyrs hanging from the lamp and a digiboard full of hand-written words. He had once been a Literature Master, but after marrying Mamá he had been demoted to work in the cleaning and repairs department. It wasn't a big thing, that, he *was* the department.

He took in reports of whatever stuff was faulty and then arranged for it to be fixed. He worked at it all day long. But don't worry, 'cause to combat his frustration he had his sugar addiction, oh sí. That's how we found him, looking at his deskreen, chewing caramelised nun-tits. He raised his eyes too slowly. He hated when I entered his office without knocking first. But when he discovered Mamá behind me, oh Hermanas, the caramelised nun-tits turned into gasoline in his mouth.

"¿What are you doing here?" He switched his deskreen off.

"My job," Mamá said.

Father settled into his chair and placed five nun-tits on the deskreen in a perfect row.

"It's the third day I come to work and they send me home because of this." Mamá raised her hands, still covered in black bandages. Wounds from her last corrida. "I can work alright; it doesn't slow me down."

"Well…You've to deal with that." Father smashed the nun-tits with his thumb. "See, we can't be responsible if you end up losing your fingers."

"I need to work."

"You got what you deserved. I can't ask them to give you special treatment." Father sucked his sugary thumb.

"I know. But I can't lose my job, we need the money."

"¿Do my children need anything?" Father kneaded the smashed nun-tits together using a pen. "*My* children, not that fat girl."

"Don't talk about Ree like that," I said.

"It's ok, Kerry, just shut up," Mamá cut me off.

Father shook his head while he ate that disgusting

amorphous thing that wasn't a nun-tit any more.

"Look, I'll provide for *my* children as I've always done. I'm having a new wheelchair sent for Alcalá. And they can come here and live with me. That's probably the best thing to do, given your current situation." He was catching bits of caramel with his nails.

"I'd rather die." I crossed my arms.

"I'm not asking you to take them away. And you were the one who brought Alcalá to that awful place where she almost drowned," Mamá replied. "I'm just asking for my job. I thought compassion was what Jesus taught us all."

"Don't pronounce His name with your impure lips," Father interrupted. "Compassion is tolerating the presence of a whore in such a sacred place. And I'm not even telling them about your bullfighting. Don't ask for too much, woman."

Mamá walked towards the door.

"Don't call my mother a whore."

Blood was burning beneath my cheeks. I was always waiting for a chance to get Father. I took a step towards him.

"Kerry…" Mamá's voice sounded tired.

"You're disgusting," I said, looking at him.

"Stop that, Kerry," Mamá was already at the door.

"I can't fucking stand you," I continued. Father raised his hand. "Don't even try to touch me, viejo."

We were the same height. His hands were still huge like metal planks, but my arms were full of scars. He was trembling. I wanted him to hit me so I could hit him back. I wanted to hit him back more than anything in this world.

KNOCK, KNOCK.

"Come on in," Father said.

The door opened and a woman entered.

"Sister Ciarana, ¿what can I do for you?" Father gestured us towards the door.

"Oh, nothing urgent," she said.

She was the nun who had saved Alcalá, and Sceilig's mother. I hadn't seen her since the day of the accident. Her habit was now sparkling clean with Sunnaluz and she held something wrapped in a purple towel.

"I'll come back later," she told Father.

She walked out with us. Mamá stared at her as if she was watching Jesus Christ on Earth. She knew that the Sister of Cow saved Alcalá, of course. People were still talking about it in North Liffey.

"I heard everything," Sister Ciarana said. But she wasn't pitying us. She seemed disgusted. She put a hand on Mamá's shoulder, and I'd like to say she looked friendly, or kind, but it was more like a mantis grabbing its prey. "I can help you. Tomorrow night, at El Mercado. Everyone's going to be there." </record>

<record> **DEEL 15.** *A very special kind of sun will shine on Neo Dublin soon*

When Mamá, Alcalá, Ree, and I arrived at El Mercado de San Miguel a small crowd had already gathered around Sister Ciarana. I recognised a few faces: Father, Íscar and Sceilig.

At night, El Mercado turned wild. There were still some stands, but they sold the freakiest shit, such as the mummified hands of obscure saints and other body parts that were supposed to keep evil away. People drank SugarCans and danced to ancient songs in hacked projectors, like *Livin' la Vida Loca*, mientras others opened their wet ponchos and offered their soggy bodies to the halo of the UVA lampposts.

I know this is weird, Hermanas, but Sister Ciarana didn't look strange at all sitting in a corner, on an empty box, drinking a SugarCan, passing the beads of her rosary with her free hand. Her black tunic blended with the darkness. I don't think anyone had seen a nun in El Mercado before. I mean, normal nuns would have left their habits at home before coming.

"Welcome, Hermanas, Hermanos," she said. It was then I realised that Sister Ciarana, Father, Ree, and Sceilig were the only Irish in a multitude of hundreds.

A little girl was throwing up in a corner (regretting having drunk so many SugarCans, I bet). Ree looked the other way.

"I won't sit on the floor," she said.

For once, she was right. The place was covered in mierda, fishbones, piss, and dried, sticky cum (sí, there was some fucking going on somewhere, possibly in the places the UVA lampposts didn't reach). Everyone dragged boxes and buckets close to Sister Ciarana's seat. Sceilig helped Alcalá so she could place her wheelchair next to the nun.

"That alright, ¿señorita?" Sceilig asked.

"Sí, sí, ponme ahí. There. Gracias," my sis said.

Alcalá hadn't taken her eyes off Sister Ciarana. She wanted to stay close to the nun. That's why she was being all nice to Sceilig, like.

Father brought two broken plastic chairs so we could sit together. He offered me a SugarCan and opened another for himself. He wanted to stay far away from Mamá. I slurped the sugary liquid. There was a man selling them going around, shouting prices whilst a brain-cripple followed him, carrying a bunch of cans. It would have been so easy to steal a couple, but I bet Father paid double for them just to be pious.

"She's Deus's messenger," Father whispered to me. Talking about Sister Ciarana, of course.

"Another Maria Inoculata?" I laughed.

"Your mother is a bad influence," Father said. "Be blasphemous and you'll go to Hell, just like her."

Hermanas, don't get this wrong. I had faith in Deus. It was because of faith that we all gathered in El Mercado that precise night. We all had witnessed Sister Ciarana's miracle: she had revived Alcalá and given her the gift of breathing Neo Dublin's noxious air. The nun's presence had been haunting us, just as blood haunts sharks and makes them chase the prey they took that delicious bite from.

"It's the paperbook. She has the paperbook that explains everything," Father said, and then started biting his nails. I bet he was fighting the need to jump on another SugarCan. I'd seen so many empty SugarCans in his apartment before, hidden in drawers, cupboards and inside the electric fireplace.

Everyone went silent.

Sister Ciarana finished drinking her SugarCan, burped behind her hand and looked at us. "Hermanas, Hermanos. What I say must be said in our ancient language, Spanish. Because this is the language of Iberia and Iberia is where we all come from."

And she started talking in perfect Spanish (no joke):

"Neo Dublín está podrido."

Silence.

I started shivering as I realised why she could speak the two languages. She was a half-bred mongrel. Just like me.

"Neo Dublín está podrido en barro y herrumbre, como el Infernum." Neo Dublin sucks, she basically said.

Silence.

I was surprised to hear her speaking like that. After all, Spanish was banned, ¿no?

"Solo hay una manera de destruír este pecado: el sol. Poderoso y terrible, como Deus." The city is full of shit and we need the sun.

"Si no hay sol, Deus nos dará el poder para crear uno. Un sol poderoso y terrible."

I was getting a bit confused, because she was talking about the sun, and how Deus would give us the power to create one, but at the same time it seemed she was saying something completely different.

"The sun…" Ree whispered, pulling at the cross-neck-lace-ID around her neck. After having lived in North Liffey for a few years, she understood the odd Spanish word here and there.

"Llevaremos nuestro sol al corazón del New Trinity College y, una vez allí, su ardor consumirá el edificio maldito en un suspiro. Esa es la voluntad de Deus."

We'll take our sun to the NTC and then it'll make the building disappear because that is Deus's will, so—

I was getting more and more confused.

"Y el sol arderá, el sol que—"

Then I understood.

"It's not a sun, for fuck's sake. ¡She's talking about putting a bomb in the NTC!" </record>

`<record>` **DEEL 16.** *Y finally, I get something. I get a story to tell*

We were all, whoooo, like, ¿what?

"Our saviour is not Jesus, but St. Ciarán," Sister Ciarana continued, this time in Irish, "and he came from the peninsula that is now under the waters, and he spoke Spanish. The Domini didn't conquer the Spanish, because the Domini are Spanish too. We all came from here, millennia Before The Flood."

"¿What? That can't—"

"She's telling the truth." Father stood up. His eyes were bright with tears. He'd been waiting for that moment to make the revelation. "She shown me the paperbook, weeks ago, when she first came from the Vatican Boat. The Book of Cow."

"The Book of Cow…" Íscar gasped.

"We have enslaved our own race for far too long now," Sister Ciarana continued. "¿Do you think that was what Deus wanted? Deus is angry at us. That is why the waters are rising, every day. Neo Dublin will soon be gone, and our sins will finally be punished. The New Trinity College is a monster, built on lies and suffering. A monument to human greed and lust for power. We must destroy it."

"She's right. It's all in The Book of Cow," Father spoke over her. "And as a Literature Master," tears started running down his cheeks, "I can verify she has the *real* document. And it explains the rains, the flooding, why we are here. Everything. The Pope has been hiding the truth for too long. Starving us out with SugarHosts and Vitamilk to keep the population in manageable numbers, and controlling us by means of V-D. And now that the water levels are rising again he's leaving us here to sink, with no food, nothing that can save us. There are all lies." He stamped on the floor. "They. Are. All. Lies."

Silence.

"¿There's no more Vitamilk?" Ree cried.

"No, I'm telling you, the Pope is gone, with his Vatican Boat, and his cows, and the Vitamilk. Gone to look for other floating cities because Neo Dublin is already dead," Father replied.

"But we're hungry," Íscar complained.

"The Pope can't leave us now. We're hungry," Ree repeated. "¡We're so hungry!"

"I know," Sister Ciarana said.

And then she performed the second miracle. She took something from under her habit. A piece of meat.

Now, ¿can I just stop here for a moment? I'm feeling dizzy...Sí, sí. I know you have all kind of fancy foods here. No, I don't want rundvlees. I want more sinaasappelsap, yes. More. Bedankt. Thank you.

In Neo Dublín we just got the Vitamilk, this warm flavourless liquid. Or the SugarHosts for a good boost of energy. Nothing else. Well, and the fish, that tasted great in comparison, gummy and salty, but we tried not to eat fish, because we were afraid of cancer and the Excommunicationes.

We'd never seen real meat, not even smelt it. Never, like. Edible animals were long gone. The closest thing left was Dominus Domitius's paper-like calf, or the Pope's cows that no one but the Sisters of Cow had permission to come close to.

So that piece she was holding, it was a fucking miracle. ¿Do you get it? That was the only proof we needed to believe she was holy. That did it for us. Sí.

That meat had the most rabid red colour. It was

drenched in blood. It was disgusting and mouth-watering. Like having sex for the first time. The smell of it. I'll never forget it. I knew it was food. My stomach was screaming for it.

I had to swallow hard. My mouth filled with saliva. The meat had lumps that looked soft, like they would dissolve in my mouth. Yellow streaks of oily fat. It smelt of warmth, fulfilment, life. My muscles tensed. My body was dying to throw itself at that precious food.

Sister Ciarana separated the meat from the white towel it was wrapped in. A dark substance dripped.

Dizziness.

I fought the need to lick the meat juice straight from the floor.

Everyone, Irish and Spanish, looked the same under those UVA lampposts: grey faces and hollow cheeks. Mierda.

Sister Ciarana held the miracle of the meat a while longer and finally she gave it to Alcalá. "Corpus Christi," she said.

Alcalá's fingers nursed the meat and she lowered her head to kiss it. She passed it to Ree.

"Sanguis Christi," the nun said.

Ree licked it. Y passed it to Sceilig.

"Corpus Christi." Sceilig gave it to Father. "Sanguis Christi."

"Amen," Father cried, and he passed it to Íscar. "Sanguis Christi."

Íscar passed it to Mamá.

"Corpus Christi." Mamá gave it to me. "Sanguis Christi."

I knelt, like everyone else. Pero I was so hungry. I bit it.

When I tasted the meat, my blood warmed after what seemed like a thousand winters. It was better than the Sunnaluz. My stomach was finally content. I felt drunk and full of energy. My eyes itched. I was still chewing when Ree took the piece from my hands. She stuffed it in her mouth.

Father struggled to take it from her.

Hands, blood, teeth.

Íscar started crying.

"Deus...I knew...He'd never leave us...sinking..."

The meat was gone and we were all covered in red now.

Sister Ciarana stood up. She was a tall woman. She raised her arms and closed her eyes. It was funny but I didn't laugh. I didn't want to. There was something in her voice, her eyes. She felt true. She was a half-breed. She spoke Spanish and English. She was going to end the hunger. She had to come from Deus.

"To hell with the NTC." Íscar knelt in front of the nun, his chin glittering red.

"We'll follow you." Father knelt in front of her too. "Show us the way. Please, show us."

Sister Ciarana opened her eyes but instead of looking at Father, she walked among us and grabbed Mamá's bloody hands. You should have seen Father's face. Well, everyone was jealous as fuck.

"Your talents have been wasted for too long. Tú vas a crear la bomba."

Sí. She asked Mamá to create the bomb.

You know what, ¿Hermanas? Mamá was the only one who didn't tremble. She wasn't afraid. She wasn't even angry. She just sighed. Deeply. She looked the nun in the eye. She nodded.

"You will translate the Book of Cow, so everyone knows about the wonders of St. Ciarán," the nun told Father. "You are a Literature Master; you were born to do this. And when the time comes, you will let us into the NTC."

He started sobbing.

Sister Ciarana went to Alcalá.

"I saved your life once. And now the flesh shall save you again. You will help your father with the translation so our most important paperbook doesn't perish in the floods."

"I'll do anything for you," my sis answered.

"You have always been treated as an outsider. But here you are with your family," Sister Ciarana spoke to Íscar. "You will get us the materials to make the bomb."

"To Hell with the Domini, those fat bastards," Íscar smiled.

"And you…" Sister Ciarana approached Ree. She was the only one who avoided looking at the nun, scared shitless, like. "I know about your father. I know the Domini murdered him. There will be a reckoning, my child. You will carry the bomb, and place it inside their NTC."

Ree nodded. Still pale.

¿Y me? ¿Y me? I mean, the nun had spoken to everyone, but I was left. After all, she had also betrayed me.

Then, ¡praise Deus!, she turned to me. She hadn't forgotten our deal. She had saved my sis and now I was prepared to do anything for her. And (pay attention to this) she said:

"You'll press the detonator." (Grandiose silence). "So you'll have a story to tell afterwards." </record>

<record> **DEEL 17** *Flamenco-dancing fluorescent lobsters*

Let's fast forward a bit here. I don't want to bore you.

Sister Ciarana taught us Deus in a way we'd never heard before. She didn't talk about suffering, sin or repenting. She kept us fed and asked us to make a bomb.

¿What? Sure, you have trouble believing this. Ja, ja, I understand. But let me tell you something: you've never starved. You may know hunger, sure, but I'm talking about something different here. Days and days with only bits of SugarHosts diluted in water. The emptiness that you feel is like a void that devours everything: your stomach, the warmth of the blood that still runs through your veins. Your good mood. Your ability to care for others. Hope. Because when you're starving you are so fucking cold all the time that you don't feel at home in your body anymore. This, sí, all this has become a cage you can't escape from. Así que at this point, you may as well give up all the hope and die. ¿Get what I mean?

So when Sister Ciarana gifted us the flesh, we became her followers. I swear that's how it happened. Without her and her miracles, we'd have died. We knew it.

Además, we'd never felt it before, you know, the euphoria, the holiness. It was as if our bodies had been frozen for decades, poisoned by hunger, and rain, and now they functioned as they should for the very first time. If you ate too many SugarHosts, you started seeing weird things, like gigantic fluorescent lobsters dancing flamenco. Pero meat not only kept the hunger away, it also made us lucid.

Every day we all gathered in Sister Ciarana's house to listen to her reading *The Book of Cow* and then we devoured the meat.

I was there for the second part, really.

It was all a ritual, a Meat Missa. Famine was killing everyone else in Neo Dublin. Parents even prostituted their kids to pay for SugarHosts. And there we were, feeding on Sister Ciarana's mysteries.

We were the chosen ones.

Oh, glorious chunks of meat. Like the miracle of the five loaves and two fish, she always had enough for us all.

"Corpus Christi."

"Amen."

"Sanguis Christi."

"Amen."

We buried our hands in the redness. We brought the melting flesh to our mouths and licked it and let it dissolve under our tongues so it lasted longer.

One day (yeah, I just remembered this now) I slurped a bit of rubbery fat and I heard a giggle.

Sceilig.

The red was on his lips, cheeks, forehead. It was revolting and sexy. I dipped my fingers in the blood and touched his nose. I wanted him. I wanted him so much it made me nauseous, because it was so sick, to want another boy like that, but I just did. I did.

"Fuck off," he whispered, giggling. Grey drops of meat juice clung to his hair.

"You two, be quiet," Father ordered. "Show some respect. This is Deus's mystery."

He went back to his piece of meat and tore off a tender bit to offer it to Mamá. She didn't look at him, but took it from his hands all the same. I'd never seen them like that before, so quiet, so comfortable in each other's presence.

Sister Ciarana's scapular always remained white. She tore the flesh with her long nails and ate it like that, in small pinches.

"But..." Ree swallowed. "The bomb...it...it will kill people. It will destroy..." Her eyes were two green glasses full of anguish.

It was difficult to think about death when our stomachs were so gloriously full. Ree grabbed another piece of meat and gulped it down.

"Deus, this is so good."

She was ravenous, like everyone else.

Eating flesh had only one downside: you always wanted more. </record>

<record> **DEEL 18** *Ripped clouds, singing stars y dancing boats*

After each Meat Missa, we always walked around Neo Dublin, all together. Father pushing Alcalá's wheelchair, Íscar and Mamá chatting about the corridas, Sister Ciarana and Ree, Sceilig and myself.

The wind was wild and the rain felt electrifying. My body was full of savage energy. The bridges clinked. Over us, purple clouds raced across the sky, moving faster, way faster than us.

CLINK.

CLINK.

The stars were singing. There were stars, there, ¡and there!

"¿Can you see them?" I grabbed Sceilig's arm.

Once every one hundred years or so, the clouds moved so fast that one ripped, and you could catch a glimpse of the real sky above. Stars. Planets. Worlds and worlds beyond ours.

The NTC's clock was shining, a full moon, saying goodbye. The waters sparkled and smelt of salt and deep mud.

Orcas whistled in the distance.

The barcos attached to the rusty piers danced. Like they could also hear the stars singing. We all laughed. We were full and I felt damn good.

The crucifix farms waved at us in the distance, a collection of white skeletons (Da, I still missed him, and it made me sad, so I sent that thought away). Many of the windmills didn't work anymore. School had stopped. The inquisitors didn't arrest people. Power failed all the time those days. ¿Who cared? The windmills deserved a rest. I felt their pain. Their weariness. I felt so many things since I had tasted the flesh.

Far beyond the waters, a shadow moved. ¿A blue whale? ¿The Vatican Boat? I drank the rain. It was alright.

We were all connected. The huge tower in the NTC, the clinking bridges, the dancing barcos, the millions of fish making the waters alive, the nourishing rain born from the fog, the singing stars. I looked at my life from the outside and it was a musical score, every note had its place and the tune was perfect, like.

I grabbed Sceilig's hand, and Ree's hand, and they grabbed other hands, and more hands, and we were all connected then, physically too. Flesh. It was better than being drunk. It was better than being loved. </record>

<record> **DEEL 19.** *Mamá dreams of her own Spanish*

Rover

I helped Mamá set some of the small explosives. We were doing a trial before detonating the real bomb. Alcalá spent her time with Father, they were working on a translation of *The Book of Cow*, porque it was all in Old Spanish. I preferred doing handiwork. Sí, I saw Mamá putting The Bomb together, but that happened way later. ¿Was it big? ¿The Bomb? No, not really. Just a silver suitcase with guts made of wires and tiny things that buzzed and whizzed. No, I have no idea how it worked.

At this point, Mamá's hair was all silver ¿you know? Pero she looked younger than ever. Glowing, just like Saint Lucía carrying her own eyes in a tray and still ecstatic. Mamá was wearing a sleeveless top and I could see her tattooed arms, showing how many corridas she had survived so far. Many of them etched into her skin way before I was born. She handed me the deskreen.

"My thesis," she said. "I submitted it to NTC Intellectual Property Office sixteen years ago. MarTren."

"¿MarTren? ¿A sea train?"

"Sí, a train that goes over the water. The fastest vehicle on Earth. The idea was that it'd help us contact other floating cities, if any of them had survived the rains." Mamá grabbed the deskreen and started passing the pages. "Everything is in there, the numbers, the plans, the engine…"

"¿What happened?"

"Those assholes…They sent me home. They laughed at me. They didn't even look at it. They just said, woman go back home and raise your family. I was seven months pregnant with you. That didn't help."

She gave me the deskreen back. I looked at the mathematical formulas and incredibly detailed drawings.

"I was thinking about making something similar. More like a barco," she said.

"¿A boat?"

"Not very big, so that we can hide it. Pero a barco fast enough to take us all away before the explosion, far away from this poisoned place."

"¿Where to?"

"Anywhere."

I wondered if she regretted taking Alcalá and me back to Neo Dublín. She missed our days in the ocean as much as I did, I knew that, even if we never talked about it. The whole thing with her creating this new *barco* made me think of The Irish Rover, sí, the barco in that annoying song Íscar loved.

"¿Who'll be on this boat? ¿Sister Ciarana? ¿Us?"

Mamá grabbed my hands and I froze. It'd been ages since she'd touched me, she'd been probably scared I'd bite if she tried to give me a hug or something. Couldn't blame her, really.

"Us," Mamá said. "Sister Ciarana knows that some have to survive. There's still work to be done to cure the rains. Everything can be fixed. Everything but death."

I imagined the MarTren, a silver eel rushing through the black sea.

"Give me back the thesis now. Let's work on the bomb," Mamá said. "Let's see if the guys from the NTC like it better."

Sí, lo sé. The barco we arrived in was the one Mamá designed and built. Impressive. You liked it, ¿uh? You liked it sooo much you kept it. Fuck no, I don't remember how she designed it. You'd need to ask her. I told you, I'm the dumbest in my family. And now everything is gone. No. It can't be fixed. </record>

<record> **DEEL 20.** *Poisonous mud y warm SugarHosts*

Sí, we hung out sometimes. I mean myself, Ree, and Sceilig. No, Alcalá didn't come anymore, she was deep down in that translation of the *Book of Cow* she was working on with Father. Paperbooks, yes, that was her drug.

So Sceilig, Ree, and I used to go the abandoned Windmill Farm, the one that didn't work anymore. We kept coming back. It's funny, sí. Da had been killed in that same place and there we were, drinking SugarCans and Rioja. The dizziness felt so good. It was also a big FUCK YOU to the Domini, if I'm honest, indulging in all those sinful things in a place that had been so sacred. A place of punishment and atonement.

"The NTC is going to Hell," I said.

"Yes, but..." Ree said, between gulps of SugarCan. "The bomb...will destroy everyt–"

"¿Who cares?" I passed the Rioja back to her, but she didn't take it. "What's wrong, ¿you don't like it?" I asked.

"It's too sour."

She looked to the other side and burped.

"¿Is it because it's Spanish?"

Sceilig burst out laughing.

"This Rioja is just bad, Kerry, there's no decent alcohol left, is there."

"Go to El Mercado to fetch something else if you don't like it," I said. "I exchanged seven packs of Sugar-Hosts for this shit. Nah. ¿You know what her problem is? Her Da treated her like a princess, buying all sorts of gourmet bits to stuff her and now she can't cope."

"That's not true," Ree said. "This Rioja is sour. Even Sceilig said so. Stop spiralling down, Kerry, don't go all crazy on me now."

That word set my brain on fire. I don't know how else to explain it. *Crazy.* Being in the Windmill farm was making us both remember Da, sure, but being there with Sceilig too made me think of what Da would have said about him. Da would have laughed about how clean and put together he always looked. His ironed uniform, his blonde hair, perfectly brushed. But I'll tell you something, Da wouldn't have laughed if he'd ever known what thoughts crossed my mind when I saw Sceilig. No, ah, no. Da would have gone berserk, same as Father. Because any time they took men like that to the Windmill farms, men that were, you know, like me, Da and Father and all the other men I'd ever seen would nod to themselves. That was the one crime they could never understand. 'Cause it was *crazy.*

"¿You calling me crazy, vaca?" I pushed her away. "¿Because I'm Spanish? Sister Ciarana is Spanish too, like us."

"She's Irish," Ree replied, pushing me back. "She speaks Spanish, yes, but she doesn't look Spanish."

I smashed my SugarCan against the floor until it spat all its juices. The small figurines of Jesus Christ on the windmills didn't want to witness what was about to happen.

"Kerry, chill…" Ree said.

I got the SugarCan back. It was empty. I couldn't drink it. But I could throw it at Ree. Now, Hermanas, I didn't want to hurt Ree. I wanted to hurt so many people, but not Ree. Not really.

I threw the SugarCan at her.

"¿What are you doing?" She screamed.

I grabbed the Rioja bottle.

"Kerry…" Ree said. She got on me and we struggled until the bottle slid off my hands and exploded, the booze pouring onto the floor, like blood.

"Vaca de mierda."

Ree ran away. I grabbed a handful of mud and threw it at her. I grabbed another one and chased her.

Someone pulled at me me from behind.

"Stop…Stop." Sceilig said.

"Vaca, gilipollas de mierda," I said, kicking Sceilig's ribs. I threw more mud at Ree.

Sceilig pulled my arm.

"Stop."

"¡Vaca!" I shouted at her.

I kept throwing things until she was gone. Scrabbling in the mud like a worm. "¡Fuck the NTC!" I said. "¡Fuck Neo Dublin!"

"¡Fuck it!" Sceilig echoed.

It was then that I realised Sceilig was still holding me from behind so I couldn't run for Ree. I tried to move backwards and he stumbled on me, and I turned, and suddenly my mouth was on his mouth. It was wet and sticky but his breath smelt of warm SugarHosts, sweet, warm SugarHosts.

I pushed him away.

I was afraid.

He tried to kiss me again.

"¿What the fuck?" I said.

I smacked him across the face.

His arms were all over me and he kissed my lips. It felt like being high on SugarHosts, but three hundred times better. I kissed him back. I'd never kissed anyone before, but it felt so instinctive, like lapping fresh water from a tap when you're dying of thirst. Our bodies collapsed onto each other. He was hard too. I felt his sex on my stomach, curling inside his trousers. Hermanas, I know you don't see the problem here, but the Domini would have said that El Diablo got me there, right there, at that moment when I pulled Sceilig's hair and bit his lips.

They tasted so good, though. </record>

<record> **DEEL 21.** *Pearls y dangerous constellations*

And then a few days came when everything was fine. I can't believe I'm saying this, but it was. Instead of unpacking what it truly meant to kiss Sceilig, Hermanas, I just went with it without questioning it. Like we'd all done with the meat. We never asked where it was coming from, nobody really cared when we'd all been starving.

Sceilig took me to a party in a submarine under Dolphin's Barn. The few Angeli and Inquisitors that were left couldn't spot us there because the submarine changed locations constantly, like a whale shark lurking under the mud.

It was crowded and hot. Everyone was half-naked. I'd stepped into the hall of the Infernum, that dangerous place full of the temptations Domini had warned us about. But all the stuff Domini had told us were lies, dirty, ugly lies. Neo Dublin was sinking. Here there were people getting drunk and kissing, and touching each other's bodies as if there was nothing else left to do in the whole world. The air was SugarCan-sweet, not like that shit we breathed every day in North Liffey. People were dissolving V-D tablets, ready to inject them into their bloodstream. ¿Were they Irish? ¿Spanish? I couldn't tell. They were of all ages and colours. The music mixed them all.

Sceilig took my hand and I messed with his blond hair. He smiled, winked an eye, and moved following the sound of the music.

A woman was singing in the background. I got a V-D shot.

"Ven aquí, Kerry," Sceilig said in his heavily accented Spanish. "Vamos."

I refused to move. The lights changed from pink to green to blue to yellow. I wondered where they got all the power to make them work. Sceilig's white shirt (he'd lost his uniform jacket) revealed his neck and part of his collarbone. I wanted to lick it. I took his hands and he wrapped his arms around my neck. He stood on tiptoes to look me in the eye. The curve of his neck was delicious. He was wearing a pearl necklace under the white shirt. The lights created mini constellations in each of the beads. He rubbed his hips against mine.

"It's ok," he said. "Nobody knows anyone here."

"Mmmm…"

He wasn't right, though. In this ocean of people, I kept recognising faces: Dominus Domitius, completely naked, riding his scooter and breastfeeding his calf, like, while an old woman opened her dress and tried to put her boob on Domitius's mouth.

There were other people from North Liffey right next to them. I think I saw Íscar with another man. Kissing.

The Matadores were there too, the top part of their overalls tied around the hips. Mamá was with them, drinking and laughing, her arm extended whilst another woman tattooed it. The old guy with no legs from El Mercado. The children with wasp-seaweed on their faces...¿Was that man wearing a silver suit and a necklace of hooks Father? V-D was making me see things.

I drank the Rioja someone offered me.

I tasted Sceilig's yellow hair, his ears. He had the most perfect ears I'd ever seen, Hermanas. They were small, curled on the sides of his head. Perfect snail shells.

"I like you," I heard him say.

My tongue on his neck. On his chin. My fingers caressed his soft nape feeling the smooth cavity there. His pearls shone like stars. Sceilig was a galaxy. An exotic galaxy I should have never come across.

I dropped the glass of Rioja. I was an instrument; he was playing me. I kissed him.

"I like you," he would say, every time he had to catch his breath. "I like you..." </record>

<record> **DEEL 22** *Barcos howling in the ship graveyard*

I took Sceilig to see The Spanish Rover when it was almost finished. We'd hidden it in the Matadores' headquarters, where they created their drone-bulls.

The Matadores had claimed for themselves the ship graveyard in Fairview, the only place in Neo Dublin where Domini didn't bother to put Angeli. That place was cursed, I'm telling you. The water looked like coagulated blood because of the rust and spilt fuel. To that, you've got to add the fetid explosions (shark farts, we called them) and black bubbles popping all the time.

Barcos lay on top of each other, like whale carcasses. The rain had a metallic sound there, and when it was windy, the barcos screamed like mating seagulls. Sometimes you could even hear words, I swear. Those barcos wanted to get out. They'd been made for fishing and travelling; the two things Domini hated the most.

I guided Sceilig to the Matadores' headquarters, located inside a huge cruise ship with faded grey letters on its hull that read "Transmediterranea". I keep wondering what that meant. I liked to think that barco had seen cool things, Europe Before The Flood, like. ¿Did you know that the Domini used to tell us that Europe didn't exist any more? Europe, yes, all gone, forever. Europe. We'd get hit in the mouth just for saying that word. They also told us we were the only floating city left. In the entire planet, like.

Inside the cruise ship it was cold as fuck, but the smell got bearable: synthetic oil and fried SugarHosts.

We passed by the pools that were the bullfighting rings and headed down to the workshops where the Matadores created the drones.

"Spooky." Sceilig caressed a mess of wires and screws. Bulls always looked scary to me, even when they were switched off. Some Matadores gave them animal features: eyes, limbs, hooves and all. I hated bullfighting. Not only because I hated seeing Mamá diving in the ring before the waters turned red with her blood. I always felt disgusted when bulls got destroyed. Those machines moved like they were alive. Surely they suffered too.

"Come."

I opened the door to the bunk with Mamá's code. Inside, The Spanish Rover looked like an old bulky barco, but I knew its guts (the engine) was where Mamá was focusing on.

"¿You guys did this?"

"Yeah. It's going to take us far," I promised Sceilig.

The smell of new paint and Sunnaluz made me dizzy. Íscar was getting us tons of Sunnaluz those days, and we used it all on the barco.

"It's so small," Sceilig said, looking over the railing into the darkness.

"That's so it can jump the waves."

I sniffed Sceilig's nape.

"You can't tell your mum about this," I said. For all that we trusted Sister Ciarana, I feared her. Mamá feared her too. Sister Ciarana talked about death as if it was just the next stage of life. And that made me sick.

"I know," he whispered back. "I won't."

"¿For real?" I was breaking Mamá's rules by bringing him there. But even then, I already knew I wanted to take Sceilig with me no matter what happened. If we were leaving Neo Dublin after the bomb, he was coming with us.

We started kissing. I grabbed him, knelt down and opened his trousers. He pulled my hair and pushed his hips forward. Suddenly he pushed me away. Rage hit me, but when I turned back, I saw Mamá was there, at the door, with a mess of green and red wires in her hands.

Sceilig had already zipped up his trousers. I stayed on my knees. I wanted to shout at her, but my voice was lost.

She smirked.

"No pasa nada," she told me. All was fine. Then she was gone. The sound of a nailing gun started coming from the barco's bridge.

No pasa nada.

She was not calling the Inquisitors. She was not telling Father. Nobody had to know Sceilig and I were going to the Infernum. I mean, Mamá was going to the Infernum too, after all that bullfighting. Jesus. The whole city was going to the Infernum in less than a month. ¿Why worry? </record>

<record> **DEEL 23.** *Welcome to Centipede City*

Sí, those last weeks were all about putting the explosives in place. Me, Ree and Sceilig did that. No, for the last time, I don't know how the explosives were made, or how they worked. You would have to ask Mamá. I told you already, I—"

<...>

We started with the NTC foundation. That's how we blew up the whole thing. It was pretty easy, because the NTC had been already sinking little by little and the classrooms on the lower floors were already infested with living things. There were all sorts of hazard signs.

DO NOT CROSS.
ENTRANCE FORBIDDEN.
DANGER.

The Domini had evacuated these places and thrown arsenic into the waters, trying to get rid of the plagues. Afterwards, they'd forgotten about them.

We slipped through corridors and staircases always going down, down, down, until the chants of the Domini were replaced by the waves smashing against the walls. It stank of wasp-seaweed. Cold water licked our ankles and reached our knees in some places. We placed the explosives in all the places Mamá had marked on the map. Here and there, here and there.

Now, Mamá had done beautiful work with these explosives. They were all in water-proof capsules and could be activated remotely. Ah, they were noiseless, just like the worst farts. And before you ask again, that's all I know about them.

We saw a classroom close by. It didn't reek too much.

"Kerry, ¿what do you think lives in there?" Sceilig asked.

"Centipedes, ¿what else?" I said.

Sceilig laughed.

"Let's get this done," Ree said. "Come on, we have to go back."

We opened the door in two, three kicks. The water inside felt viscous. I switched on the torch attached to my hatraguas.

"Wow" I heard Sceilig scream. "Have you seen that?"

SPLASH.

I moved just to see a long shadow diving down, through the water.

"Here," Ree screamed. The water was full of them.

"It's like centipede city," Sceilig said.

"Careful. They're venomous," I said.

"¡Wow, wow, wow, holy shit, look at that!" Sceilig ran through the water. "Hey, bring the light."

I followed him slowly, Hermanas. I was afraid. What a pussy, ¿right? Pero centipedes had already bitten me twice in my life, see. ¿Do you have centipedes here? Then you don't know what I'm talking about, you have no idea.

Finally, I got to see what Sceilig was gesturing towards. A little maroon mountain growing on a rotten desk.

"¿What the f–?" Ree gasped.

"It's a centipede colony." Then it occurred to me. I'd been kind of angry for a while, since Mamá discovered me with Sceilig, even if all she said was no pasa nada, and she hadn't treated me differently since or anything. But I hated she'd seen me like that, being all crazy like for another boy, which was wrong no matter how good it felt, it had to be, that's all I'd heard from Da and Father and all of them men. Disgusting. Crazy. I didn't want to be like Íscar, no, no I was already the half-bred mongrel with the freaky arm and goggles, I didn't want to be crazy too.

"Give me the flamethrower, Ree," I said. "Quick. Quick.".

"Let's go," Ree said.

I took the flame-thrower from her hands and pressed the trigger as hard as I could, Hermanas, directing it towards the mountain. The classroom turned white and then sparkles were everywhere, petards, like.

The centipedes started to squirm out from the colony base, their segmented bodies contorting into weird forms, their antennae moving frenetically, trying to understand where the fire was coming from. Hundreds of them, small and big, started falling into the water. Half of their bodies were already charred. The colony melted like earwax, but that didn't stop the flames. Some big centipedes appeared. Hermanas, those were real monsters, and I swear I heard a noise, like fainting screams. The smell was unbearable. The mountain had disappeared, and in its place was a mixture of mud, boiling water, and centipede parts. I wanted to puke *pero* I didn't, because Sceilig was there, and **Ree**. I pretended to enjoy myself.

There was a **CRACK** and the rotting desk caved in, and the centipede mess sank into a hole. Dark salty waves formed around it. We ran and ran up the stairs. Sí.

¿Can I tell you something? Burning live centipedes didn't feel as good as burning things. `</record>`

`<record>` **DEEL 24.** *Flowered dresses y sugar martyrs mark the end of a dream*

Palm Sunday came, foreshadowing Jesus Christ's murder and marking the beginning of Easter. The Bomb would explode on Resurrection Sunday, a week later.

We went to Phoenix Lake that Palm Sunday in Mamá's barco right after Missa. Sí, our dear Spanish Rover, the other barco Mamá had been building, was almost ready, still hidden in the Fairview graveyard. It looked quite clapped-out and old from the outside, made from loose bits and pieces that Mamá had been storing for years. Pero the engine was tight and sweet, and the hull, covered with rusted planks, harder than shellfish teeth.

That afternoon, the rain was but a caress. The air smelt of blue mushrooms, mussels and gasoline. The sky was white for the first time in months.

Primero we organised a mud race at Phoenix Lake (the mud there was less toxic). The one that reached the obelisk in the middle first would win. I carried Alcalá on my back. We were an awesome team, and we won. We laughed at the others, next to the obelisk, sinking in the mud slowly, slowly, like when you fall asleep.

Íscar shouted at us when we threw mud at him. He lay on a mat on the deck of the boat, his hatraguas off, to let the light rain fall on his face. He'd said some shit about rain being good for the skin. ¿What? Everyone knew rain was radioactive and made things mutate. Well. Íscar's brain was probably affected beyond hope at that point.

Covered in mud-freckles, Mamá sat next to him. Ree came to show Mamá her new dress. Ree wasn't wearing her poncho either (they were all going to develop tumours after that day, I was pretty sure about that). The dress had a flowery pattern and it was short so I could see Ree's white legs. And her knees. Her knees were like soft bundles of dough.

"¡Let's do another race! ¡Come on!"

Ree's copper hair was covered in mud pero her eyes were bright, like new moss.

"Let's go!"

I shook my head. My arms were still hurting from the last race, and every time I coughed, mud came out of my nose.

"¿Sceilig?" She asked.

"Nah," he said.

Ree laughed and then took Alcalá on her back and ran down back to the mud with her. Alcalá laughed too, so hard. Going up and down on Ree's back, screaming.

"Careful there…" Father warned them, from under a gigantic hatraguas. He was licking a sugar martyr on a stick.

When nobody was looking, I grazed Sceilig's hand, so I did. It was just a second.

Sí, this was the moment. We were all content then, I think. We were so used to nightmares, but that day at

Phoenix Lake was our sweet dream.

It stayed like that until Siser Ciarana summoned us, and we were all back in the barco.

The nun was wearing dark goggles: she said light days hurt her eyes.

She related the old stories from *The Book of Cow* one more time, from when cattle grazed free, and Saint Cia-ráin brought light with him, and then he came back to Spain, where the sun shone every day, and people were covered in golden dust and rain was a rarity. ¡Imagine…!

Pero that time she didn't celebrate any Meat Missa. Instead, the nun's face darkened, as though covered by thick blue clouds, and she said: "En verdad, en verdad os digo, que uno de vosotros me hará traición."

Someone among us is a traitor. </record>

<record> **DEEL 25.** *Crazy Dutch Gardens*

Sceilig wanted to show me something. He got out of bed and took a pocket-size projector and pressed some buttons. FLASH, there it was: a hologram came out, on the bare wall in front of us. I wasn't paying attention to that. I liked to study Sceilig's naked body. His narrow shoulders, his smooth hips, his fleshy thighs. The golden fur on his stomach.

"Hey, ¿isn't it pretty?"

"¿What?"

I sat on the bed eating SugarHosts. I wanted to be happy. To laugh.

"Look at this, Kerry. *The Garden of Earthly Delights*."

He meant the hologram, which was a mess of colours

and all things, like. I bent over to look at it more closely.

It was made up of three parts. The most colourful one was in the middle: it shown a lot of folks fucking and playing around an artificial lake, or something. There were flowers and animals, and beasts. These guys looked all pretty dry, they couldn't possibly have known the rain, I thought. Lucky them.

"¿Is this some religious shit?" I asked, because the first part looked something like the Garden of Eden.

"No, this was painted by a weird Dutch. A very old one."

"The Dutch were weird," I agreed.

"Well, if they live in a place like this," he pointed out the lake, "I wouldn't blame them. I like it, though. The Dutch, they know the sea, they've lived with it for ages and ages, and they're alright. ¿Did you know they have many floating cities up there in the Low Countries? They were the first ones in Europe to build them and I bet they're still having fun."

"¿What do you mean? The Dutch don't exist any more. All the floating cities are gone."

Sceilig stared at me.

"¿Do you really believe all the Domini tell you? There are many floating cities around. Venice, Paris, Porto, Berlin…But Amsterdam is the biggest of all. The Dutch built the best floating cities because they were never on land to start with. I heard they even have trees and all."

"Trees?"

He nodded.

"And cows, red cows like this one," he pointed out a little animal in the central scene. It had evil eyes and reminded me of a skinny water-rat with horns.

"¿How do you know?"

"They traded real cow embryos with us. For the Vita-milk. We gave them Sunnaluz."

"But the Domini said…" I didn't quite believe Sceilig. I mean, I wanted to, but it all sounded bonkers. The thing is, I was so chilled I just went with it.

"¿Have you ever seen the Dutch?"

"No, but their parcels arrived on the Vatican Boat all the time when I lived there. This came with one," Sceilig said about the painting.

I licked my fingers. They were sticky. I could also taste something more spicy, real, like Sceilig.

"See," he kept going, "Infernum is in the flames, ¿right?" He shown me the last part of the picture. A ruined city and its monsters burning in orange flames. "Not in the waters. Domini are making us afraid of this world. Of what this world really is."

"I hate the water." I sucked one of Sceilig's fingers. "Water is killing us."

"Sure, Neo Dublin is a wet dumpster. But Amster-dam, that should be alright, I'm telling you. I want to go up there."

He came back to bed and I lay under him. Our legs locked.

"¿To that lake? ¿ Do they have these super big birds and all?"

"Possibly. And they don't have religious shit, you know what I mean. They've got an atheist state. They have real freedom up there."

"¿Do you want to leave Neo Dublin?" I felt sick. Too many SugarHosts. Pero I wanted to have Sceilig. I wanted him all. A life without him…¿could that be a life at all?

"Yes, I want to leave, we'll make it there, ¿right? In

the boat, in The Spanish Rover your mum is building, after the—"

I covered his mouth with my mouth. I didn't like him saying the word "bomb' when we were alone. </ record>

<record> **DEEL 26.** *BLING, BLING, BLING... CHACKS*

Good Friday. Jesus Christ's ghostly funeral service.

When the day got darker, the Irish started their Holy Processions. They all flooded the bridges dressed in black cloaks and capirote hoods. ¿What? Sí, capirotes were pointy hoods with just two holes for the eyes.

I was working with Mamá at the Fairview graveyard but I got sick of messing with wires, so Mamá sent me back home to bring her a large electric screwdriver she had left there. I heard orca whales fighting. It was mating season. I took my poncho out as soon as I got in. There was another noise. BLING. ¿Water rats? I squeezed through the corridors inside the barco. It smelt of dried oil and Alcalá's paperbooks rotting.

I started looking for Mamá's screwdriver but it wasn't in the toolbox she'd left open on the table.

BLING. BLING. BLING.

The noise came from Alcalá's cabin. The door was half open.

Alcalá was lying on the floor. Ree was on top of her, her copper hair falling on Alcalá's face so I couldn't see anything much apart from Ree's tiny white nose. Pink freckles. I smelt her: cheap synthetic cologne and sour

Vitamilk sweat. Her enormous thighs were bent under her flowered dress, fat trembling like jelly. Ree's dress was open at the front. She had a phosphorescent yellow bra that could barely contain her massive boobs. Oh Hermanas. And Ree opened her bra and her boobs poured down Alcalá's face.

No, no, I wasn't angry, Hermanas. It was way beyond that. I can't even describe it, exactly, I can only say that it burnt, it burnt like the flames I'd used to exterminate those centipedes, ¿you get it? No, it wasn't that I wanted Ree. No, no, she was my sister too, ¿right? Maybe that's not how I usually talk about her, sure, but she was. No. It was more about them, they were two girls, and they were fucking, and I'd wanted to do that for so long with Sceilig, to just do it, and feel good, and I had, but a part of me had been rotting since the first time I touched him. And that part of me, rotting, whispered things to me in Father's voice, you have to get El Diablo out of your soul, Kerry. I was sick in the mind, crazy. Poisoned by the rain. But that was me. Not Alcalá. Not her. No. And Ree. No, no, no, no. </record>

<record> **DEEL 27.** *Our tearless Holy Mother*

I came out from the boat panting, nauseous, shaking. I could hardly breathe. I kept seeing my sister with Ree. It was playing in my mind, on a loop.

Putas, putas, putas.

The Holy Week Procession came down North Liffey.

People wore black and marched along, beating the

drums. They had been repeating the same tune forever, like drones. Just one thing made them human: the blood drenching the drum heads. Sí, they beat them that hard. There was something weird in this Holy Week Procession, though. Instead of a cross, the capirotes in the front were carrying a glass reliquary embellished with golden chains and plastic flowers. There was a child lying inside, his hands tied up with a rosary and arranged in a praying position. His skin was blueish. I wondered if the wax was old or if it was a *real* child. Children had been dying all over North Liffey for months, pero now the same was happening in the Irish houses.

Skelpers. Scurvy. Starvation.

The capirotes walked barefoot, and their feet were claws. Experiencing any part of Jesus Christ's suffering was a holy act. Some of them dragged shackles. Those were the ones who had done very bad things, Mamá used to say. Inquisitors. Excommunicators. All of them repenting through blood.

It was all about blood.

More glass reliquaries with children and then, guess who. The Steel Maria appeared in the mist and rain. The drumming went mad. The Holy Mother was standing on a palanquin that had space for six to hold it, pero there were just two capirotes struggling to carry it on their shoulders. She was eyeless. Her metal sockets were empty. I don't think she could see our pain. It was all a big lie. Our Holy Mother was not crying for Jesus Christ or her deceased children. She was not crying for us, either. ¿Why would she care? She was made of steel. She had never been alive.

Ree and Alcalá.

I had something in my hands. The iron bar we used

as an oar to move the *barco*.

Ree and Alcalá.

I stepped into the Procession.

We were all starving again. No more Meat Missas, because there was a traitor among us. I raised the bar.

And the NTC kept sinking.

I hit the Steel Maria as hard as I could.

A metallic wave swallowed the drumming. The palanquin fell in the mud.

I hit the statue again, and again, and again until the metallic face started denting.

Screams.

Cries.

"Kerry…"

Some of the capirotes tried to grab me, pero they were all too weak, like made of paper. The Steel Maria's face was all bent. Monstrous.

"Kerry…Kerry…"

It was Íscar. He was not wearing his hood. He was crying. "Kerry, don't…"

¿What did the Steel Maria mean to him, to them all? It was just a statue. Hands grabbed me back but I kept hitting. The Steel María's head fell off; one of her arms went flying.

I went for the glass reliquaries.

Fucking child martyrs. They were already in Heaven, while Neo Dublin turned into the Infernum. Domini had turned it into the Infernum.

Hermanas, as soon as I broke the first reliquary, the screams turned to wails. You should have seen the way the capirotes fought me. But there were no Inquisitors close enough to stop me. They were all dead already, or too starved to fight.

Íscar held one of the reliquaries.

"You can't…" His eyes were about to pop out. He embraced the glass as if the child inside was alive.

"Drop it," I told him.

"Kerry, please…"

"Drop. It."

He didn't.

I beat the glass and it burst. The pieces, like daggers, sank into Íscar's face. The child inside the reliquary. I've not stopped thinking about it since.

Fuck, fuck, fuck. `</record>`

`<record>` **DEEL 28.** *The doctor y his stapler gun*

Father came when Mamá was curing Íscar's broken face. She had kicked everyone else out of the barco but made me stay to watch. Father brought along a young Dominus with ears as big as fins. He carried a little suitcase of medical equipment.

"¿You did that?" Father asked me.

I looked over my shoulder. The young Dominus had a stapler gun in his hand. It looked fancy.

"Jesus Christ…¿Why son, why?" Father put his hand over his mouth.

"He–" Mamá interjected.

"It's your fucking fault. You've got him here, living with scum, and he's turned into scum," Father said.

"Don't you–" Mamá started.

"You selfish woman."

"You wanted to take him away from me."

"Yes, I wanted to take him away because–"

"We've got to take Íscar to the NTC hospital," Mamá interrupted. "Stop that," she said to the young Dominus, "do you know what you're doing?"

"We can't take him to the hospital if he's not Irish" the young Dominus stuttered.

"You go and pay your fucking money so they fucking take him into the fucking hospital," Mamá said to Father. "Or I'm taking your son to the Inquisitors."

"You spoilt him."

I let the screams pour down on me, like rain in a purple storm.

"¿Me? You spoilt him with that shit about the NTC and religion. He's not one of them." "Because you took him."

"I couldn't leave him with you."

"You…you should never have had children," Father said.

"¿Want to know why I took you away, Kerry?" Mamá grabbed my arm. "Your Father here was a V-D addict. He was so high, all the fucking time, he didn't even know who he was. You were little, Kerry. You cried when he hit me, you cried so much, and he was so annoyed that he threw you down the stairs from our fancy NTC flat. He broke your arm. He almost killed you."

I'd always thought that my right arm was shorter since birth. I told you, Hermanas, deformities were so common, and I was lucky compared to my sister. I couldn't remember the time Mamá was talking about, though. I couldn't remember anything from when we lived in the NTC. I wondered why Mamá was saying all this now. A part of me wished she were lying. But Father's anger dropped from his face to the floor. He went pale with horror and regret. Mamá was right. She was right.

"Kerry, listen…" Father's voice sounded weird. Dry.

"Why are you so afraid?" Now Mamá was tall, immense, not scared of Father at all. "It's the truth. ¿Is not that what obsesses you all, Domini? The truth. Sí, your son took it all from you. All from you."

"Shut up. Kerry can be saved. He can still be saved. Not like you. You'll burn in the Infernum, you whore, you'll burn in there forever."

"¿Save Kerry? ¿You still want to save Kerry? ¿You know about him and Sceilig? You know they fuck, ¿sí? ¿Is he going to be saved by your Deus after that? He's beyond salvation," Mamá shouted at him.

Joder.

My head buzzed. Deus.

"¿What?" Father's eyes filled with real tears. He looked at me without actually looking at me. It seemed like he was finally seeing the side of me that was rotting. That part of me that was more nauseating than a corpse left to dissolve in our polluted waters, eyeless and bloated.

I wished I could tear Father's face with my hands, so he couldn't look at me like that ever again.

Instead, I came to Mamá. Íscar whimpered, maybe he knew what I was about to do. Shame burnt my chest, shame for all the disgusting things Sceilig and I had done. I slapped Mamá's face and ran away kicking the door so hard it came off its hinges.

Sceilig.

I needed to get to him before Father killed him. </record>

<record> **DEEL 29.** *Tungsten, hallowed be thy name*

The door trembled inside Sister Ciarana's house in an empty wing of the NTC. She and Sceilig looked at me. The door trembled. Drumming. Thunder. Lightning.

"Open the door, Kerry, open the door, open the blasted door," Father roared outside.

I looked at Sceilig. ¿Would Father kill him? Father hated anything impure. He hated sex. Me and Sceilig, that was way too much for him.

"Open the door now, open the door or I'm going to burst it open now, Kerry. Kerry, right now, ¡open the door!"

Sceilig came closer to me and reached for my hand. His fingers, like an insect, stayed for a second then flew away.

"¿What's going on?"

Sceilig looked so scared.

"He won't touch you," I reassured him. "But–"

He looked at his mother.

Sister Ciarana was in a corner, in the dark, passing the beads on her rosary, humming,

"*AO-comeherebringyourgoldencattlebringthesunthemoonandall-thebeautifulthingsyouhavecreated…*"

"Your father has to go. Please," Sceilig said.

I nodded and went to the door.

"Go away," I screamed. "Mamá is a whore and you're an asshole and you're not touching Sceilig, so go away you fucker."

"Kerry," Father answered and I understood then that replying had been way worse because now there was some crazy hope in his voice. "Kerry, please, please…"

One thrust.

"Kerry, you know he needs to go," Sceilig screamed. "He needs to go now."

A second thrust.

The door fell down. Father was inside the house.

Sister Ciarana darted towards him.

"You," she said, trembling in what I thought was fear, "you are…"

"Freak," Father said, and he punched Sister Ciarana's face so hard that her body bent and she almost fell. Blood ran down her nose.

"No, no," Sceilig ran towards them.

Father grabbed his arm and twisted it. Sceilig screamed and kicked, Father punched him in the stomach, shoved him backwards, and when Sceilig fell into the floor he stepped on his chest and—

"You."

Sister Ciarana grabbed a horned Virgin Mary figurine set on a glass table and hit Father in the head. It was so fast it seemed unreal. I froze.

CRACK.

She hit him again.

CRACK.

CRACK.

"Stop stop, stop," Sceilig yelled.

Hermanas, ¿you understand it now? Sceilig was not concerned about Father hurting Sister Ciarana: it was the other way round.

Sister Ciarana's golden hair was all over the place, her veil around her neck.

I froze.

"¡Stop!" Sceilig cried.

Sister Ciarana's hands were red but she didn't falter. She raised the figurine one more time. Holy pure tungsten.

I forgot to breathe. </record>

<record> **DEEL 30.** *The horned Virgin Mary hosts our Last Dinner*

I don't know if I want to continue. Yes, my father died. He died. He died, I went mad, so mad that Sister Ciarana had to tie me to a chair and then she called everyone but I don't remember any of that, because I was blind with rage. ¿Do you have enough now? ¿You want more? ¿Still? Fuck you. This is everything.

<...>

"He was the one," Sister Ciarana told us. "He was the traitor."

Mamá cried. I felt something in my chest. A fish-bone piercing my throat, like. My face burnt.

My arms burnt.

My legs burnt.

Being tied up to the chair burnt like the Infernum. Like the sun. "Kerry…" Mamá said.

I looked at the bundle of green clothes dirty with blood. The statue of the horned Virgin Mary was among them. She had a contented expression on her tungsten face.

I didn't want to look at what lay on the table.

If they'd tried to force me, I'd have hit them, bitten them, anything. I was not going to look.

"Kerry…"

Those clothes on the floor. Father's clothes. Like a pile of rubbish. "Kerry…"

Mamá hugged me. Her body was warm and smelt of the sweet whale resin that she used to clean the barco's gears. After five or six years, I felt I was coming back home. My goggles got misty. Oh, Deus, I stopped seeing. What a blessing…

<…>

So Sister Ciarana started telling another story:

"Apart from being a nun, I am a cattle keeper. And a butcher, too."

She opened a reliquary that had been sitting on the table all that time. A lacquered box decorated with happy calves grazing on golden grass. Inside there were no old bones or pieces of fabric. Just knives. Weird-shaped knives.

"Sí, there were cows in the Vatican Boat," she continued. "Real cows. Where did you think the Vitamilk came from?"

She started organising the knives on the table.

"Well, technically they were not alive. They were… designed." She took a serrated knife and started cutting the dead limbs from him. From that body I knew so well.

The noise made me sick.

"They sure breathed, but they didn't look like cows anymore. They didn't have eyes. ¿What did they need eyes for? Or legs. They didn't have those, either. A waste of space. And no, no horns. Actually, they didn't look much like cows at all. Like the cows in the deskreens, I mean. They were big lumps of hairy flesh with veined udders hanging on the side."

I retched.

"They told us they were our manna. And we all needed food. So I took care of them. I gave them pills whenever their udders had ulcers. I butchered their bodies to burn them when they stopped producing milk.

But one night…I swear by Deus, I heard them crying."

Alcalá was studying the table with wide, bright eyes. "¿What did you do?" she asked.

"I finished them. The cows. It turned out, they were alive. They were suffering. And then, I purged the other Sisters of Cow. To erase their sins."

"¿You killed them?"

"The Pope would never allow that."

"What you did…you murdered…" Ree was pulling her cross-necklace-ID so hard that she tore it.

"¿The Pope?" Sister Ciarana made a weird noise. Half a laugh and half a snort, like. "I *ate* the Pope."

A lump of bloody flesh landed on Ree's dish.

"My sinful body purged them. That was my sacrifice. And your sacrifice, too. That's what we've been doing. Purging everyone in Neo Dublin. Making them Holy. We all deserve to be Holy."

Sister Ciarana buried her teeth in the bleeding flesh.

<…>

"I'll do it," I said.

"We cannot trust you anymore." Sister Ciarana cleaned her mouth with the back of her hand.

"I'll pull the trigger."

It was so hard to move. My arms and legs were numb.

"I'll pull the fucking trigger."

"You're the son of the traitor."

"You don't get it." I swallowed. Tears and snot blocked my throat. "To hell with humanity. To hell with them all. I'll pull the fucking trigger."

In my mind, we were once again at the bridge, where Sister Ciarana had saved my sister and I'd promised her

I'd do whatever she wanted me to do. This was it. She knew it, too.

"You're right." She got a knife and cut the ropes. "Humankind is the monster." The white horns of her cornette were enormous. Black and white, she was a nun-cow. "The only way to turn humankind into something good is by eating it, transforming it into manure to heal the Earth." Her hatred poured over me like boiling water. Not her words or what she meant by them: her hatred. Hatred made my blood boil too. She hated people as much as I did.

I got off my chair and crawled to the table.

I buried my face in my father's body. I embraced it. I nursed it with my own body, as if it were a baby. It smelt of wet hooks. I licked the blood. The pain. `</record>`

`<record>` **DEEL 31.** *That forgotten body in the bottomless waters*

The day after it happened, I woke in the middle of the night, the wounds from the knots Sister Ciarana had made to tie me up to the chair still fresh. There was some screaming, and I thought maybe it was Alcalá, until I realised it was me, my hands hitting the floor of the barco, and my head. I was screaming louder than the women and men on the public Excommunicationes, Hermanas.

It was so cold in my bed, like swimming across the sea. When Mamá ran to calm me, I hit her. Someone took me into their arms. Sceilig was there. He didn't mind the blows. My body was so cold. It'd been like that since the last dinner. I had trouble breathing, so much trouble that I considered using Alcalá's respiradero, but there was no power to charge it. All the crucifix farms had stopped and turned dark by then.

Sceilig felt so light. His bones were fragile. Sceilig. He smelt a bit of V-D pills, the ones you put on Vitamilk to make it orange and fizzy. Father always gave Alcalá lots of those to chew, thinking they'd make her stronger.

He held me tight until I calmed down.

I pointed towards Alcalá's room.

"She's fine," Sceilig said. "And so is Ree."

I let him hold me for a little bit longer. His right arm was covered in bandages. I wasn't angry or annoyed at anything right then, knowing that someone loved me, that someone needed me as he did. (Sceilig held one of my curls and squeezed it).

"Tomorrow, I'm going to drive The Irish Rover right to Rory O'Moore bridge," Mamá said after a while. She slowly put her hands around my shoulders. "I'm taking them with me," she said, referring to Sceilig, Ree and Alcalá. "Íscar too."

I hadn't been able to say a word since the last Meat Missa.

"Remember," Mamá's voice was flat, detached, but her body was shaking. "You will have five minutes to escape the moment you activate the bomb. Make your way to us. Rory O'Moore. We'll wait."

I shook my head. The cold kept spreading, and my body felt as if it had been left at the bottom of the ocean.

"You have to do it," Sceilig said. "It's the last thing before she lets us all go."

His face was wounded. I knew who had done that to him, and the arm too. But I remembered he'd always looked a bit like that: bruises and bandages, a bit too pale sometimes. Sister Ciarana and her tungsten Horned Mary.

Hermanas, I'm not sure any of us really thought we could escape Sister Ciarana like that. She hadn't said to us what we were meant to do after The Bomb. Maybe because there was no after for her. I understood everything then. I did, oh I did. The meat we'd been fed wasn't what we thought. We also believed she spoke of hope, but that was our own lie too. </record>

<record> **DEEL 32.** *White dolphins shout at me: you're so lucky*

Resurrection Sunday. Everything around me was quiet. The UVA lampposts were dark.

The sea was furious.

I dragged my body towards the NTC. The school uniform hid all the purple rope marks. My throat was still on fire. I spat out bitter blood.

The detonator was in my backpack. The card that gave access to all the corridors, Father's card, was tucked inside my shirt.

SPLASH.

A group of three white dolphins leapt out of the water. Following me, screaming. I stopped, couldn't believe what I was seeing, Hermanas. Those white dolphins. I'd never seen them in my life, water was way too polluted here to allow for anything more than orcas and skelpers. And yet, there they were, like Alcalá had said. Three of them, like a pack of ghosts.

It was a nice thing to be watching before The Bomb.
```
</record>
```

```
<record>
```
 DEEL 33. *There is one amongst us who will betray us (y I know who it is)*

That ladder. It was that same place (sweat started running down my nape) where Dominus Domitius had punished me once. I was supposed to climb that ladder to get to the clock room, set the detonator, and press it so The Bomb, hidden inside the entrails of the NTC weeks ago, would go BOOM.

I talked to Deus then, Hermanas. For the very first time in my life, I put my hands together and called for Deus up in the clouds, higher than the rain, closer to that sun we could no longer see. I told Him what I was about to do. But I wasn't praying. I wasn't asking. I was just mocking him. Because all the Domini were floors below, in the main chapel, in the middle of the Resurrection Missa, celebrating that Deus was going to bring his celestial son back to life. Well, they would be the first ones to burst into flames.

Sister Ciarana promised me that The Bomb would purify their bodies. Hermanas, I just wished they would all burn. Sister Ciarana was right in just one thing: humankind was the monster. We had been eating it because we were monsters too.

Pressing my eyes closed, I climbed the ladder. Flames crawled up my leg. I bit my tongue to deceive the pain. I trusted that the next step would be there. It was. So was the next. And the next.

I arrived. There was a little skylight and a repetitive noise, a heart beating, like. The inner mechanism of the NTC clock. That huge clock had marked every second of our torture: living in that hideous, sinking city. I took the silver suitcase from my backpack and placed it on the floor. Mamá had made me memorise the combination of buttons just by touching the detonator's surface. I caressed the left side.

I pushed the buttons.

Five minutes to go.

I rushed down the ladder back to the first room. I had to get to the balcony in the corridor and jump down into the water. A chill in my nape. I wasn't alone.

CLICK

I looked all over.

CLICK.

CLICK.

CLICK.

Thirty seconds went. Nothing. I was alone. ¡But I wasn't! I considered ignoring the fact I'd just seen another human shadow with me in the room. I just wanted to get the fuck out.

CLICK.

"Hey…"

CLICK.

Time did stop at that moment.

CLICK.

"Ree, what the…?"

I wanted to die right there. CLICK.

"Kerry, is not what you think, I promise."

She rushed past me and climbed up the ladder.

"What are you doing, ¡just come back here! Let's get the hell out of here."

I tried to follow her.

CLICK. CLICK.

She was already in the upper room.

"¡Don't touch it, joder, it's dangerous…!"

CLICK.

"I just want to stop it," she shouted back.

CLICK.

"¿What…?"

"It's not fair, ¿you know? Killing hundreds of people, even if some of them are evil. It's not right. I can't do it. I've told everyone to escape, to run away to the boat."

CLICK.

The room spun around.

CLICK.

"¿You what…? Ree, please, please, just come here. There's no time for this."

CLICK.

My legs were lifeless and the ladder infinite. I wouldn't get there in time.

CLICK.

"Yes, they're all gone, and now I'm going to stop it, and we'll go home, and nobody will know."

CLICK.

"Ree…Ree, listen, you don't know how to…Don't touch it, joder, come here now, I tell you. ¡Let's go!"

CLICK.

I couldn't go up.

CLICK.

"It's not that difficult, I've been observing Mamá and…" She sounded like she really knew what she was doing, like. I could almost see her smiling faintly.

CLICK.

I couldn't go up.

I couldn't. CLICK.
"There we g…" `</record>`

`<record>` **DEEL 34.** *And the sun shone in Neo Dublín for the very first time*

They said:

- That the rain stopped. Some chemical reaction from The Bomb created a light-mist that took over everything, and during three minutes and thirty-three seconds there was no rain at all, just light, shining all over the city.

- That the NTC had a purple glow around it that turned white. Deus had blessed all the Domini at the same time, lifting the whole building to the sky and the stars and beyond, so the Domini would be higher than the Angeli.

- That the NTC started melting, and it was like when you throw a photo into the flames. It was a strange but beautiful effect, and the people who saw that still thought Deus's hand was in all that and it was some sort of miracle.

- That the NTC crumpled and disintegrated. It disappeared into a big ball of fire, an artificial sun created for Neo Dublin and Neo Dublin alone. The sun shone over the whole city, and they said that all the city seemed made of gold, like the chalices in the NTC. All was perfect, pure and sacred under Deus's sun.

- That the sun sank into the waters. The barcos trembled violently, some of them went flying through the air. Barcos here and there, dancing like crazy. The floating houses had already sunk deep down but the barcos were like dolphins and so they kept jumping over the waves for a while.

- That a tsunami, bigger than the NTC, originated. Deus's monstrous tongue, they said, ready to devour this city of sins. The people who saw it knew their hour had come, so they grabbed their children and lovers and closed their eyes, and didn't even bother with screaming because they knew they wouldn't be heard once the wave hit the city. The wave swallowed everything, and the bridges broke and sank, like veins of a collapsing body. Without its heart, Neo Dublin was nothing more than a corpse.

-That the waters reigned all over That – listen closely, Hermanas – that was Deus's true will. And when the calm returned again (because it certainly did) there was no city,

no bridges,
no NTC,
no barcos,
just quiet golden blue waters.

I didn't see any of this, though. Ree's massive body disintegrated instantly, but I was sent flying through the air, through the glass windows, and landed on the waters, which saved me from burning.

That was Deus's last joke.

I didn't die.

And when I opened my eyes, Neo Dublin was no more. </record>

CAMERA 553 – THE ROOM

The boy finishes telling his story. His body is scarred with third-degree burns. He wears white overalls and a pair of rudimentary goggles.

One of the tall women sitting in front of him switches off the recorder. There are three women in total. Two of them wear military uniforms.

"Dank je wel, that was good, Kerry," the woman with the recorder says. She's the only one in civilian clothes. Her name tag reads "Anouk Boul. Literatuur en Geschindenis Archief". "Thank you very much for agreeing to contribute to our records. The Ministerie van Buitlandse Zaken will be informed and this will certainly be taken into account for your application. We are aware of the environmental conditions that accelerated the disappearance of Neo Dublin. However, it was the most prosperous floating city in Southern Europe, and your testimony will help us understand what really happened."

On the chair, the boy folds his knees against his chest. "Are you going to send me to jail?" he asks.

"You are a refugee in the floating city of Amsterdam and Joined States. You have committed no crime here. And, as an underage person, you cannot be taken to court. Besides, you're one of the few survivors from Neo Dublin. You're a valuable historical resource and you will be protected. Failing to do so would be like burning pages from our annals. And we might need you further."

"Will I get citizenship?"

"Well, it's not that easy, I'm afraid. But some special arrangements will be made."

"Am I free to go, then?"

"Not yet. You'll have to go back to the camp for the time being."

CAMERA 278 – THE CAMP'S GARDEN

A small concrete square. The sky is grey. It's raining, but the drops are very thin. The boy puts his hood on and walks, with wobbly legs, like someone who is used to living on a boat. Water flows over his clothes without touching them. He's covered in Sunnaluz. He heads towards a blonde boy sitting under an apple tree next to an ornamental pond in the middle of the square.

"Ya está?" the blonde boy asks. The boy nods.

"It was kind of…It felt good," he says. "You?"

"I kept silent." The blonde boy's eyes are of the bluest sky in summer. He's wearing similar white overalls. "So they have trees here," he adds.

"Yes, all over the place, like."

There are twelve apple trees surrounding the pond. The boy picks up an apple. Water can be heard flowing under the pavement. Light comes from the transparent dome.

The boy leans over the pond and touches the water. He licks his finger. "It's salty," he mumbles.

"This place is not *The Garden of Delights*, or whatever that painting was called," the boy says to his companion. "There's no Eden here. No Infernum. No Deus either." He stands on the edge of the pond. It has stopped raining. He looks at the apple he's holding. He's about to throw it into the black waters.

Instead, he keeps it in his hand and bites in, and again, and again, devouring the fruit right under the white sun.

Acknowledgements

This book was written in the very specific context of a Creative Writing PhD, which I undertook at Lancaster University (when I thought that all a PhD would entail would be three fun years of writing whilst providing me with a clear reason to stay in England as an immigrant). Of course, it was way more complex than I envisioned in my naïvety, which is why I want to thank my supervisors, Jenn Ashworth and Eoghan Walls, both of them talented authors and the kindest, most generous mentors I could have ever asked for. Thanks as well to the wonderful staff and students at ELCW in Lancaster who provided friendship, good conversations, food and overall love while I was working in this project. I experienced many challenges during my PhD, but I always had a community by my side. It truly takes a village.

To my mother, who not only gave me financial support at the start of this journey, but has always been my greatest cheerleader. I was already attending literature classes when I was in your belly, so I guess it surprises no one that this is the career I decided to embark on?

To my sister, the clever one in the family, who, like my mother, has always believed I am a writer way before I did and didn't doubt, not for a second, that this book would be published.

To my beautiful yaya Pilar, who shared with me her memories of the Spanish Civil War and passed on her love of storytelling and books.

To my inspiring community of writers and companions in the craft who read many drafts of this project, helped me proofread and provided generous advice every time I asked; I specially want to thank my dearest friends and writing pals Teresa Garanhel and Anne Cleasby.

To my PhD-sisters/mentors Naomi Krüger and Yvonne Battle-Felton who are always so generous to provide guidance and comfort in the writing life.

To Ivar, who doesn't really read fiction but tries to read my strange, twisted books nonetheless.

To my Irish family for welcoming me in their home back in 2010 – yours is a beautiful country where I've always felt like I belong, and without your love these stories would have never been written. Thanks as well to the amazing staff at the Clonmacnoise museum who were so helpful and enthusiastic when I visited them and asked them questions while I was writing the book.

To friend and historian Ana Rosa Domínguez, who provided very useful information about the Spanish Second Republic and the Spanish Civil War, and shared with me the stories of her father and the arrival of the International Brigades in Madrid. ¡Viva la república!

To the incredibly talented and hardworking team at Blackwater press. This is the weirdest book I've written (so far) and I wasn't sure it was ever going to find a home. But then it did. Thanks especially to Vivien Williams, my editor, I can't quite believe I got so lucky I found someone who speaks both English and Spanish to edit my work. Your suggestions and thoughtful advice made this story better. Thanks so much for believing in this project and choosing to work with me.

The writing of this novel and my PhD was funded by the AHRC and Lancaster University – a privilege I am very thankful for.

And last but not least, thanks to my cats, Nori and Luna. You have no idea what I do and you won't ever read this book but you make my life so much better – so, obviously, you deserve a place here too.